JAM

JAM

Jake Wallis Simons

First published in Great Britain in 2014 by Polygon, an imprint of Birlinn Ltd.

Birlinn Ltd
West Newington House
10 Newington Road
Edinburgh
EH9 1QS

www.polygonbooks.co.uk

A CIP catalogue record for this book is available from the British Library.

ISBN 978 1 84697 280 5
eBook ISBN 978 0 85790 783 7

Typeset by Hewer Text (UK) Ltd

Printed by Bell & Bain Ltd, Glasgow

For my grandfather
Tony 'Gramps' Simons (1922–2012)
who loved cars almost as much
as he loved a good story

Jamming

The day was closing. The world was revolving gently, easing a new portion of its surface to the sun; London was moving along with it, towards the great darkness. Shadows were puddling under trees, stretching out from buildings, carpeting the streets. On the southern flank of Trafalgar Square, at the foot of the statue of King Charles I – which for centuries had been considered the dead centre of London, from which all signposts were measured – a young man covered his eyes before opening an email on his phone. If it was a rejection, well, he'd be sunk. A third of a mile away, a dog looked up at the Cenotaph. On Waterloo Bridge, a middle-aged gentleman chewed his fingernail to the rhythm of a dreadlocked busker's bongos, snipped it clean, and flicked it spiralling, a tiny comma, over the side. A woman from Leeds, struggling with a broken high heel, was late for a trip on the London Eye that was paid for by her clients, and arrived to see familiar faces looking at her from the oval capsule as it arced away into the gloaming. In Gordon's Wine Bar on the Embankment, a manic-depressive discovered he had won £210 on the National Lottery. Although it was a Sunday, the occupants of an entire floor of Slaughter & May, which inhabited the grand building at Number One Bunhill Row, were still at work; a dispute between two mobile phone giants had entered a critical phase. In the suburbs, a million kettles were being boiled. People everywhere were looking out of their windows, drawing their curtains against the gathering night.

Suppers were cooking. In Marylebone, a woman suffering the onset of flu opened a can of Heinz Cream of Tomato soup to remind herself of her childhood. In Southwark, a man heated up a Waitrose Lamb Rogan Josh and strummed his fingers on the microwave. A fifteen-year-old behind Elephant & Castle Station – whose mother, at home, was cooking a chicken – gasped as a knife slipped between his ribs. A child fell over: the pause before the howl. In St Wilfrid's Residential Home, Chelsea, an old lady who had worked as a codebreaker during the war let out her final breath. On the seventeenth floor of the Royal Free Hospital, through the windows of which a vista of the city could be seen, a nurse was forced to wait a full fifteen minutes until a lift arrived to carry her down for her break. In Fortune Green, a schoolboy, who had been thinking all day about becoming a Gooner, decided to join the army. An estate agent arrived home to an empty house. His broadband, for some reason, was down. The Prime Minister misbuttoned his coat; a baby began life in a taxi on the Goldhawk Road; a chicken nugget fell to the ground; a young man who had once grown a moustache for charity cut up his credit card with a blunt pair of scissors. An obese resident of Bromley, face bleached by the light of the television, changed the channel, then changed it back again. An escort, on the way to her last job, climbed the stairs of a Twickenham hotel. People texted and tweeted and emailed and Skyped, texted and tweeted and emailed and Skyped. People ignored these messages. Everywhere immigrants strived; everywhere crime seethed; everywhere people were eating, drinking, flushing, fucking; everywhere people made supplications to a variety of gods.

Such was the wormery of London, encircled like a fortress by the sluggish moat of the Orbital, which, now and at any time of the day, was grey, and relentlessly so, though spangled with millions of headlights. A tail-eating Thames, straining against itself while vehicles in their millions ghosted past in a pageant of colours, with all the randomness of fish against the monochrome of the ocean. The M25 had no beginning, no end, and did not go anywhere but back, eventually, where it was. This was an environment one would endure to reach one's destination quickly, nothing more; land for passing through; a dream which, upon awakening, could only be remembered in fragments, each identical to the others, and all so unremarkable that they were soon forgotten. The London Orbital, although scoring through 117 miles of Britain, lay on the surface of the earth like a snakeskin, as if one day it might be scraped up and discarded.

But: as the sun turned copper, the traffic began to slow. Drivers, squeezing their brakes, created scarlet constellations of warning. Something had happened. A tumour developed, hundreds of living cells amid gauzes of exhaust. Got to be an accident, said the driver of a Mazda MX5 to his wife, who was reading something on an iPad; she was hoping to make partner at her law firm, hoping to be the second female this year. Shall we turn off? Or sit tight? Several cars behind, a woman who had grown up on an army base outside Berlin said, hope there hasn't been an accident or anything. Dad? But he was asleep. A motorbike passed them, weaving its way along the queue, the driver turning his antlike helmet. A group of teenagers watched it as the bass-notes of their hip-hop thumped in their souped-up Corsa. One of them tweeted. A mile back, on the seat of a BMW, a woman wearing man's clothing slept uncomfortably, her face pinched into a frown as if gripping her burden even in sleep. In the next lane, a man who still thought of himself as young cursed his irritable bowels. The van behind: two men in leather jackets – the first had the face of a schoolboy, the second looked more like his mother than his father – were speaking on their mobiles, each in a different language. One of them knew in passing the man with the irritable bowels, though they were not on first-name terms. Two exits behind, in the front seat of a Honda FR-V, a man, fearing he was too old to be a parent, peered over at the two slumbering toddlers in the back seat, between whom was an empty packet of sweets, and said, just when the little monkeys had finally conked out, Jesus. Keep the engine running, his third wife replied. Behind them, a container lorry loomed. The driver, who had a broad and pallid forehead, spread a tabloid across the steering wheel and rubbed his chin. He'd promised the missus he'd do WeightWatchers, but not done anything about it. The song 'Dancing Queen' was going round in his head, he couldn't get it out. Will be late home now, pain in the arse what with Sue's operation in the morning. Sod's law. Fancy some bacon.

Standstill. The sky was tarnishing as black-winged night accelerated its descent. Over the swarms of grubby, gleaming machines, a fug of fumes sighed.

Max and Ursula

'This'll clear soon,' said Ursula. 'Don't you think?'

'It's all I need,' said Max, heaving up the handbrake in his meaty fist. 'Fucking pain in the arse.'

Ursula didn't respond. She was looking out of the window at the city of vehicles that had sprung up around them. They were in the middle lane, flanked on one side – as she often thought – by the daredevils, and on the other by the meek. Here I am, stuck in the middle with you. When did cars get like this? It felt like the last time she looked they were made of rectangles, squares, lines. Now it was all ovals and bulges and curves. Cartoon bugs.

'When did cars get like this?'

'Like what?'

'You know, all buglike. All rounded. Like sucked sweets or something. Jelly Babies. Sucked Jelly Babies.'

Max didn't respond. He tended to ignore his wife's remarks when they didn't make sense. He was an IT consultant, a systems analyst; he couldn't relate to her when she was in this sort of mood. Cars like Jelly Babies.

'I mean, if you didn't know,' said Ursula, 'you'd have thought we were all in capsules.'

'Capsules?'

'If you were an alien.'

'Well, you're not,' said Max. 'At least, I'm not.'

It never used to be like this. Not when they first met, not even in the first years of their marriage. They used to have a lot in common. When had it started, then? Like this?

'I told you it was stupid to drive back to London on a Sunday evening,' said Max. 'I knew it would be like this.'

'I suppose even our car probably looks like a sucked sweet, if you think about it,' said Ursula. 'They used to be all boxy and sort of friendly. Now they're like jelly moulds. You turn around and everything's changed.'

Max didn't respond.

They were sitting in the womb of a Chrysler Voyager, a car which, Ursula now thought, looked like it had been inflated with a bicycle pump. It was four years old; they had bought it when Carly was born. Carly was sitting in the back of the vehicle, in the sixth of its seven seats, on her booster seat, leafing restlessly through *Where the Wild Things Are* and talking to herself. She was a good girl, generally, and charming; Max's black and Ursula's white had given her toffee afro hair, light brown skin and – Max thought – eyes like the first light of dawn on a freshly laundered tablecloth. Next to her, in the fifth seat, was Bonnie, her friend from pre-school, a blonde and freckled girl with a perpetual stickiness about her, who was asleep, one hand clutching a doll, the other resting in a packet of crisps.

Ursula and Max knew the Chrysler had been a mistake, a result of the heightened state of excitement that had gripped them upon Carly's birth. We'll need something with a bit of space, they had said. A family car. For all the kit. And for when we have more children. But now that Carly was four, there wasn't so much in the way of kit. Or more children.

'You all right in the back?' said Ursula, twisting round in her seat. 'You all right, Carly?' No response.

'No news is good news,' said Max. 'She looks all right in the mirror. Bonnie's asleep. Thank God. Better let sleeping dogs lie.'

'If this goes on much longer, we'll have to call her parents,' said Ursula. 'They'll be worried.'

'I haven't got a signal,' said Max. 'Fucking mobile's useless.'

'Me neither,' said Ursula, looking at her handset. 'I got the sim-only deal from you, remember. Same network.'

'You can't blame me for everything.'

'Nobody's blaming anybody, Max. I was just saying.'

'Saying what?'

'Saying that we're both incommunicado, and we have some-one else's child in our car. That's all.'

'Just thank God it's asleep.'

'Don't be so nasty.'

Max felt foolish and enraged, a trapped bull. He was a big man, and felt uncomfortable in cars, even a seven-seater. Nothing moved. The traffic around them fumed. There they were, in a little world of moulded plastic, padding, fabric, reinforced glass, a giant crash helmet. It was stuffy. It smelled of air freshener, the result of a recent valeting. Ursula hated that smell. The engine throbbed idly to itself as a succession of police cars caromed down the hard shoulder.

'Shall I turn on the radio?' asked Ursula. 'There might be something on about it.'

'Please don't mention . . . that,' said Max. 'That would be the final straw. We don't want to set Carly off again.'

'What do you mean again?'

'Again. First time, second time. Again.'

'I want TV,' said Carly.

'Not going to say I told you so,' said Max.

'She said TV, not radio.'

'One thing always leads to another with her, you know that.'

'If you'd only let her watch another film, we'd be all right,' said Ursula.

'She's watched one already. That's what we agreed.'

'But these are exceptional circumstances.'

'Rubbish. It's only a traffic jam.'

'Fine. You deal with her then, if you're such a genius at childcare.'

'Daddy, I want TV,' said Carly. 'I want TV.'

'You're not having any more TV,' Max said. 'God, what was I thinking buying a car with TV screens in the headrests?'

'It keeps her quiet,' said Ursula. 'You've got to learn to relax.'

'And have our daughter going to hell in a handbasket? That would be relaxing.'

'It's a DVD, Max, not bloody heroin.'

'I thought you wanted me to deal with it?'

'I do want you to deal with it.'

'I . . . want . . . T . . . V.'

'For the last time, Carly, you're not having TV,' said Max.

'Aaaw!'

'You can't have TV now, darling,' said Ursula, 'Daddy isn't in the mood.'

'Not in the mood?' said Max.

'I can have TV if I want to.'

'No, you can't,' said Max. 'Just read your book, OK?'

'I don't want to read my pooey book.'

'Carly, I've told you. Carly! Carly! Don't you dare throw that book! Carly! Right.' He took off his seat belt and turned to face her full on. Ursula shook her head gently, then froze under Max's glare. For a moment he was torn between directing his wrath at his daughter or at his wife. 'You're not having TV,' he said, 'and that's final. So do you want your book? Or not?'

'Yes,' said Carly sullenly.

'Good. Here it is. Now just be quiet and look at your book,' said Max.

'I don't want my pooey book.'

'Look, if I hear any more from you, I'm going to open the door and put you out there on the road all by yourself.'

'Aaaw!'

'Do you want to be put outside on the road all by yourself?'

'No.'

'Then not another peep out of you.' She fell into a dark silence. He glared at his wife.

'What's the death stare for?' said Ursula.

8

'It's not a death stare.'

'Why are you so upset?'

'It's nothing. All right? Nothing.'

Last week they had – on Ursula's insistence – finally signed up to the Marriage Course at the church in Onslow Square. For months, Max had resisted. Number one: he suspected it was run by those Alpha Course weirdos. Number two: it would involve revealing personal – and potentially compromising – details of their relationship to complete strangers. Number three: it was fundamentally cheesy.

But Ursula, having softened him up with the fact that the course included a candlelit dinner, had addressed each of his three points in turn. (She had grown used to this with Max.) Firstly, the website stated that there would be no prayers or dogma, and very few mentions of God. Secondly, it said that at no time would participants be required to reveal anything to other members of the group; they had only to reveal things to their spouse, and what could be embarrassing in that? Finally, although she could not deny that the thing would have its share of cheesy moments, wasn't that worth enduring for the sake of their relationship? They both wanted their marriage to work, and it had been under a lot of stress recently. Anyway, all vehicles need a regular service to keep them roadworthy. (A promotional video for the Marriage Course featured a couple taking a camper van to a garage.)

'Bloody traffic,' said Max, 'bloody bastarding M25 traffic on a Sunday evening. Should have known better. Bloody fucking bastard balls.'

'I wonder where we are?' said Ursula.

'No idea,' said Max. 'That's freaking me out as well. I don't even know what junction we're at. We could be anywhere.'

'Why don't you look on the satnav?'

'Out of battery, isn't it? Or have you forgotten?'

'Charge it up, then.'

'What, and die of carbon monoxide poisoning?'

Max turned off the engine, and a profound silence fell. Their future seeped by degrees into the present.

'It'll clear,' said Ursula. 'Just relax until it clears. It's probably a minor incident.' She looked out of the window at the cars stretching into the distance. The end of the queue, where new cars were joining, was out of sight. All around had sprung up a densely populated autopolis. People, people, all nested in their own little cars. People, people, everywhere, and not a drop to drink. Actually, she was thirsty. The children would be OK, they had their beakers. She slid half a bottle of mineral water from the glove compartment, drank some and offered it to Max. He made a sardonic comment about the saliva at the bottom. She shrugged and finished it herself.

'If this goes on much longer, we'll miss the Marriage Course tonight,' she said. 'Miss the first session.'

Max didn't respond.

She remembered their wedding.

One of the bridesmaids, a school friend called Lillian, had become dehydrated throughout the morning and, just as the vows were being exchanged, had fainted. Not uncommon, that. She went down stiffly; the sound of her coiffed head striking the floor resounded through the chapel like a thunderclap. A single flower, Ursula remembered, detached itself from her hair, completed a single revolution and came to rest in the nape of her neck. Ursula hid behind Max's bulk as people clustered around the fallen girl. Max stood his ground, commanded the chapel, made everyone feel that things were under control, until the emergency passed and the ceremony recommenced. It was the sort of situation in which he thrived. He was a manager by training and by instinct, good under pressure; he was six foot two, and broad, imposing; he had the gift of leadership, she knew that; that had been part of what had attracted her to him. This was a man who, even as his own wedding was being disrupted by forces unseen, could be a rock in the storm. Or so she thought then. Mad Max. She turned the sky-blue lid of the bottle until it closed, and put it – empty and weightless, ridiculous – back into the glove compartment. Max was sitting motionless, looking out of the window.

That world outside the car: did it really exist? That seething landscape of machines, clouds of exhaust, distant fields and trees? The far-off city, in a corner of which the Marriage Course would already be under way? It seemed so remote from here in the Chrysler. Like sitting in a jeep on safari, looking out at another planet. She noticed the silhouettes of people in car windows. Some speaking on their phones, their faces lit up by the screens. Some gazing listlessly into space. One man eating from a packet propped on the steering wheel. There, a couple kissing, they were even kissing. An old lady reading. Some bicycles, like trophy bucks, on the back of a Volvo. A caravan. A lorry painted in supermarket livery – Waitrose? – with a homely slogan on the side that she couldn't be bothered to read. A canoe, upended, on a roof. There was a white van beside them; she couldn't see the driver. She flipped a switch. The doors of the Chrysler responded by locking, simultaneously, with a satisfying clunk. She closed her eyes.

No signal

But sleep evaded her. She readjusted her position again and again, but it only made matters worse. After some time, she opened her eyes and sat there looking at the cars, the road. The atmosphere in the car was heavy. A long time passed before she looked around. When she did, Max, lips pinched sourly, was doing his stress thing, picking at his nails with that horrid little penknife. Ursula felt briefly sorry for him; he looked even larger than usual, very cramped. He was grappling with something, she could feel it. Why wouldn't he tell her what it was? She hadn't asked him, granted; but she would never have needed to before. She looked at her watch. The course was well under way. The babysitter would have come to the house, waited for a while, gone home. Ursula would pay her anyway, keep her sweet, good babysitters were hard to come by. But for what? The end, she thought, must be nigh. Ah, it was stuffy in the car, there did not seem to be any oxygen. The only air available had been filtered through fabric, plastic, leather, circulated and recycled many times, polluted with air freshener. But she knew he wouldn't open the windows, even if she asked him to.

Outside was an endless universe; inside everything was constricted. She looked at the kids in the mirror. Carly, bless her, had fallen asleep, the book tented on her tummy as if she was an old man at the beach. She looked flushed – not ill? Surely not. Bonnie was awake now, looking out of the window as if she had had been born in a state of stickiness and boredom. She had finished her crisps, and her face was smeared with orange food dye. In the half-light her mouth looked like a gash in the centre of a bruise. But she was quiet. With a bit of luck she'd nod off again.

Ursula looked away, looked down at her hands, at the dashboard, out of the window. In a silver car in the next lane – a Golf, perhaps, she thought – a man was looking at her. Immediately they both turned away. When she looked back he was hidden behind the headrest.

Her sense of time was starting to skew. She hadn't been watching the clock. Men had got out of their cars, craned their necks like meerkats, then got back in. Max had done this on three occasions, periscoping absurdly in an effort to catch sight of the obstruction. He had even asked another motorist if he had any idea what was going on. He hadn't. Ursula wondered if his pride was preventing him from turning on the radio. Perhaps that was the cause of his stress. There he was, picking away, pick, pick, pick, pick, pick. He had across his chin and neck a dark smudge of bristle, now; amazing that men got that. Pick, pick, pick, pick, pick. It was as if she didn't exist.

Max folded his penknife decisively and stashed it away in his pocket. 'Big day at work tomorrow,' he announced, scratching his neck. 'Starting at the CCCS.'

'The what?'

He sighed, still did not look at her. 'Consumer Credit Counselling Service. You know, consumer debt. I've only mentioned it a million times. We're starting a six-month analysis of their customer records system.' He sat back, rubbed his eyes.

A strange quietude reigned in the vehicle. It was as if, Ursula thought, the car was newly inanimate. The growl of the beast had been silenced; the audacious roar of the technological age had stopped. Everything was dying around them.

More emergency vehicles howled past on the hard shoulder. A helicopter throbbed overhead. Max twisted and looked at the children, then fell heavily back into his seat. He rubbed his eyes again. Then he took his phone out of his pocket, unlocked it, held it at various angles of elevation. 'I tell you what's really stressing me out,' he said, 'is having somebody else's kid in the car. That's what's really stressing me out.'

'Don't worry,' Ursula began, 'it can't last for ever. I'm sure we've got off lightly compared to the people involved in whatever's going on up there.'

'That's not the point, Ursula,' said Max, opening the window – at last – and raising the phone into the night. 'The point is that Bonnie's parents are going to be worried sick. And there's no fucking signal.' He gave his phone a final flourish and put it awkwardly back in his pocket. Ursula gasped at the freshness of the air. The window hummed shut. There was a pause.

'Isn't it quiet in here,' said Ursula, 'without the noise of the engine?'

'Hmmm.'

'How much longer do you think we'll be stuck here? We could be sat here all night.'

'Possible. Unlikely.'

'What would we do for food? And water? Shit, I've drunk all the water.'

'There'll be shops around here somewhere, if it comes to that. I'll go and explore, if it comes to that.'

'Do you think that Waitrose van would give us any water? And food?'

'Don't be stupid.'

'Where will you go, then?'

'I don't know. I'll find somewhere.'

'What if the traffic moves while you're away?'

'I'll only go if we're stuck here all night.'

'How will we know? There'll be no way of knowing.'

'We'll know. We'll make an educated guess. We'll take a view.'

There was a pause.

'What about the kids?' said Ursula. 'They'll have to eat something at some point. They haven't had any supper. They'll be dehydrated.'

'Hmmm.'

'And James and Becky will be worried sick.'

'Oh, stop going on about James and Becky.'

'They'll be worried. They might have called the police by now.'

'I doubt it. I doubt their brains work fast enough.'

'Max, please. I'd be worried sick if it was my child.'

'Well, you're not exactly known for your level-headedness.'

'Perhaps we should try and borrow someone's phone.'

'Whose phone?'

'I don't know. One of the people in the other cars. We could offer them a couple of quid.'

'I'm not going to embarrass myself by begging,' said Max. 'Because that's what it amounts to. Begging.'

'It doesn't. It's paying for a favour.'

'It's begging.'

'I'll do it,' said Ursula. 'I don't mind.'

'You don't mind begging?'

'It's not begging.'

'I thought you had more self-respect than that.'

'It's not begging.'

'I'm not having you embarrassing yourself.'

'What difference does it make to you?'

'We're married. You're my wife. What embarrasses you embarrasses me. I'm not having you beg.'

'It's not begging.'

'You'll make a fool of yourself.'

'Why do you care what I do? I'm not embarrassed by what you do. When you make a fool of yourself, I don't feel embarrassed.'

'That's because I don't tend to make a fool of myself,' said

Max. 'Maybe I should make a fool of myself for once, just so you can see what it's like.'

'Ha ha ha,' said Ursula. 'What about the other day, when you told that poor guy on the Tube to turn his music down? That was embarrassing.'

'Why should I be embarrassed by that? I didn't find it embarrassing. He should have been embarrassed by that, not me. Stupid twat.'

'All he was doing was minding his own business, listening to his iPod, and you had to go and bloody interfere. The poor sod thought you were about to mug him.'

'He was being anti-social. It was disturbing everyone in the entire carriage.'

'It wasn't disturbing me.'

'That's because your head's in the clouds half the time.'

'It was embarrassing, Max. You were embarrassing.'

Max sighed. 'You can't do any better than that?'

'What about when you served dessert wine with the fish when Bob and Laura came round? Or when you fucked the tyre up by clipping that wall on the way to Surrey? That was expensive as well as embarrassing.'

'Why was that embarrassing? That wasn't embarrassing.'

'It was embarrassing because of your careless driving. Your carelessness was an embarrassment.'

'You know full well my driving had nothing to do with it. That wall was nigh on invisible, by the side of the road like that. Behind the turn. Under the bush. We could have sued.'

'This is so typical, Max. You just can't ever accept that you've made a mistake.'

'I'm perfectly willing to admit when I've made a mistake. But I don't see why I should say I've made a mistake when I haven't made a mistake.'

There was an acrimonious pause.

'You know what *is* really embarrassing, Max?'

'I've got a feeling you're going to tell me.'

'The fact that you've never once in your life admitted that you've done something wrong. And it's even more embarrassing that you never get embarrassed when you make a fuck-up. That I find truly embarrassing. And so would you, if you had even a modicum of self-awareness. Which you don't.'

Max, as their conversation gathered animosity and momentum, had started to feel like a spectator. Here was the globe, scarred by war, fouled by inequality, blemished by the ugliness of industry, modernity, technology, and the cruelness of nature underlying it all; here were the little chips of land called Britain; here was the seething bearpit of London; here was the M25, cobbled with vehicles; here was the jam; here, his own car; beside him was his wife; behind him two children. Here was the magic tree, dangling from the mirror. Here was the logo, coined in the centre of the steering wheel. Here was the car seat. Here was his body. And within that he crouched, confused and tiny and alone, looking out.

Why was he behaving like this? He, who prided himself on his high-mindedness? And how could he explain this visceral hatred he felt towards his wife? He had long admitted, to himself at least, that he no longer wanted her. They shared the bonds of circumstance – they had a joint mortgage, joint car, joint child – and once, before the darkening mists of time descended, they had experienced something that could be called love. But now it was duty, nothing else. It came in two parts. Number one: he had promised never to leave her. Number two: the responsibility for Carly was on his shoulders. His own father had worn his responsibilities lightly, and shrugged them off the first time they were tested. And the decades that followed had proved beyond doubt his mistake. Max would never do the same. Number three: despite everything, he was determined to be a good man.

What would Ursula say if he were to just turn away and pull out a book? He should do it. He should simply pull out a paperback and begin to read. But he didn't have a paperback. Either way, he wished he was the sort of man who, cognisant of his wife's anger, could concentrate on a paperback. He had tried it in the past, not with a paperback but with a magazine, managed it for one sentence, for two. But he had never even made it to the end of the paragraph. No, his emotions were not his own.

How long could he live with this conflict inside? How many more nights would he have to endure before he could lay his head on the pillow knowing that he would sleep easily, and through the night? Ursula was talking to him now. He could hear her as if from a great distance, as if through a wall of water. She was trying to return them to the conflict. To their natural state. Had she really suggested that they borrow a phone from a stranger? Why was he so resistant to the idea? Was it simply because Ursula had come up with it? Perhaps his reaction had been knee-jerk. Perhaps it demonstrated his lack of trust in humanity. He had to admit, if only to himself, that should some poor soul knock on the window of his Chrysler asking to borrow something – a phone perhaps, or something equivalent given the fact that his phone does not have a signal – that he would, out of hand, refuse. And that Ursula, in contrast, would be magnanimous. Perhaps she was, as he had suspected all along, simply the better human being.

Now that he had started a confession, he might as well admit, to himself at least, that he was quite relieved to have missed the marriage guidance session. Would it be going too far to suggest that he was glad of this traffic jam? Perhaps. But only just. Either way, his chances of avoiding the next one were slim.

And of course, he was aware that underpinning it all was a single issue. No, not a single issue; a single woman. That was wrong – the games words play! A *married* woman. She was on his mind all the time, from the moment his eyes peeled open in the morning until they lowered at night. And throughout the night. He confessed to himself that he missed her terribly, even though they had met, in secret, only last week. And the married woman's name – the name that was driving him crazy – was Nicole.

Night had fallen profoundly now. All ambiguity had faded from the sky. Ursula rested her head against the window, feeling numb and dead like a puppet.

Waitrose Jim

Max slammed the car door behind him and looked around. He was trembling. He took a deep breath; the night air had cooled, it entered his lungs like a balm. Another deep breath, a third, and he was better composed. He made his way along the long lines of traffic, negotiating wing mirrors and half-open doors with awkward rotations of his hips. Most of the engines were quiet now, and the few that still grumbled were sending wispy smoke signals into the atmosphere. He glanced into cars as he passed them, hoping for a friendly face. Everybody seemed to be groping their way towards sleep. Many dozed already; many gazed listlessly into space, trying to make themselves vulnerable to sleep's approach. All were emotionless. He walked on.

At times like these, it was his habit to remind himself of his wedding speech, as if to conjure up the love that had expressed itself then. He still knew parts of it by heart: how they had met through a mutual friend, all those years ago. How he had fallen head-over-heels almost overnight, how he had even given up a trip to Spain with the lads for her. They had loved it, the wedding guests. And now he tried to remember it, as if, like some ancient amulet, the recollection of that previous man's emotions could ease his suffering now.

The previous night, Carly had been unable to sleep. After more than an hour of comforting – for Ursula had given up – he had lain beside her on her bed, his hand on her fragile shoulder, and waited as the room darkened, its shadows multiplying into a smothering thicket, and her breath slowed into that particular rhythm of sleep. And he had been struck, all at once, by the imperfections of the days of his life, of everyone's lives, all sullied by concerns about the past, about the future, insecurities and angers and unrequited passions, while the moon shone on and the breeze passed unheard above the trees overhead. And he had remembered the members of his family who were gone, realised how rarely he thought of them now. And he had thought that his heart would break.

Night clung to his shirt in the sour streetlight. The people in their vehicles seemed so remote; they might as well be waxwork dummies, seated there for effect. He was just about to return to the car, when he caught somebody's eye. It was a delivery man, clad in a uniform, skirting the Waitrose van. The man paused, looked about to bolt, then smiled weakly. Perhaps it was his obvious consternation that infused Max with a sudden courage.

'Awful, isn't it?' said Max. 'I've never seen anything like it.'

The man nodded, sweeping his eyes along the cars and into the distance. 'We're all going to be late now, like,' he said. 'Thousands of us. Hundreds of thousands, like. Think there's a million here?'

'No. Not a million.'

'Think it's solid the entire way round the M25? The whole sort of ring?'

'Doubt it.' Max sighed. 'The volume of frustration that's building up, it's enough to fuel a rocket to the moon.'

The man laughed nervously. 'I was just checking that the back doors are locked,' he volunteered, as if trying to slip an explanation in under the radar. 'I'm like that, me, having to check things all the time.'

'I know what you mean,' said Max. 'I'm a bit like that myself.'

They fell awkwardly into companionable poses.

'Do you know what the problem is?' said Max.

'The radio said it was flooding, I think,' said the man.

'Flooding? But it hasn't been raining.'

'Don't know, mate. There hasn't been much on the radio. Difficult to get reception here, like. Bit of a black spot. I've buggered all my timing anyway. I'm supposed to be doing three more drops tonight. But instead I've just got to sit here and stew.'

The man was short, much shorter than Max, with the kind of face that seemed to cling to its skull, as if in a strong wind. His uniform hung sacklike on his frame, and his eyes were two sparkling pebbles; the voice was high-pitched, constricted. Max thought he must be forty; a bachelor, probably, for he wore no ring. Imagine, sitting in a jam like this for the sake of someone else's shopping.

'Sorry,' said the man, 'didn't offend you, did I?'

'Offend me?'

'Christ, I did, didn't I?'

'What? How?'

'When I said . . . you know . . . the b-word, like.'

'What b-word?'

'Black spot. God, I'm cringing.'

'Black spot? Why should I be offended by that?'

There was a difficult silence.

'What time is it?' said the man.

'Nine,' Max replied. 'I hope this isn't going to last all night.'

'No way,' said the man. 'It'll clear in an hour, max.'

'How did you know my name?'

'What?'

'My name. Max.'

'Oh, I see. No, I meant it will clear in an hour, max. Maximum, like.'

'Ah. Sorry.' Max chopped his heel into the tarmac. 'I just want to ask you a favour. My wife and I have somebody else's little girl in the car, and we need to tell her parents about the hold-up. But neither of us have any signal.'

'Somebody else's little girl,' the man repeated.

'It's completely above board. Completely,' said Max, aware

that his protestations were implying the opposite. 'She's a friend of our daughter's. We've taken them out for the day.'

'I see,' said the man. 'So what do you want from me?'

'Just to . . . to borrow your phone. Just for one minute. It was my wife's idea. I'll pay you. Sorry. This wasn't my idea. Sorry.'

The man turned and climbed into the cab of the van, where he slid across to the passenger seat and began to rummage in the glove compartment.

'I do have a mobile, somewhere,' he said over his shoulder. Max peered into the cab and saw that the door of the glove compartment had broken, and needed to be propped open.

'Do you want me to hold it for you?' said Max.

'If you wouldn't mind.'

Slowly, and without expertise, Max levered himself into the van. Instantly he found himself surrounded by a familiar fug of bodily odours, stale exhalations, and the suggestion of fried food and beer.

'Can't seem to find the bugger,' the man said, as Max held the glove compartment open. 'I was sure it was in here somewhere, like. Work's not going to like this . . .'

'Oh, don't worry,' said Max, 'please. Don't go to too much trouble.'

The man continued to search, cursing with frustration. Max asked him to stop – then implored – but no. This had become a matter of honour. In the end, however, the man had no option but to admit defeat.

'Sorry mate,' he said. 'Pain in the bloody arse, that's what it is.'

'You're very kind,' said Max. 'I appreciate it. What did you say your name was?'

'Waitrose Jim,' said the man.

'Waitrose Jim?'

'That's what they call me. It's not my real name, like. I mean, Jim's my real name. Not Waitrose.'

'I see.'

'Because I work too hard, like.'

'Right.'

'And you're Max?'

'That's right,' said Max. 'Max King.'

'Good name.'

'Thanks.'

'Sorry I couldn't help,' said Jim. 'It's bollocks that. If this goes on any longer, what you want to do, I reckon, is walk up that hill. Give it a go up there. Reckon there's reception up there.'

'Looks like a bit of a hike to me.'

'You could do it. If you're desperate, like.'

'Yes, I suppose I could. Though I'd be rather reluctant to, just for the sake of James and Becky.'

'James and Becky?'

'The parents. Awful people.'

'Right.'

A silence filled the van. Max found that he had no wish to move. Jim seemed contented just sitting there. Like a confessional, Max thought.

'It's a bit frustrating,' he said. 'My wife drank the last of the water a couple of hours ago. There's nowhere for us to go to the loo. Apart from in the bushes, and we're really short on tissues. None of us had a proper supper. And with two kids in the back . . .' He shook his head. 'Anything could happen out here.' He glanced at Jim, gauging his response.

'Sorry, mate,' said Jim. 'I can't go opening the van up, even in a situation like this.'

'Oh God, I wasn't suggesting that.'

'Can't say it hasn't occurred to me, like. It occurs to me all the time, truth be told. Driving round all day with piles of groceries in the back and that. Samosas, pork pies, chocolate, croissants. Milk, Coke, beer. Brie. Pasties. The works, like.'

'That's all back there?'

'Tip of the iceberg, mate. It's a right torture, having it all there all the time, having to deliver it to these swanky houses and that.'

'But you've never opened it?'

'No, mate. Devil's work, like. And I ain't going to start now.'

There was a pause. Max looked out at the traffic. All these people with mouths to feed, places to be, people they loved, enemies they hated, problems, futures, pasts. If he threw away what he had, could he join them?

Jim rummaged under his seat and pulled out a ripped cardboard box. 'Crisps,' he said. 'And Coke. I always keep a little stash in the front. Take some. To see you on your way.'

Rhys, Chris and Monty

'Oi-oi,' said Rhys, over the noise of the radio. 'That black bastard came away with a stash of fucking crisps, didn't he? And a Coke.'

'What?' said Chris, his brother.

'There. See him?' They peered out through the windscreen of the white van, straining their eyes against the orange-bleached darkness.

'Reckon there's any more?' said Chris.

'Course there is. It's a fucking supermarket van, innit? Bound to be full of stuff.'

'We'll be moving soon, I reckon,' Monty interrupted. 'We'll stop at services and stock up.'

A police car whined into view then shot past them, siren blaring; as one, they turned their faces away until it had disappeared.

The three men sitting shoulder-to-shoulder in the front of the van – the two brothers, the comrade – felt trapped. This was how it was: however action-packed today had been, they were all to start work early tomorrow. They had been hoping to wind down with a few drinks at the boozer in Newham before bed. A debrief. That wasn't going to happen now, was it? Fucking traffic.

'Weren't bad today, eh,' said Rhys, the older brother, for the umpteenth time. 'The boys left their mark and no mistake, eh?'

'Fucking great, bruv, fucking great,' replied Chris. 'Kings of the town. The pigs couldn't get anywhere near us.'

'Didn't get a scrap in, though,' said Rhys. 'Got to get a scrap in soon, innit. It was kicking off everywhere, but we were nowhere near. Sod's law, eh? Been too fucking long.'

Chris nodded, like a sage in a school play. 'Too fucking long,' he repeated.

Rhys stretched out his fingers as if taking stock of his hand span. They were outlined against the windscreen, which was framing a sweep of twinkling scarlet lights on the rear bumpers of cars, stretching off into the distance; thousands of little cars and big, hulking lorries, a Hindu elephant parade. 'Fucked off with this traffic,' he said, hitting the dashboard with the heel of his hand. 'Fucked off with it. Overcrowded fucking England. Just look at this shite. This lot'll be claiming fucking Jobseekers tomorrow morning and all.'

For a while they sat without saying anything. Music hung dully in the air. Chris pulled out his iPhone and resumed a game of Angry Birds. All day he had been facing a tricky level, which had pockets of green pigs in far-flung parts of the screen, all of which were to be destroyed with just four red birds on the catapult.

Monty, the third man, the driver, passed his hand across his face. Look at this shite, he thought. Got to be back on the site at six tomorrow. Can't be late. Gaz thought it was important that he didn't lose touch with the foot soldiers; a good general, he said, leads from the front. Personally, Monty didn't think it was worth it; he didn't think anybody noticed either way. They would love him or hate him, the foot soldiers, on their own terms, regardless. And he tired easily, that was his problem. The other leaders seemed to be able to go on for ever. But he had less stamina. He got hungover easily, and was inevitably exhausted two hours before the end of the working day. Anyway, he had more going on than them. In the past month alone he had visited groups in France, Germany and Norway. It was exhausting; it was all he could do to hold it together. And for what? This endless, petty struggle against the sweeping waves of history? He saw Rhys with his outstretched hands, and looked down at his own fingers. The whorls and creases were picked out in white paint from the week before, still not off. All busted fingernails. Shite life this is, he thought. Shite life.

'I reckon,' said Rhys, 'we should pay that van a little visit.'

'You what?' said Chris, not looking up from his phone.

'A visit. You know, mate. Get the bloke to give us some stuff. Like he did with that black cunt. It'd be a laugh.'

There was a pause. Chris looked up from his game, and appeared to turn the idea over, a smile spreading across his face.

But it was Monty who spoke into the silence. 'There's only going to be shite food in there,' he said hesitantly.

'Shite food? That's a Waitrose van, mate. That's posh, that is.'

'But it's not hot, is it?' said Monty.

'Hot?'

'You know, hot. Proper hot grub.'

'Course it ain't hot.'

'Exactly. I reckon we should send Chris off to find a Macky D's.'

Chris, hearing his name, and wishing to make it clear that he didn't have anything against anyone, flipped them both the bird, jovially. But he didn't look up from his game.

'Not a bad idea,' said Rhys. 'I reckon you should fuck off and find a Macky D's, Chris.'

He looked up. 'Why me?'

'Why not you?'

'Nah, man. We should toss a coin or something.'

'Look, bruv,' said Rhys, 'you could do with the fucking exercise.'

'Come on . . .'

'Plus,' said Rhys, 'you'll be quick. You can sniff out a burger three miles away.'

'I ain't going nowhere,' said Chris. 'What if the traffic moves?'

'You'll just have to be quick, then,' said Rhys. 'Large Big Mac meal for me, bruv, with a Coke. And an apple pie. And make sure you get enough fucking ketchups this time.'

'Same for me,' said Monty. 'But I want two apple pies. And extra cheese. And barbecue sauce.'

'All right, same here, bruv,' said Rhys. 'Two apple pies, innit. And all that. Plus onion rings.'

Chris looked bewilderedly from one to the other.

'Get going, go on,' said Rhys. 'Or we'll be gone by the time you get back.'

'Give me the dosh then.'

'We'll pay you back,' said Rhys. 'You've still got that twenty quid on you, haven't you?'

'Yeah.'

'Use that then.'

'You'll pay me back?' said Chris. 'You swear?'

'Course, mate. Now fuck off. Quicker you go, quicker you'll be back.'

Chris looked from his brother to Monty and back again. Then he heaved his bulk out of the van, closed the door carefully, and lumbered off.

'Mind if I kill the radio? There's nothing on about the hold-up anyway,' said Monty. 'We've been listening for ages.'

'Whatever, bruv,' said Rhys.

Monty did so and the vehicle assumed a cavernous, morgue-like stillness: no music, no engine, no shuddering vibration in their bones. No human voice.

Rhys rummaged in the scarred glove compartment and found his cigarettes. They wound the windows down and smoked. Monty picked up the paper, which they'd all read several times today – they'd agreed on her tits, a seven or eight – and turned to the sports pages.

Rhys broke the silence. 'Wonder what the fuck's going on. Accident or what?'

'Accident probably,' said Monty.

'Nina'll be wondering where I am.'

'Oh, Nina tonight, is it?'

Rhys laughed. 'Yeah.'

'Give her a call, then.'

'No signal, mate. Can't be fucked to piss about.'

They smoked, listened to the sizzle of the cigarette paper burning down.

'Surprised you didn't get a scrap in, Monty,' said Rhys, after a time. 'Must of been plenty of chances what with your experience, innit?'

'If it's not there, I won't look for it,' said Monty. 'No point doing it for the sake of it.'

'There is, mate,' said Rhys grimly. 'Defenders of England, innit. Show them who rules our fucking streets.'

'Yeah,' said Monty, folding up the newspaper and tossing it onto the dashboard. 'But if I got banged up it'd be a disaster. The pigs'd start nosing into my business and all sorts.'

'Don't be a cunt, Monty. You're a big-balls with the boys now. You can't be dicking around worrying about your own skin. You got to be setting an example to the young 'uns, innit? People without fucking jobs, without fucking money. People like Chrissie-boy . . .'

'Anyway, I did have a scrap, didn't I?' said Monty quietly. 'I did have one.'

'You had a scrap?' said Rhys.

'Yeah.'

'Go on then,' said Rhys sceptically. 'Dark horse.'

'Well, it were when we got separated,' said Monty. 'Remember?'

'That were only for twenty minutes.'

'Long enough, mate.'

'Why didn't you say nothing?'

'Don't need to, do I?' said Monty. 'Got nothing to prove.'

'Go on then,' said Rhys. 'How many did you scuff? You obviously came out all right, innit? Not a scratch on you.'

'It weren't as simple as that,' said Monty. 'It were, like, you know, chaos.'

'Course it were,' said Rhys. 'It weren't like a duel or nothing, were it? Or the fucking Queen's fisticuffs.'

Monty fell silent. Rhys waited for him to respond; when he didn't, he snorted and stubbed out his cigarette in the van's ashtray. After a moment, Monty did the same.

'We'll be here all night,' said Monty. 'Must be an accident. A spillage. Or a shooting or something.'

'And we ain't got nothing to eat or drink,' said Rhys. 'Going to run out of fags soon. Imagine what's in that fucking van. Just imagine.'

'Chris'll be back in a minute.'

'Come on, let's do it. Go over there, tell the cunt to open it or we'll cave his fucking head in. What's he going to do?'

'The chopper's still up there, mate. Police chopper.'

'Paranoid prick.'

'I told you, Rhys. I got to be careful.'

'That van's an Aladdin's fucking cave, mate. There'll be all sorts in there. Booze. Fags. Condoms.'

'What the fuck are you going to use a condom for?'

'Dunno, bruv. To shit in.'

'What?'

'That's what the fucking SAS do, innit.'

'Shit in a condom?'

'Yeah, man. So they don't leave a trail.'

'Fuck's sake.'

'Nah, man. Whatever. But condoms are fucking expensive. Be prepared, innit?' Rhys laughed.

'The pigs'd be here in no time, I'm telling you.'

'It's all posh food in there, innit?' said Rhys. 'Posh food for fucking posh cunts. Even the delivery men got to be posh.'

'How do you know?'

'Never mind how I know. Prick.'

There was a pause.

'What's wrong with you, Rhys?' said Monty.

'What's wrong with you, Monty?' said Rhys. 'You're a pussy.'

'Bollocks.'

'Bollocks, bollocks. The pigs this, the pigs that. Never mind the pigs, bruv. What about the boys?'

'You don't get it, Rhys. I got given responsibility. There's a lot I'm doing.'

'Bollocks.'

'Nah, mate. If I got banged up, the demo next month wouldn't happen . . .'

'Course it would. Prick.'

'Whatever.'

Monty picked up the newspaper, put it down again.

'Anyway,' said Rhys slowly. 'About that scrap today.'

Monty sighed. 'It were one of theirs,' he said. 'Got separated from the rest of the pack. Down this side street. Raghead. A couple of lads spotted him and started getting stuck in. He weren't bad though, gave as good as he got. The two lads were backing off. So I had to have a go, didn't I?'

'And you got him, did you?'

Monty nodded. 'Sorted him out something proper. Didn't even need to go back to the van for the toys.'

'Probably still there, the cunt,' said Rhys. 'Scum on our fucking English streets.'

A cloud came over Monty's face. 'It were self-defence, though,' he said. 'The bloke had this bit of piping, innit? Like an iron bar.'

'You're talking bollocks now.'

'Bollocks, bollocks,' said Monty. 'I sort of got it under my arm and smacked him like that. You know, over the top. Nobody came back for him, neither. Least, I didn't see no one. He were just left there, fucked, on the pavement.'

'Let's see the knuckles then,' said Rhys.

Monty eyed him warily, then held up his hands.

'Them are old, them grazes,' said Rhys. 'From the site and all.'

'Bollocks they are.'

'Yeah, look. That's a scab, innit? That's a scab and all.'

'I scab over quick, all right?'

'I'll say you fucking do.'

There was a pause.

'We could sort it out here and now,' said Rhys, dreamily. 'You and me. Nobody's about. Nobody would know. We could go up into the woods up there and sort it out.'

'What?'

'Man to man,' said Rhys. 'Queen's fisticuffs. Pass the fucking time.'

'Don't take the piss,' said Monty.

Rhys lit another cigarette. He didn't offer Monty one, and Monty didn't ask.

'Looks like we'll be here for a bit,' said Rhys. 'There's still time. If you change your mind.'

Monty looked out of the window. Outside, darkness had unfurled like a shroud. Cars were everywhere, dull and unmoving. There were lots of expensive vehicles on the road, no doubt about that. The one next to them, a Chrysler, probably cost a packet. Wouldn't look at it twice, but what – twenty grand? At least. A family in there, probably. What wouldn't he give to have a family like that? To drive your kids around in a twenty-grand Chrysler? Normal, that's what it was. Not for him. He rested his forehead on the glacier-cool glass. He saw his own reflection, his own eyes looking sadly back at him, windows into his soul. I'm fucked, he thought. Fucked.

'Fuck me,' said Rhys. 'Look. That black bastard's going back to the van now. Loads of people are there now, innit? That toff van.'

'Go on then,' said Monty. 'Nothing's stopping you.'

'I will,' said Rhys. 'Once I've finished this fag.'

Monty turned his face away. He couldn't hear properly, as if he were underwater; Rhys's voice sounded muffled and remote; the world seemed eerily fuzzy. What would his father say if he could see him now? Through the window he could see a woman in one of those microcars, the ones that could be parked side-ways. He could see her shoulder, blanched by the dull glare of the motorway lights, and a cascading mass of blonde hair. He felt a stab of pain. The darkness was deepening, he noticed that, growing like a fungus, like someone changing the contrast on a telly. Must be the exhaustion. He closed his eyes.

Stevie, Dave and Natalie

After Max had gone, Jim sat for a few minutes in the cab of the van, looking through the windscreen at the darkness, thinking about nothing at all. A breeze passed into the cab through the open door. He was tired; it had been a long shift, and the traffic just compounded the exhaustion. If this lasted all night, he thought, and he didn't return home until daybreak, who would notice? Answer: nobody. Next Thursday he was supposed to be playing chess with Warren, and the following weekend he had promised to visit his mother. Apart from those two social engagements, his days stretched out before him in a chessboard of work – spent mainly on the road – and leisure time, which he passed by himself.

But he was not unhappy, or he did not think he was. He had grown used to it. The job appealed to him because it was simple; he was not one of those delivery men who built up, over time, relationships with the customers. He did his job, delivered the groceries, and left. On the road it was just him, his van and his thoughts. All the normal things – intimacy, marriage, friends – had passed him by almost without him noticing. He had expected these things to just happen, as they seemed to just happen to everybody else; only they never just happened to him. It has always been just his work and his home, a static routine. One day he had looked about him and found that he had fallen into that twilight land of the disenfranchised, the shadow people. And now, gazing out at the thousands of individual cars sitting nose-to-tail all along the motorway, he was reminded acutely of this.

He levered himself up from his seat and positioned himself on the step, with his legs stretching out of the van and the soles of his trainers on the tarmac. It was uncomfortable, but sometimes one needed discomfort, a contrast with the soft stuffiness of the van. He reached under the driver's seat and pulled out a small Waitrose bag, folded to form a rough oblong. This he unfurled, and a packet of cheap cigars and a lighter gleamed in his hand. He didn't smoke as a regular habit, but he kept the equipment on standby for times like these. Carefully he unsheathed a single cigar and put the rest away. Then he lit up, closing his eyes to savour the instant hit, the musky, bitter-sweet fumes brushing the taut skin of his face. I could get the sack for this, he thought, as he always did.

It was when the cigar had burned down to half its size, and Jim was contemplating going for a piss, that he noticed three figures coming towards him, weaving their way around the vehicles. He drew his legs into the van, huddled into the cover of the open door, drew secretively on the cigar. But it was him they were after. They stepped awkwardly into view and hailed him with wavering smiles. They looked like students: two young men with remarkably messy hair and teenage slouches, accompanied by a black girl with plaits. Had they singled him out?

'Hey, man,' said one of the boys in a loud voice. 'What's up?' He peered forward excitably, his eyes like marbles in the half-light.

'Nothing,' said Jim. 'Just sitting it out. Same as everyone else, like.'

'Yeah,' said the boy. 'Shit, isn't it? Shitty shit shit.' He was smiling stupidly.

'Any idea what the hold-up is?' said Jim.

'No. We've just been chilling.'

'I asked Twitter,' said his friend. He had a fringe that was swept diagonally across his forehead, obscuring one eye; he kept tossing it to the side like a colt.

'Twitter?' repeated Jim.

'Yeah.'

'Find out anything?'

'Apparently it's floods.'

'Weird it isn't raining, like,' said Jim.

'Someone else reckoned it's an accident,' said the boy with the fringe, 'though that could have been a joke.'

'A joke?'

'Yeah. You know.'

Jim didn't. He took a long drag on his cigar. Beneath the smell of the smoke was another, barely perceptible aroma that these kids had brought with them. He couldn't put his finger on it. A smell from another time.

'Where are you from?' he said.

'Mars,' said the lanky, glazed-eyed boy. 'No, Uranus. Uranus.' He giggled. 'No, man, we're students. Sheffield.'

'Right,' said Jim.

'I'm Stevie,' the boy said, 'and this is Dave.' The other boy tossed his hair.

'Is the girl with you?' said Jim.

'Oh yeah,' said Stevie. 'That's the sket.'

'Sket?'

'Just joking around. That's Natalie. She's from the year below.'

The girl gave a small, self-conscious wave.

'Want a cigar?' said Jim, despite himself.

'A what?' said Stevie.

'A cigar, like. This, look.'

'Is that a real cigar?'

'Course. Only a cheap one, mind.'

'I thought they were proper fat and shit.'

'Don't have to be. Though I'm not an expert.'

'We don't smoke,' said Dave, pinning his fringe back, briefly, with his hand.

'Not tobacco, anyway,' said Stevie, and they both laughed. And Jim recognised the smell.

'I'll try one,' said the girl.

'She's up for anything, she is,' said Stevie.

Natalie leaned into the cab to receive the cigar, and Jim lit it for her.

'Don't inhale, love,' he said.

'Don't inhale?' she said. 'What's, like, the point in that?' Behind her, Stevie was making little mocking noises.

'If you inhale, you'll know about it,' said Jim. 'Just hold it in your mouth, like, and just puff it out.'

They caught each other's eyes for a brief moment.

'You all right, love?' said Jim.

She nodded and stood back. 'It's like . . . it's like burnt chocolate?'

Stevie made a grunting noise that seemed to embarrass her, and fell about laughing. Dave joined in, uncertainly.

'Talking of that,' said Stevie, 'we were wondering. You're a delivery van, right? For Waitrose. Waitrose.'

'That's right,' said Jim, pulling on his cigar.

'Is that cigar thing from Waitrose?'

'Yeah.'

'What about them crisps and shit?'

'What crisps?'

'Over there.'

'Where, here? Oh, they're just empty packets, like.'

'But they're from Waitrose, are they?'

'Yes.'

'I suppose you get all free shit from Waitrose, eh?'

'Sometimes.'

'OK, cool. Christ, I've got terrible munchies.'

Before Jim could reply, his attention was stolen by another figure appearing out of the gloom.

'Sorry,' said Max.

'That was quick,' said Jim.

'Yeah. The missus has conked out now – she gets terrible insomnia, so it's best to let her sleep when she can – and I couldn't face sitting in that car any longer. I saw these guys here, and I thought I might ask them . . .'

'Ask us what?' said Stevie.

Max avoided their eyes. 'It's just,' he began, 'Christ, this doesn't get any easier. Look, I've got someone else's kid in the car.'

'A kid?' said Stevie.

'She's a friend of my daughter. Look, it's all totally above board.'

'I thought you meant a goat and shit,' said Stevie, and laughed.

'So what I really need to do is call her parents and let them know she's safe. Right? Only my phone has bugger-all signal. Fucking piece of shit.'

There was a pause while everyone waited for somebody else to fill the silence. In the end, Max passed a hand across his face and, though he knew there was no hope, took the plunge. 'OK, can I borrow someone's phone? I'll give you some money for the call.' He looked from one to the other.

'Not mine,' said Stevie cheerfully, with a strange contortion of his gangly frame. 'Mine's in the car. Probably got no signal, either,' he added. 'Black spot.'

Jim glanced warily at Max.

Dave shrugged. 'Likewise,' he said. 'Plus my battery's dead.'

Natalie rummaged in her pockets and pulled out a battered phone with a crack across the screen. She turned it on, and her face was up-lit by a white glow. Then it went dark again.

'Sorry, mate,' she said. 'Nothing.'

'Are you all right?' said Max. 'You're shivering.'

'It's nothing,' she replied. 'I just, like, feel the cold.'

Max felt that odd pang of identification. He never normally felt black. Not with a capital B, anyway. 'Would you like my jacket?' he offered.

'No, no, I'm all right.'

'You're shivering. Here.'

He glanced back at his car – Ursula could just be seen in the passenger seat, still asleep – and swung his jacket across Natalie's shoulders. Dwarfed, she wrapped it around her body like a dressing gown; he saw her, then, as a child, trying on the clothes of a parent. She hasn't got a father, he thought.

She sniffed. 'Think I might be getting a cold or something.'

'Oh, I've got the munchies sooo bad,' said Stevie.

'Me too,' said Dave, tossing his hair. 'I could munch my way through a whole supermarket.'

Jim finished his cigar and scuffed it into the motorway. The boys were watching his every move.

'Look,' said Max decisively. 'This man can't open the van. He can't get anything out of it.'

'Why not?' said Dave.

'He just can't,' said Max.

'That's right,' said Jim.

'But it is full of stuff and shit?'

'I don't know,' said Jim.

'What do you mean, you don't know?' said Stevie. 'It's your van, isn't it?'

'Look,' said Max, 'just drop it, OK? You're not getting anything out of this van, and that's final.'

'Don't see what it's got to do with you,' muttered Dave.

'What's that?' said Max.

'Nothing,' said Dave, adjusting his fringe. 'It was nothing, OK?'

Natalie sneezed. 'I'm going back to the car,' she said. 'I'm, like, frozen solid.' She took off the jacket and handed it back to Max.

'Come on,' said Stevie. 'Let's get back for another toke and shit.'

He walked off along the line of cars, prancing and laughing. Without a word, Dave went after him. Natalie gave Max a half-wave and followed them into the darkness.

Max shook his head. 'I never thought I'd say this,' he said, 'but young people today. Makes you worry for your own kids.'

'There was something . . . going on with them,' said Jim. 'Something wasn't right, like.'

'They were off their heads, that's what. One of them was, anyway.'

'I know,' said Jim. 'But there was something else.'

'Do you have kids, mate?'

'Not me. Would have liked to. That's life.'

Max put his hands on his hips and stretched his back. 'What a night. What . . . a . . . night. This traffic really is the absolute limit.'

The wail of another siren stood up tall on the horizon, then a police car shot past on the hard shoulder, followed by two more. Silence returned, and Max noticed that the helicopter had gone.

Jim shook his head. 'It's like,' he said, 'I can't describe it. It's like . . . it's like . . .'

'What's like what, mate?'

'I don't know. It's like living in a computer. That somebody else is controlling. Know what I mean?'

'What is?'

'Life, mate. Modern life.' He reached into the van and brought out the pack of cigars. 'I'm chain-smoking now,' he said.

Max hesitated, then accepted and placed one between his lips. 'If this isn't the right night for a smoke,' he said, 'I don't know what is.'

Shahid, Kabir and Mo

It was not long afterwards – their cigars were still alight – that the feeling arose in both men that they were being watched. Neither of them said anything, but their skulls were prickling, and they started scanning their surroundings. Max caught the eye of a tired-looking man, seat reclined, curled up against the window of his silver Golf, trying to sleep; the man, protecting his privacy, turned his back. Many people were trying to sleep now. One or two were reading, and lots were playing with their phones. Some, even now, were standing next to their cars, trying in vain to catch a glimpse of the obstruction. Everything was as one might expect. But the feeling of being watched was unshakable.

'Hey,' said Jim, 'what's that?'

'What?'

'Thought I saw something moving, that's all. Over there, like.'

'I can't see anything. It's difficult to make anything out. In this light.'

'There, there it is again. See it?'

'What?'

'Someone's coming. I think.'

'Just your eyes playing tricks on you.'

'Is your car locked?'

'My car? Yeah, I think so. Yeah, it is. Ursula was asleep, so I locked it.'

They continued to look in that direction for several minutes, while their cigars burned down. Eventually, simultaneously, they shook themselves to their senses and stubbed them out.

'I've got the willies,' said Jim. 'Freaking myself out, like. Feels like the end of the world.'

'Come on,' said Max. 'It's not like *The Road* or anything.'

'It is. It's the sodding M25.'

'No, I mean the book. *The Road*.'

'I've never read a book, mate. Not outside school, anyhow.'

'It was made into a film too.'

'*The Road*?'

'Yes. Apocalyptic disaster sort of thing. Man and a boy.'

Jim thought for a moment. 'Nope.'

Then there was a noise, and they turned to see three hooded men emerge from the shadows. As one, they straightened up.

'All right, brah?' said the leader.

'All right,' said Max.

'Know what's going on?'

'No. You?'

'Nah.'

The three men spread out in a semi-circle around the van door. Max saw that they were Asian, and in their late teens. The one who was speaking pushed his hood back from his head; he was taller than the other two, with what seemed to be a habitual haughtiness.

'This your van?' he said.

'It's mine,' said Jim. 'At least, it's my job to drive it.'

'How much do you want for a Coke?'

'What?'

'A Coke, brah. A Coke.'

'For Christ's sake,' said Max, 'he can't open the van.'

'He's the driver, isn't he? No point in having a guy who can't open the door, innit?'

'Look,' said Max. 'The van cannot be opened, and that's final.'

'All right, mate,' came the reply. Then, after a pause: 'I'm Shahid.' He extended his hand, and his grip was firm. 'This is Mo, and this is Kabir.'

46

'Max. And Waitrose Jim.'

'What Jim?'

'Look, just – just Jim.'

'Nice one. OK, I hear what you're saying, right. But we got to help each other out, you know. Times like these.'

'It's a traffic jam,' Jim said. 'We've just got to sit it out, like.'

'Yeah,' said Shahid, 'but we've been here for what, two hours? Three hours? It's not a joke no more. People need food and stuff. Water. All that.'

Jim shrugged. 'There's nothing I can do. I'd lose my job.'

'Really?' said Shahid. 'Even if it was, like, extreme? If we were here all night or whatever?'

Jim hesitated. 'I'd lose my job.'

'Anyway,' said Shahid, 'we should, like, work together. Anything we can do for you boys?'

'There is, actually, now you come to mention it,' said Max. 'Think you could lend me your phone.'

'You got no phone?'

'No signal,' said Max. 'Dead.'

'Mine's no good, brah,' said Shahid, pulling out his phone. 'You can try it if you don't believe me.'

'Sure, sure.'

Shahid gestured to his companions, who brought out their phones.

'I ain't got a signal either,' said Mo.

'Me neither,' said Kabir.

There was a pause. The world tightened around them like a noose.

'What about that?' said Shahid, pointing at a small orange box mounted on a pole with a telephone painted on the side. 'Tried that?'

'It's only for emergencies,' said Jim.

'This is an emergency,' said Max. 'I might be able to find out what the hell's going on. You never know.'

'You two go and check it out,' said Shahid. 'We'll watch the van.'

'Thanks,' said Max. 'I don't need anyone to hold my hand.'

He walked around the van, squeezed between two cars and made his way across the hard shoulder. On the way, some instinct told him to check his own mobile. He did so, and although there was no telephone signal, the 3G sign was appearing; he could send an email. Forgetting everything else, he composed a hasty email to James and Becky, copying them both in, and pressed *send*. Relief. He looked back: Jim and the three boys were still watching him.

'Got a signal then?' called Jim.

He shook his head. 'Only 3G. Only email. Not great, but at least it's something.'

'Check the BBC site,' called Shahid. 'They might have something about it.'

Max tried, but this time he could not find the exact angle at which he had been holding the phone, and the 3G eluded him. He shrugged, walked over to the phone box and held the receiver to his ear. He tapped the receiver against the box a few times, and listened again. Then he hung up, checked his mobile – still no signal – and walked back.

'Dead,' he said.

At first, nobody spoke.

'Something big must've happened,' murmured Shahid.

'Bollocks,' said Max, 'it's just a dead emergency phone. Don't tell me you're actually surprised.'

'I don't know,' said Jim. 'The whole thing creeps me out.'

'This is England, mate,' said Max. 'Nothing works in England.'

'Where you from?' said Shahid.

'Ealing. You?'

'Belsize Park, brah.'

'Belsize Park?'

'Yeah.'

'I used to live near there. Down the hill from the station, you know? Towards Chalk Farm?'

'I know.'

'You live with your parents?'

'Yeah. It's on the Northern Line, so it's good for my dad's job.'

'What job?'

'*Guardian.* Executive editor. Or some shit.'

'Oh, right.' There was a pause. 'London,' said Max. 'It's a curse. My wife is always talking about moving out to Cheshire or Hampshire or Kent. But something in me can't do it. I'm like some sort of abused woman.'

'You're London's bitch,' said Shahid.

'You said it,' Max replied. 'London's bitch.'

'What about trying the others?' said Jim.

'The other what?' said Max.

'The other emergency phones. They're all along the motorway.'

'That's a point,' said Max. 'But I don't think I can be bothered to go on a massive mission. And I don't want to leave the kids.'

'I'll go,' said Mo. 'Need a piss anyway.'

'I'll come with you,' said Kabir. The two boys jogged off along the motorway, leaving Max and Jim alone with Shahid.

'Cigar?' said Jim.

'Can't,' said Shahid.

'Can't?' said Jim.

'Not allowed. Training. Football.'

'Are you a footballer, then?'

'Trying to be.'

'Where do you play?'

'Wing usually. Sometimes up front.'

'No, I mean who do you play for?'

'Long story,' said Shahid. 'Who do you support?'

'Nobody, really,' said Jim. 'I'm not into football, like.'

49

'I used to support Liverpool as a kid,' said Max. 'Steve McMahon? Bruce Grobbelaar? Alan Hansen? Ring any bells?'

'Alan Hansen,' said Shahid. 'Isn't that the commentator geezer?'

'Yeah, that's the one,' said Max. 'But he used to be a player. Great defender.'

'Lies,' said Shahid. 'A player? Alan Hansen?'

'Yeah.'

There was a silence. Jim lit another cigar.

'That smells nasty,' said Shahid.

'It is a bit,' said Jim. 'That's sort of the point.' He blew a thin jet of smoke horizontally in front of him and watched as it dispersed gradually in little feathered clouds. For a moment he fancied that a face appeared in the smoke, a female face with hair pulled back into a rough ponytail. Then the smoke cleared, but the face remained.

'Hello,' said the woman. 'Sorry. Can I . . . are you . . . any idea what the hold-up might be?' She was slim and pale, with dark smudges under the eyes and an oversized woollen jumper that reached almost down to her knees.

'We've heard various theories,' said Max, after sizing her up. 'Crashes, flooding. That sort of thing.'

'A chap further down said he thought it was a terrorism thing,' said the woman. 'Have you heard anything about that?'

The men exchanged looks.

'If that was the case we'd know by now,' said Jim. 'It'd be all over the news. Someone would come and tell us. A police officer, like.' At this, Max and Shahid scoffed.

Max glanced over at the Chrysler, craning his neck. Through the windscreen he could still see Ursula. Still asleep. Still in the same position. 'Where you from?' he said.

'London,' said the woman. 'Fulham. You?'

'Ealing,' said Max.

'Oh, I used to live in Ealing. Near the Broadway?'

'Not far. Between there and the North Circ.'

'Yeah, I know. Nice round there.'

'I was just saying I'd love to move out of London, in a way. But it's in my blood too much.'

'You've got to get out a lot,' said the woman. 'You can only survive in London if you get away on the weekend. My parents live in East Sussex, so I'm lucky.'

'That where you've been?'

'No, no. Wedding. Hence the fact that I'm rather . . . delicate today.'

'Must have had a good time, then,' said Max.

'Disaster, actually,' said the woman. 'Complete and utter fucking disaster. I completely humiliated myself.'

'I'm sure nobody will mind,' said Max. 'Everyone's a bit silly when they're drunk.'

'Trust me,' said the woman, 'I made a complete arse of myself. It was not funny in the least. At least, not to me.'

'I feel your pain,' said Max. 'I'm Max, and this is Waitrose Jim and Shahid.'

'I'm Shauna,' said the woman, glossing over Jim's nickname. 'How do you do?' Nobody moved to shake hands. With a quick flick of the wrists, Shahid flipped his hood up.

'So, where are you guys off to?' said Shauna. 'Not that anybody's off to anywhere, of course.'

'We're not together,' said Max. 'We've only just met in the jam. I'm on my way home. At least I was. I imagine you guys are as well, aren't you?'

The other men nodded.

'I can't wait to get home,' said Jim wistfully. 'When I was a kid, and we got stuck in traffic, my mum would let me press all the buttons on the dashboard and pretend the car could fly.'

'Are you with anybody?' said Max. 'Boyfriend or anybody?'

'No,' said Shauna. 'Just me on my lonesome.'

'Have a cigar,' said Jim.

'Um, no thanks,' came the reply. 'But I'll have a cigarette if you've got one.'

'Sorry,' said Jim.

'Oh well. So, do you think we'll be here all night?'

'Surely not,' said Max. 'You never get traffic jams that bad.'

'What if we are, though? It's been hours already. And it's getting cold. Loads of people won't have eaten. We'll all get dehydrated at the very least. I've a good mind to call 999. But I can't get any reception on my phone. It's a bit like that book, isn't it? That one with the father and son . . .'

'*The Road*,' said Max.

'That's the one. It's just like that.'

'Oh, come on. It's nothing like that. There are no cannibals here for one thing.'

'I wouldn't count on it,' said Shauna. 'If this carries on, and there's no chance of getting any food or drink, I wouldn't put it past people.'

'*The Road* has a happy ending, anyway,' said Shahid. The others turned to him, surprised. 'It's a shit ending, if you ask me,' he added. 'Just my opinion.'

'I just have this awful thought, I can't get it out of my head,' Shauna continued. 'We're on the M25, right? So it's circular. What if the entire ring road is solid? What if the traffic jam goes all the way round the M25 and joins with itself at the other end?'

'It can't,' said Max.

'Why not?'

'It's not logical. Look at the opposite lane. See?'

'It's deserted.'

'Exactly. That means that up ahead there's an obstruction that's crossing both sides of the motorway.'

'What's that got to do with it?'

'Think about it. If the traffic was solid all the way round, it would be solid on the other side as well.'

'I'm too hungover for this,' said Shauna, passing her hand across her brow. 'My head's killing me . . . and I'm totally out of supplies. No water, no painkillers, no olives . . .'

'Olives?' said Max.

'Don't you find they help? I always have a craving for olives after I've been drinking. I fantasise about them. Oh, olives!'

'It's the salt,' said Shahid. 'That's what your body needs. The salt.'

'You know what the best hangover cure is?' said Max. 'Watermelon juice and milk.'

'Not mixed together, surely,' said Shauna.

'Yeah, mixed together. It's great.'

'Oh god, that makes me feel ill,' said Shauna. 'Doesn't it curdle? Ugh.'

'I'm telling you,' said Max. 'The milk lines your stomach and the watermelon juice takes the heat away. Everything you need.'

'That's nasty,' said Shahid. 'What you need with a hangover is salt.'

'I agree,' said Shauna. 'Crisps would do, if olives weren't available. Oh for some crisps! And some olives! And some water!' Her eyes wandered to Jim's van.

'Before you ask,' said Max, 'He can't open the van for anybody. For any reason.'

'Sorry?'

'The van. It's a no-no.'

'Oh god, sorry. I wasn't even suggesting that,' said Shauna. 'I was just prattling on. Making conversation. Jesus.'

'No, no, no, I didn't mean it that way,' said Max. 'Sorry. I was just pre-empting any embarrassment.'

'You've done a good job of that,' said Jim. 'Christ, go on then. I've got a few things. Emergency rations, like.' He reached under the seat, pulled out several packets of crisps and a few bottles of Coke. They were received with cries of delight.

For a few moments nobody spoke, and the crunching of crisps and the hiss of Coke bottles opening filled the air. Then there was the sound of a door slamming nearby, followed by footsteps. All four looked up, mouths full: a wiry man in faded jeans and a rumpled T-shirt was swaggering towards them. One of his hands was running across the shaven dome of his head, and he was grinning. He was being doubled, trebled, stretched, warped by the car windows around him.

'Oi-oi,' said Rhys, fixing his eyes on the group. 'What we got here, then?'

Coke and crisps

Jim cleared his throat. 'Can we help?'

'You can, bruv,' said Rhys, a smile on his face. 'I want a packet of crisps for starters. A few packets. And a Coke.'

'Sorry, you're out of luck.'

'You what?'

'They were all I had. I'm all out.'

'Well, get some more, then.'

'Where from?'

'You got a whole van load there, innit?'

'I can't open it.'

'Bollocks. Where did you get this lot from then?'

'Look, mate,' said Max, in a voice not dissimilar from that he used with his daughter, 'this traffic is shit. We're all pissed off. But there's no reason . . .'

'I'm fucking starving, bruv,' said Rhys. 'You had a job lot earlier on and all. I saw you. Come on, relax. Spread the love.'

'Fine,' said Max. 'If you want some crisps, have mine.'

'No, mate,' said Rhys, 'I'm not touching your dirty, fucking, infected crisps. Or yours,' he said, jabbing a finger at Shahid. 'But I wouldn't mind hers.'

Before Shauna could react, he had scooped the contents out of her crisp packet and filled his mouth. She backed away several paces.

'Mate,' said Max, 'that was out of order.'

'Come on, bruv,' said Rhys, swallowing with some effort. 'It's only crisps, innit? We're all human. Now, what about your Coke, love? I'm thirsty now.'

The van door slammed again, and a man appeared through the gloom: tall, sinewy, vulpine face. Jumpily, he took up a position beside Rhys.

'Ah, Monty,' said Rhys, 'nice one. You didn't pussy out after all. Look, we're fair and square now.' As one, their eyes locked on to Shahid.

'Nobody wants any trouble, brah,' said Shahid.

'Who said anything about trouble?' said Rhys. 'I never said nothing about trouble. All we want is some food, yeah? You got a sense of humour, mate.'

'Rhys,' said Monty in a low voice. 'This ain't the time, mate. Let's get back to the van, yeah? It's been a long day. I don't want trouble.'

Before Rhys could reply, two hooded figures emerged from the night and flanked Shahid.

'What have we here?' said Rhys. 'Called for reinforcements?'

'They're not reinforcements,' said Shahid. 'They're my mates, innit.'

'Where've they been?' said Rhys. 'Having a fucking bacon sandwich?'

The Asian boys bristled. Monty placed both hands on Rhys's shoulders, as if giving him a massage. 'Come on, mate,' he said into his ear. 'Let it go. Save it.'

Nobody moved. Black shapes in the orange light, like insects locked in amber, they had nowhere to go; the jam had enforced a strange stasis on the world. Here was a place that could be accessed only by car, and only by car could one escape.

Shahid and Rhys both started to speak at the same time, and, strangely, each gave way to the other, leaving a fraction of a second of silence; and at that moment came the sound of a man calling 'Rhys? Monty? Rhys?' Monty, without taking his eyes off Shahid, yelled, 'Chris? Chris, mate. We're over here.' And through the gulley between the lines of stationary cars, carrier bags rustling, came Chris, a faithful hound, laden with burgers and chips and onion rings and apple pies and ketchups and Cokes.

'Fucking nice one,' said Rhys excitedly, 'fucking nice one.'

'Course, mate,' puffed his brother, wiping his brow with his wrist. 'Got the lot. And more. I was the last one in before they closed. Fuck-all else for miles.'

'And you been burning some calories and all, by the looks of it.'

'Come on,' said Monty, 'let's get back to the van. While it's hot.'

Like a child, Rhys abandoned his game in favour of food. He seized Chris's bags and returned to the van, one arm slung across his brother's shoulders. Chris was carrying his hoodie under his arm, and something was bulging underneath it. Monty hung back.

'Look,' he said, quietly, to the group. 'I'm sorry about him. He's pretty, well, excitable. And he has a weird sense of humour. Just don't provoke him, OK?'

'We didn't provoke him,' said Shahid in a thin voice.

Monty glanced around. 'Shit way to spend a Sunday evening, eh? Wonder what the hold-up is. Anybody know?' There was no response. He caught a glance from Shauna. 'You all right?' he said.

'I'm OK,' she said. 'That man's a nutter.'

'He's just . . . like that. Let me give you some money for the crisps.'

'No, no, honestly. Don't worry.'

'I'd like to. Here, a quid. Is that enough?'

'You should give it to Jim, really. The crisps all came from him.'

'You're shaking.'

'Sorry, it's . . . I'm a bit freaked out, that's all.'

'I'll keep an eye on him, OK?'

'OK.'

'I'm sure the traffic'll be moving soon, anyway.'

Monty looked around the loose semi-circle of faces, from face to silent face, seeing matching expressions of fear and disgust. He didn't want to go back to the van.

'Monty?' came the call. 'Monty! We're going to eat yours and all, you cunt.'

'I'd better go,' said Monty. 'You're sure you're all right?'

'I'm fine,' said Shauna. 'Thanks.'

He turned and disappeared into the darkness, a fish into the depths of the sea.

There was a universal exhalation of breath. Each of them put their crisps and Cokes together on the tarmac, as if making a pyre, as if they had become infected with some plague. Jim made way for Shauna and she sat on the step of the van, trying to suppress the trembling.

'Fuck me,' said Max. 'What is going on with this country?'

'You're not surprised, mate, are you?' said Shahid.

'I would have called the police,' said Jim, 'if I could.'

'The police couldn't have got through the traffic,' said Mo.

'Hard shoulder,' said Jim. 'But those blokes could come back any time. We'd better watch ourselves.'

'The emergency phones down there are dead too, by the way,' said Kabir.

'The whole system's down, innit?' said Shahid morbidly.

Shauna was sitting with her head in her hands, massaging her temples. Max glanced at Ursula; still asleep. He removed his jacket and slipped it over Shauna's shoulders.

'I'm fine, I'm fine,' she said. 'It's only a packet of crisps.' She drew the jacket around her.

'We'd have had a good chance,' said Shahid. 'That fat bastard wasn't worth nothing. And there's more of us than them.'

'It was only a packet of crisps,' said Shauna.

'You're all mouth now,' remarked Max. 'After the event.'

'Christ sake,' said Shauna. 'I keep saying, it was only a packet of crisps. That other one was all right, anyway. The tall one.'

'You're joking,' said Jim. 'He was worse. Sinister, like.'

'Oh,' said Max, 'looks like my wife's stirring. I'd better go.' He looked at the people around him, as if unsure of what to say; then, with awkward apologies, he removed his jacket from Shauna's shoulders and hurried back to his car.

Shauna

Half an hour earlier, before plucking up the courage to approach the little group by the Waitrose van, Shauna was sitting in her Smart car, in the middle lane of the endless lines of traffic, prodding out an email on an iPhone. She was still getting the hang of it; she was used to her old BlackBerry, which she would hold up to her face like a goblet, thumbs racing; but when she tried the same technique with the iPhone, the result was unintelligible. Even now, working slowly and methodically, her shoulders gibbous with tension, she was inputting error after error. It was like typing on a mirror.

'Dear Chloe and Seedie,' she typed, 'congratuoariojd on your wedding, which was Li dog. Have a super iknetmokn. I do hope to see you so on, when you get bCk to blights. I'll biby you both a oint. With all my liver, S x.' With all my liver? Biby you both a oint? Despite herself, she smiled. With all my bile, more like. For a moment she sat, the screen glowing in her palm like that piece of radioactive material in the opening sequence of *The Simpsons* that ends up in the collar of Homer's shirt by mistake, classic. She should just send it as it was, she thought, without correcting the typos. That would be true to form. Absurd. From now on, she thought, all of her actions would inevitably be seen as absurd. What a fool she had made of herself at the wedding. What a fucking fool.

Nevertheless, she went through the typos laboriously. And when finally it said, 'Dear Chloe and Seedie, congratulations on your wedding, which was lovely. Have a super honeymoon. I do hope to see you soon, when you get back to blighty. I'll buy you both a pint. With all my love, S x' she sent it. A mock aeroplane sound-effect accompanied it into the darkness. Or at least, into her Outbox. There was not a glimmer of signal to be had.

The worst thing was a hangover after a wasted night. Understatement. And she was cold. She removed her seatbelt – it sprang back with the enthusiasm of a puppy – and wrapped her caramel-coloured jumper around her body, snuggling into its folds. She had bought it on the King's Road last week, and it had become an indispensable companion. Generally, when other people felt hot, she was merely warm; when they were warm, she would be cold; and when they were cold, she was downright hypothermic. Her mother, her sister, certain of her friends, were always telling her to eat more, to 'pad out' and then she wouldn't be so cold all the time. But her friends didn't count. Her mother didn't count either.

Who did count though? Him. *He* counted, and his opinions. Who? Him. Hubster. She knew not what he would look like exactly, but she knew very well the feel of him. He would wear good quality shirts with crisp creases, shirts that smelled of a traditional cologne, not too musky, not too sweet; his chest would be hairy, but not his back, and the hair would form dark crescents along the contours of his muscles. His personality, she knew that too: he would be quick to laughter, quick to anger, quick to forgive and forget; he would be impulsive, the sort of man who on a dull Saturday morning would whisk you off to Venice; yet he would be dependable, the foundation stone on which a family could be built. He would be into cars but not too deeply, into his job but not too deeply. He would be a small-c conservative (she was willing to negotiate on this). He would be a lover of the great outdoors, and nights at home on the sofa with a bottle of wine, and non-fiction. He would be a reasonable dancer, not a babe-magnet. His voice would be booming and well-trained. This was Hubster. She could see his silhouette in her mind, though his face was always dark. He had to be out there somewhere. When he made his appearance finally, she would recognise him. There would be an instant connection. And his opinion on her figure would count.

And now this traffic! This was all she needed, a reminder of life in this accursed city. If she lived in a nice village in the countryside, or even a town or something, this traffic would be a thing of the past, only to be negotiated on her own terms, whenever she chose to take a trip to the Big Smoke to see friends or a play or a concert. The truth was, she was split down the middle, black and white, like an Othello counter. Could you still get Othello? Could you play it online now? Was there an app? She took out her iPhone but, not being able to face that fucking skiddy keyboard yet again, she put it back in her pocket.

Yes, she was split. Half of her wanted the life she had, and the other half wanted something altogether different. It was time for her life to enter the next phase, she felt that deeply. She was on the cusp; but unlike 'normal' people she had been on the cusp for years. Here lies Shauna Williams, she thought, who lived and died on the cusp. She was thirty-six, still living the same life as when she was twenty-four. She was even at the same law firm, fuck's sake, even that hadn't changed. Every day the same slog down to the City. Every day the same slog back to Fulham. Sure, she had more money now; she owned her own property, went on holiday at least twice a year, shopped on the King's Road most weekends, went out two, three times a week, would drink two hundred pounds of Krug in one fell swoop. One fell swoop: what was the etymology of that? She didn't pull her iPhone out of her pocket. She didn't even consider it. As it was she had a migraine. And there was no signal.

She rested her forehead against the steering wheel. It was the same temperature as flesh.

Life, she feared, was leapfrogging her. For years she had not questioned the way she lived. She had assumed that Hubster would make his appearance when he was good and ready, and when that happened she could flip the Othello counter once and for all; they would marry, she would get preggers, they would move out to the country; her former existence would be present only on Facebook, like some online ghost. Until then, she did in London what she had always done at Durham, at Bedales. Work, booze, dancing, casual flings, bacon breakfasts on hangover Sundays, shopping, the theatre, long novels read in hammocks in the garden in East Sussex, skiing trips plus sex with muscular Germans, villas in Morocco with friends. Horse riding. Yoga. *The Apprentice.* Lie-ins. In the summer, croquet and Pimm's (lots of). But now she was increasingly feeling that Hubster could do with making an appearance now, please. Yes, now would be nice. So that they could get on and move out to the country, and do what people are supposed to do. Pro-bloody-create.

To some extent, she blamed it on her schooling. Bedales was an ultra-progressive place, where students called teachers by their first names, were allowed to wear whatever clothes they wanted, and were encouraged to regularly bake bread; all the students and all the teachers would shake hands twice a week, which would take quite a while. It was fun, an optimistic and free-spirited time. But now she wondered whether perhaps it hadn't made her into an outsider. Whether, perhaps, happiness could only lie in empty-headed conformity. A horrible thought.

Or perhaps it was the fault of her parents, who had chosen to bring her up at arm's length rather than have her live at home, every day, with them. Who were concerned with her wellbeing enough to shell out extravagant school fees, but not to shell out much of themselves.

Her head was splitting, and she had no paracetamol. Her mouth was horribly dry, and she had no water. When would this traffic move? Hoping against hope she took out her phone, but then, without warning, the screen went completely black. She pumped the button, but to no avail. Stupid bloody phone. She sat up straight, looked around. Nothing but herself, her Smart car, and this crowd of machines pressing in on all sides, stretching out into the distance like some vast mechanical beach. Now she had no connection to the outside world. A frisson of panic rose in her, but then passed as quickly as it had arisen, leaving a fresh calmness, like the first light of morning. For the first time in ages – her yoga habit had died a quick and painless death – she became aware of the sound of her breathing, the rhythm of it. She felt still.

Shauna turned off the stereo – Frank Ocean had been playing at a barely perceptible level – there. If you're going to do quietude, you might as well do it properly. She was sitting in a car that now showed no sign of life. It might have died permanently for all she knew. A snippet of information swam into her mind: in a sandstorm one can survive by hollowing out the corpse of a camel and taking shelter inside. She had got it from TV, she thought, from some rugged survivalist type. It was absurd, but this car, cramped as it was, immobile as it was, yes, silent as it was, was her own hollowed-out camel. Yes, she was permanently absurd. She'd better get used to it. She had been trying not to think about it, but now she couldn't stop herself. The wedding.

It had been a lavish affair (she and Hubster would prefer something more discreet), held in the grounds of Chloe's father's house in Hampshire, following a ceremony at the village church. Vast marquees had been erected with drapes ballooning from a central point in the ceiling: one for the dinner, another for the bar, a third for a cloakroom. There were luxury portaloos too, which looked like they were made out of solid mahogany, and swarms of waiters and waitresses who seemed to be everywhere and nowhere at once.

The church was a beautiful old crumbling affair dating back to 1070, scarfed by a skewiff graveyard. When asked, she had been stumped for a moment, and had then answered 'bride'; she was (literally) ushered to a pew several rows from the front. By rights, she should have said 'groom'. After all, that was more accurate. But somehow she felt it would be inappropriate, even after all this time. After lengthy deliberation, she had decided to wear an off-the-shoulder cocktail dress in turquoise, with a fuchsia fascinator, clutch and Manolo Blahnik shoes. She had immediately regretted it. The colour contrast, which had seemed perfectly reasonable at the time, in these ancient surroundings felt gaudy, even obscene. She could feel people looking at her, and the song 'Raspberry Beret' was going round maniacally in her head, which was a bit of a disaster. When she fell prey to an earworm, there would be no escape for days. She smoothed her dress, made polite conversation, turned her phone off, breathed, breathed, tried to compose herself.

Just before the service started, she caught Seedie's mother looking at her. They exchanged nervous smiles; did hers appear as forced as it was? The mother – what the hell was her name? – looked older. Her hair, which had retained some of its blonde-ness ten years ago, was now pure white and cut in a shimmering bob. Her dress was gold, gold! Shauna laughed to herself nervously. Some of the old emotions were returning, as if they'd never left. There was Seedie, bathed in sunlight from the high windows, looking larger than life, sharply etched; his face was shading into an expression she had only ever seen when he was having an orgasm. He was scanning the congregation, but he didn't meet her gaze.

Suddenly the light left the church, as if somebody had sucked it out with a hoover. Shauna looked up at the stained-glass window; a glowering, black cloud had slipped in front of the sun, and it felt as if the whole of England had been cast into shadow. The air thickened. And, after all this time, she remembered the curse.

How could her hangover be worsening? This fucking traffic. A few cars along, she caught sight of an Oriental woman in a Prius. There was something horribly lonely about the woman, about this whole thing really. All along the line she could see men – not women, men – popping up like meerkats, half-in and half-out of their vehicles, hair ruffled as if just out of bed, gazing pointlessly into the blackness. Then she saw the Waitrose van, and a small group of people clustering around the open door of the driver's cab. And she decided it would be a good idea to join them.

Piece of meat

'Well, that was a great success and shit,' said Stevie, dropping back into the driver's seat and slamming the door. 'Operation Munchie. Way to go.'

'It was your idea,' said Dave.

'Bollocks it was,' said Stevie, laughing. 'Get some munchies from that van? Bollocks it was.'

'Whatever.' Dave began to scroll vacantly through Facebook on his HTC, and Natalie struck a lighter and applied the flame to the spliff. The tip glowed orange, then dimmed, then glowed again.

'After you, madam,' said Stevie, 'wouldn't mind a puff.'

'You're supposed to be driving,' said Natalie, coughing, 'you can't.'

'Just one toke,' said Stevie. 'We're not going to move for ages.'

'You don't know that,' said Natalie.

'You just want to keep it all for yourself,' said Stevie. 'Selfish sket.'

'Relax,' said Dave, pocketing his phone and taking the spliff from the girl. He was in an awkward position, twisted round in the front seat. His eyes were stinging. 'There's more than enough to go round.'

'I'm feeling quite sort of lean already,' said Natalie, flopping back in her seat. 'That's good blow. Where did you get it, Stevie?'

'Good blow, eh?' said Stevie, and laughed his wild laugh.

'It's different to the stuff we've been having so far, isn't it?' said Natalie. 'Tastes more tangy.'

'It's skunk, that's why,' said Stevie. 'We've been breaking you in slow. This stuff's strong as fuck. Off the scale. There's this bloke who comes round halls every couple of weeks and shit. Josie's mate, you know.'

'The little bloke?' said Dave. 'The black one? With the hair?'

'He has got hair,' said Stevie. 'If he's the one you're talking about.' He laughed again.

The car, an arthritic Ford estate splattered with mud, creaked with every movement like an old suitcase straining at the seams. It was full to the roof with backpacks, duvets, a rolled-up tent in a brightly coloured fabric tube and crates of beer.

'I can see the road and everything here,' said Natalie, bending over in a strange way, as if her head had become too heavy for her body. 'Through the floor.' She was shining a torch downwards. The others craned to see; sure enough, in a nook just under one of the front seats the rust had opened a hole the size of a thumbnail. She pressed her fingers into it and some fragments of metal flaked away. Now it was the size of a whole thumb, and the tarmac was clearly exposed.

'Hey, stop trashing my fucking car, bitch,' said Stevie in a high-pitched American accent. 'You're trashing my fucking car.'

More laughter. The spliff did another round or two before smouldering and going out. But the smoke remained in the vehicle, gathering around the ceiling in peaceful clouds. From the outside, wisps could be seen filtering through the cracks where the doors were not properly aligned with the roof, disappearing into the blackness.

'This traffic, Jesus,' said Stevie. 'It's actually not moving at all. I wonder what's happened?'

'Probably a smash-up or something,' said Dave. He pulled out his phone and opened up Facebook again. He wasn't online, but there was nothing else to do.

'A smash-up would suck,' said Stevie, still in a faux American accent. 'A smash-up would totally suck.'

Natalie, in the back seat, lifted her hand and placed it gently on the glass of the window. Then she removed it; a ghostly imprint remained, then faded. She did it again, watching as the condensation echoed her hand, dissolved. She did it again, and again. Then she sat back and gazed out of the window through half-open eyes.

'I hope she's not going to pull a whitey again,' said Stevie. 'I hate it when she does that. Natalie? Natalie?'

'What?'

'Don't pull a whitey. Don't leave us. Don't leave us alone. Don't leave us.'

'Leave you?' said Natalie slowly.

'Help me, Obi-Wan Kenobi. You're our only hope,' said Stevie. 'You, Princess Leia. I can see it.' He laughed and sat back.

It was complicated. They were friends from uni. Part of the same group of friends, anyway. All doing media studies. They had gone to the festival together. There were supposed to be more of them but everyone else pulled out, leaving just her, Stevie and Dave. And it had been fun, at least to begin with. No, no: it had all been fun, from beginning to end. They had seen some bands, drunk a lot, got stoned, watched the days haze by like a sepia film. As for the nights, there were parts she couldn't remember. But in the tent that the three of them shared, as the apple-green canvas shone in the torchlight like a lantern, white hands had slipped into her sleeping bag, followed by white arms, white legs, mouths. She had pretended to be asleep for some of it. For some of it she was unable to pretend. But she might as well have been; in the morning, when they awoke with sleeping bags twisted like silk-worms around them, nobody mentioned it.

Those cars were terrifying, all those cars, like a stream of refugees or something. Nobody was moving, but still every-thing was very much alive.

'We're like refugees,' she said, without really meaning to. 'You know, in this car. Like a family of refugees. Sort of, like, futuristic refugees. Alive but, like, not moving.' The boys were laughing at her again, but they seemed too distant and irrelevant for her to care. 'It's as if everybody is running from something,' she said. 'Only now we're having to wait to cross the border.'

Yes, it wasn't that it hadn't been fun, but Stevie wanted to keep at it and she felt she couldn't back out. Dave didn't seem bothered, it was as if he'd forgotten all about it, as if it hadn't happened. But Stevie – it was as if she owed him something now. It was his car, and his tent, even his rucksack she was borrowing, and now it was like she had to pay. It felt like he wanted to corner her or something. Trap her.

All those cars, look at them. It was completely solid now, as far as the eye could see. Before, like, a while ago, you could see movement on the motorway over the hill back there. But now it was just completely solid. Millions of tiny lights. She raised herself up from her seat, waited for the dizziness to subside, turned her head slowly to look out the windscreen, then out the back, again and again. She heard the boys laughing at her from very far away. It was amazing: red lights out the front, all white lights at the back. Swarms of red lights, swarms of white. Red, white, red, white. Cars and lorries. Vans. She sat back.

'She's out cold and shit,' said Stevie. 'The piece of meat is out stone cold.' He nudged her knee. 'She's a proper lightweight.'

'This traffic,' said Dave, updating his status as he spoke. 'This fucking traffic. Do you think there's been a prang?'

'More than a prang,' said Stevie, 'to have been completely shut down like this. It must have been shut down. Completely.'

There was a pause.

'Do you think we could get the piece of meat to perform?' said Stevie. 'Pass the time?'

Dave giggled. 'You dick. We'd get properly arrested. People can see through the window, you dick.'

'Look,' said Stevie, pulling a blanket off the back seat. 'We could get her under here, couldn't we? Bish, bash, bosh. '

'You're a nutter,' said Dave, 'as I've said many times before.'

'Come on, live a little,' said Stevie extravagantly. 'Nothing ventured, nothing gained, right? Who dares wins. She loves it, anyway. And a man could do with a bit of relief. Fucking bored. Captive audience.'

He fumbled in his pocket, pulled out his Nokia and cursed.

'What?' said Dave, smiling.

'Who you with?'

'Vodafone.'

'Cunts, the lot of them.'

There was a pause while Stevie, smiling conspiratorially, pressed some buttons. Then he held the device up, showing the screen to Dave, waggling it from side to side.

'That's a new one,' said Dave. 'You didn't text me that one. When did you take it?'

'Just last night, mate. Not bad, eh? I'm going to make it my wallpaper.'

'I thought you said you weren't going to take any more.'

'Not in so many words. Anyway, I couldn't resist. Make hay when the sun shines. Look at her there. Sexy as fuck.'

'Did she know you were taking it?'

'Course she knew.'

'Doesn't look like it.'

'It's not her phone, anyway. It's mine. It's up to me what I put on it. And I think she looks fucking hot in this one. Butters, but hot. What she got to complain about?'

Dave tried to piece this logic together, but his brain had lost its agility. For no reason he laughed, the noise peaking and then dying away. Then he gazed out of the window, unaware of the minutes as they passed. The world was muffled and spinning slightly, which he found amusing. It had been a strange trip, that was for sure. A strange, strange trip. Neither of them had expected to have Natalie land on their plate, so to speak – she had been up for anything, at least at first – and Stevie was picking up the ball and running with it. Dave, at times, found himself feeling sorry for the skinny little black girl with the oversized breasts. For all her posturing, she was unsure of herself. Still, they were nearly home. If this traffic would only clear.

Stevie wasn't a bad lad, just boisterous. They'd known each other since they were eight, but it was only at university that they had become friends. At school, it had been dangerous to be friends with Stevie. There's always one kid who attracts attention of a negative sort; Stevie was that kid. From the very beginning he was branded gay, teased mercilessly, often ended up bruised and sore on the floor of the toilet. One day the principal bully was caught in the act and expelled. Then the physical attacks diminished, but the best he could hope for was to be allowed to be on the outside looking in; often he was unable to do even that. And the names, of course, never stopped. Gaylord, Bumboy, Lord Anal. Refuses to talk about it now.

Dave rested his head back against the soft, soft headrest and felt as if he was sinking into a pool of feathers. He could see the driver of the car next door tilting back her seat. He could see a figure emerging from a car, stretching, craning his neck, getting back in. He began to wonder about something, but he couldn't take anything seriously. Piece of meat.

For some minutes his mind soared above the earth, images and thoughts passing through quickly, leaving no trace. Before the festival he hadn't smoked much, but now he felt like a pro. Life had another dimension to it: getting stoned. It was lovely. He loved it, it made him feel good. How could he have gone for so long without it? Like living without the ability to see. And this skunk was really something else. Slowly but surely, he fell into a fuzz.

'All right?' said Stevie.

Natalie heard his voice from far away. 'Fine,' she said, after a time. 'You?'

'You look pretty wasted. That shit must be good. You're a lucky sket.'

Natalie heard a girl's laugh, and realised it was her own. How strange. Nothing within her felt like laughing.

'You're a hot sket, you know that?' Stevie was saying. 'Have I told you that before? A hot sket.'

'Piece of meat?' she replied. But then she realised that she hadn't replied, she had just intended to, and she was unable to make her mouth speak.

'We've got some good times ahead,' said Stevie. 'Trust me, this has only been the beginning.'

Natalie's eyes were closed now, but she could nevertheless see Stevie in great detail; his tightly curling hair, waspish face, amber-coloured eyes; his white, white hands stained with a thicket of freckles; the quick way that his lips pulled back from his teeth into a grin; the Puck-like sense of mischief that surrounded him like a scent; the way that everything, every conversation, every gesture would turn out to be smacking of sex.

She was spiralling downwards in a velvety loop, falling into dead unconsciousness. Her parents were there, as well; her dad – a clammy-browed mechanic perpetually on the verge of collapse – and her mum, glamorous in a way that made up for her age. She saw them sitting at the kitchen table at home, arguing about the amount her mother was spending on shoes, about the hours her father was working. Both were second-generation immigrants from Barbados. Their fathers had both come to England to work for British Rail. Their families were intertwined almost inextricably; they were bound together by more than their personal affections; and such bonds, which were created as much by community as by love, were both profound and stifling. They were immensely proud that she had gone to university, but at the same time suspicious. This was the context in which she grew up. She still did not know who she was. The kitchen table vanished; the argument and its particulars vanished; her parents, too, spiralled off into the darkness. And she knew nothing more.

*

After a few minutes, Dave's power of hearing began to return, and he remembered where he was, and rose to the surface again. He wanted to tweet about being biffed, but was too biffed to do so. There was a strange sort of rhythm, a regular scraping noise. More than just a noise; the body of the car was moving gently to it. His head felt like a potato. He heaved it up and revolved it until his eyes were pointing at Stevie's seat. There was no sign of him. He instructed his neck to turn his head back and rest once again on the headrest, and for a moment he thought it had happened. But then his head was turning the other way instead – a movement on the back seat had caught his attention – and his arms were pushing his body up in his seat, and his spine was twisting, the muscles working like worms.

Stevie was sitting beside Natalie on the back seat. For a moment Dave saw only a scattering of colours, then things gradually became clear. The rhythmic scraping sound was coming from Stevie. His trousers were gaping like a gutted whale, and his penis was standing straight up. Dave could see it pale against his body even though he had made an effort to protect it from prying eyes by a blanket gathered around his waist. In his hand was Natalie's hand, which he was pressing palm-down against it, rubbing in a serious way, as if he was trying to get something done. Her arm was contorted awkwardly. Dave traced it up to the elbow and from there to her body. One of her breasts was clamped in Stevie's other fist. She was not moving at all. Stevie looked up and met Dave's eyes; he gazed at him levelly, but did not break his rhythm. He was breathing hard now. Dave looked back at Natalie. A strip of light lay across her face. Her eyes were closed, and her lips were slightly apart. Dave wheeled around and sank heavily back into his seat. The world was falling around him, falling, falling. He closed his eyes.

Outbox

'Can't you just put a sock in it?' said Max. 'You've been humming that same fucking ditty ever since you woke up.'

'What?' said Ursula.

'That ditty.'

'Ditty? What is this, the nineteen forties?'

'Ditty, jingle, whatever. That MP3 you've got loaded in your brain. That doo-doo-doo-doo tune. It's driving me out of my mind.'

'What bollocks you talk.'

'Surely you must know you're doing it.'

'Doing what? Humming?'

'Yes, humming.'

'I'm not humming, Max.'

'You are. You're doing it again and again. You've been doing it since you woke up. Ad fucking nauseam.'

'I'm probably just trying to get back to sleep. After you woke me up.'

'I didn't wake you up. You were stirring.'

'I woke up, Max, when you got back into the car. Like an elephant.'

'I'd had a stressful time out there, OK?'

'Stressful? Why?'

'Oh, it doesn't matter.'

'Fine.'

'Whatever. I just want you to stop that humming.'

'OK. I'll stop whatever it is you think I'm doing, if it'll make you happy. OK?'

'Fine.'

'But I think you should try and relax.'

There was a pause.

'And you're sure you emailed James and Becky?' said Ursula. 'You're sure? Because they'll be going frantic otherwise.'

'Of course I'm sure. I'm not an idiot.'

'They'll be frantic if they don't check their emails.'

'I copied them both in. You know what James is like with his phone.'

'Couldn't you have found a way of giving them a call?'

'There's no signal, I'm telling you.'

'Have they replied?'

'Not yet. I haven't got 3G in here, anyway.'

'But you're sure the email went?'

'Of . . . course . . . I'm . . . sure.'

A lava pool of rage welled within him. He tried to repress it like a cough, but it proved more than he could bear. He slammed his fist against the dashboard three, four times, then sat motionless.

'Shit, Max, get a grip. You're not going to turn violent, are you?'

For a long time he didn't move. Then, by increments, the whiteness of his knuckles as he gripped the wheel subsided into the palest of browns, then to a more normal colour. He raised his head, heavy on his neck, and looked at her as if she was a stranger. 'When did I ever hurt you?'

'You're out of control, Max. What's wrong? Just tell me.'

'Nothing's wrong. It's just this fucking traffic.'

'I know when something's wrong, Max. And something is seriously wrong. Why can't you just tell me?'

'Nothing's wrong. I told you.'

'Are you having an affair?'

'Don't be stupid.'

'Then why can't you tell me?'

'I have told you. It's nothing, OK? Nothing.'

'Jesus. You're such a fucking man.'

'Just leave me be, OK? I'm fine. Everything's going to be fine.'

She shook her head. 'I can't tell you how hollow that sounds.'

'How what?'

'Hollow.'

'Hollow.'

'Yeah.'

'I hurt my hand.'

'I'm not surprised. Are you over it now?'

'Don't patronise me, Ursula.'

A pause.

'How did we get like this?' she said.

'Like what?'

'You know what I mean.'

'I don't know.'

'At first I thought it was just the stress of having Carly,' said Ursula. 'On Mumsnet it seemed like everyone went through it. But then . . . I don't know. Things have changed.'

'So you're going to leave me,' said Max.

'I didn't say that.'

'But you are.'

She reached over and touched his arm once, with fluttering fingers, the way a mourner touches a gravestone. Then she looked away. 'Let's carry on talking about this another time,' she said, 'when we're not in a fucking pressure cooker. This traffic's enough to make anyone lose it.'

As one, they sat back. A pair of ambulances approached along the hard shoulder, their wails spiking then abruptly lowering in tone as they whipped past and rumbled into the distance. There was something absurd about them, Max thought. Penguin waiters on wheels. Weird image.

He drew breath as if he was about to say something, but then his sore hand slid off the steering wheel and he fell into a grim silence. A memory of Nicole slipped unbidden into his mind. They were in a deserted ante-room at the Basingstoke

Conference Centre; people could be heard passing by in the corridor outside; towers of metal and fabric chairs were stacked on either side of them. She was saying, how quickly do you think you could come in my mouth? Pretty quickly, he was replying, thinking it was a hypothetical question. And then she was on her knees, and her fingers were inside his trousers, and there was something in the act of a near-total stranger broaching his privacy, in this obscure corner of a public place, that turned him on unbearably. And something about the sight of her there, on her knees before him; and the way she never once broke eye contact, even as she was slipping him into her mouth, her eyes filled with faux innocence; this was the memory. It came into his mind like some delicious and evil gas, and he found rising through his body something he had never experienced before: a fiery hatred of Nicole, a hatred of Ursula, a hatred of every woman, and every man, every child, that had ever drawn breath and ever would. A hatred of himself.

From the back seat, movement could be heard. Ursula looked in the mirror. Carly was motionless and pure in the way that only sleeping children can be, a freshly minted child. Bonnie, however, was stirring, rubbing her eyes with fists covered in orange dye and granules of salt. Ursula leaned over.

'What are you doing?' said Max.

'She's going to get that crap in her eyes,' said Ursula, 'that crisp crap.'

'Don't. You're waking her up.'

'If she gets that crap in her eyes, we'll really know it.'

'Jesus Christ.'

'Bonnie,' said Ursula soothingly, trying to squeeze the tension out of her voice. 'Bonnie. There, there, now, Bonnie. We're in the car. It's all right.'

'Where's my mummy?'

'Your mummy's at home, and as soon as this traffic jam begins to move we'll take you straight to your mummy. OK?'

'I want my mummy.'

'I know, darling, and I'm sure your mummy wants you, and we'll get you home just as soon as we can. OK? Stop rubbing your eyes.'

'I don't want you, poo head. I want my mummy.'

'You'll see your mummy very soon.'

'Go away, poo head.'

'Bonnie, that's not a very nice thing to say.'

'I want juice.'

'The juice is all gone now, Bonnie.'

'I want juice. I want juice, poo head.'

Max passed a hand across his face and peered over the shoulder of his seat. 'Bonnie,' he said sternly, 'Ursula has told you. There . . . is . . . no . . . juice.'

'Max,' said Ursula softly, 'don't.'

'You're a fuck man,' said Bonnie.

'I beg your pardon?'

'You're a fuck man. You're a poo head. I want my mummy.'

'That, Bonnie, is unacceptable.'

'Max,' said Ursula, 'don't raise your voice.'

'We can't allow her to get away with that.'

'She's not our child.'

'I don't give a fuck. She's not getting away with that.'

'You'll wake up Carly.'

'You're a fuck head,' said Bonnie, 'you're a fuck man.'

'Let's just stick a DVD on,' hissed Ursula. 'Before she wakes up Carly. And teaches her how to say fuck.'

'Like she hasn't already?'

'I'm going to turn the TV on, OK? Bonnie, darling, please stop rubbing your eyes.'

'No, Ursula. We agreed there'd be no more TV.'

'Oh, don't be so fucking holier-than-thou. She's not even our child.'

'Exactly. Even more of a reason not to. God, that whinging is doing my head in.'

'Max, I am sure Becky would not mind if we allowed her daughter to watch a DVD. In extremis.'

'Let's ask her then. Oh no, we can't. No signal.'

'Don't be sarcastic. Bonnie! Stop crying. Stop rubbing . . . Now she's waking up Carly. Right, I'm giving her some TV.'

'I don't agree with it. You don't have my support.'

'Max,' she said, 'give her your phone.'

'I'm not giving that child my phone.'

'Max. Just do it. Just do it.'

'I'm not doing it.'

'Have you got something on there you don't want me to see?'

'Don't be stupid. She'll break it.'

'No, she won't. She'll only be playing Angry Birds or something. And all your data's backed up, anyway, isn't it? Come on. We're in extremis.'

Max, realising that he was cornered, pulled out his phone and thrust it at the wailing child in the back. Bonnie's cries faltered, then abated; she took the phone and started to prod at the screen. Equilibrium was restored. For now.

'What did we use to do when we were kids?' said Max. 'When we were stuck in a traffic jam? We didn't have televisions staring at us from every conceivable surface. We didn't have fucking iPhones. We had I Spy. We had Count The Red Cars. We sang songs.'

'You want to sing 'Little Bo Peep' with Bonnie for the next five hours?'

'She could read a book or something.'

'We only have one book.'

'Well, then. She could look out of the window.'

'Right. Well, I'll leave it all to you then. Good luck.'

From the back seat, Bonnie began to wail again. Max groaned.

'What is it now?' he said.

'Not working,' said Bonnie.

'What's not working?'

'Poo head iPhone. And my eyes hurt.'

Now Carly was stirring, scrunching up her face and making a noise like the mewing of a cat. Max plucked his iPhone from Bonnie's grasp. Somehow, she had managed to turn the handset completely off. He held down the button on the top and the Apple logo appeared.

Carly opened her eyes. 'I want TV,' she mumbled.

'Jesus H. Christ,' said Max.

'I want the iPhone,' said Bonnie. 'I want TV. Fuck head.'

'Right!' shouted Max. 'Both of you shut up! Shut up! I want total silence! Total silence, OK? Silence.'

At this, both of the girls began to wail.

'Oh, well done,' said Ursula. 'That was handled brilliantly. Absolute top-class parenting. Top-class.'

'Oh, put a fucking DVD on then,' said Max. 'Just switch the fucking thing on and be done with it.'

'It's too late now. You've set them off.'

'It's not too late. Here. I'll fucking do it. What do you want? Disney? Fucking Little Fucking Mermaid? Beauty and the Fucking Beast? Here. I'll do it. Here.'

Both screens lit up with a toxic blue light, both displaying the logo of a magical castle with a shooting star arching above it. The two weeping children were bleached the colour of an early morning sky, and began to settle down. Music filled the car, a cheerful, bouncy tune that was interrupted every couple of bars by a sound-effect, the noise of a spring, or a chuckle, or a comedy crash-bang-wallop. Max looked in the rear-view mirror, and was sure he could see in Bonnie's tear-filled eyes the unmistakable expression of triumph.

'I can't take this,' he said, 'I just can't fucking take this.'

'Max,' said Ursula in a dangerous voice.

He looked over; she was scrolling through something on his phone. His heart leaped into his mouth, and he made a futile grab at the phone.

'You bastard,' she said, handing the handset back to him. 'You fucking bastard.'

Here we go, he thought. The time has come. Drawing a shuddering breath, he looked at the phone. But, to his surprise, there was nothing from Nicole on the screen. Instead, Ursula had been looking at his email outbox. There, unsent, was the email to James and Becky.

'You told me you'd sent it!' said Ursula, raising her voice above the noise of the cartoon. 'James and Becky will be going absolutely spare!'

'Shit,' said Max, 'it must have got stuck in my outbox.'

'You said you were sure it sent!'

'I was sure. I am sure. I mean . . .'

'Did it not occur to you to check?'

'I'm sure I checked. This is really weird.'

'Christ almighty, Max. I ask you to do one thing . . .'

'Fine,' said Max, 'Fine!' I'll go back out and borrow someone's phone. OK? I'll find someone. I'll humiliate myself again. OK? OK?'

'You do that,' said Ursula, 'and make sure you tell James and Becky the reason why it's taken so fucking long for us to get in touch.'

Max heaved himself out of the car.

'Don't say anything rude,' said Ursula after him. 'Don't be arsey. Don't ruin things for me. They're nice people.'

Without a word, Max slammed the door and stalked off into the night.

Popper

On someone's suggestion, the little group relocated to the hard shoulder. Jim locked the van before going with them, and sat on the motorway barrier facing it so he could see if there was any foul play. Shauna perched on the barrier too, and Shahid sat in front of them on the tarmac. Mo and Kabir had wandered off a little way along the road, kicking a stone. There they sat, the four of them, scratching the ground with pebbles, kicking up grit, biting their fingernails. And talking.

'I just don't get it, brah,' Shahid was saying. 'We could be having a party right now.'

'I don't know what's so complicated, like,' said Jim. 'It's not my van, is it? It's not my groceries.'

'Come on,' said Shahid. 'Nobody thinks like that.'

'Course they do.'

'Look, mate, you got to open your mind. You got to think, innit. Waitrose are this massive company. They're taking over the High Street, pushing independent retailers out of business, and making billions of quid. And it's people like you who are doing all the work. What are they paying you?'

'That's not the point.'

'What are the fat cats getting at the top of the tree?'

'That's not the point.'

'Do you think their massive profits would be damaged one bit if we all had a party with the stuff in the back of the van? Do you think it would make any difference at all?'

'That's not the point.'

'So what is the point, then?'

'The point is I'm an honest man.'

'That's not honesty, brah. That's naïveté. It's people like you that maintain the status quo.'

'Proper little lefty,' said Shauna. 'What does your father think?'

'Don't matter what he thinks, brah.'

'What's with this brah business, anyway?'

'Brah, you know. Brah, bruv, bruvver.'

'Do you call your dad brah?'

'No . . . look . . . shut up, OK? We're talking about the van, blood. Mate. We ain't talking about me, or my dad.'

'He's at the *Guardian*, isn't he?'

'God, I wish I'd never told you that. You're bare jarring me.'

'Jarring you? What?'

'Whatever. Getting on my tits.'

'That one I've heard.'

There was a pause. Then Max appeared, his thunderous expression fading as he greeted them.

'What have you been up to?' said Shauna.

'Just, you know. I managed to find an old boy down there who had a signal. I borrowed his phone, but the number was engaged. I've been trying for ages.'

'What number?' said Shauna.

'Oh, sorry, I thought I'd mentioned. We've got our daughter's friend in the car . . . oh, fuck. Trust me, you don't want to know.'

'We're going to be here all night,' said Shauna.

'Surely not,' said Max.

'Do you think it's safe?'

'You're thinking about those nutters?'

'Amongst other things.'

'I wouldn't worry about them,' said Max. 'Thinking about it now, I reckon they were all bark and no bite.'

'So how much do you reckon it costs to produce, say, a typical bar of chocolate?' said Shahid.

Shauna groaned.

'I don't know,' said Jim, wearily. 'Thirty pence?'

'Nah, man. Less than three pence.'

'So?' said Jim.

'And what are they selling it for?'

'I don't know.'

'Anything from sixty pence to a pound.'

'Your point is?'

'That you should open the van, mate. That's my point.'

'Look, Shahid,' Shauna interjected, 'you've made your point, OK? This isn't going to get us anywhere. Can we now have a bit of peace and quiet?'

'You're the one who's worried about staying here all night,' said Shahid. 'There might be something you'd want in there. I don't know. Alka-Seltzer.'

Shauna shook her head. Max had stepped over the barrier and was walking off. He approached the orange emergency phone, tried it again, played with the connection and the receiver, tried again. Then he pulled out his mobile phone and held it at various angles. At first nothing. Then, suddenly – there, 3G! No, it's gone. Yes, it's back! It's back! Swiftly, he opened the fateful email to James and Becky and made sure it sent, holding his phone at an angle of thirty degrees to the ground. Then, leaving the receiver dangling, he returned.

'Seems like the world's stopped,' he said. 'There haven't even been any emergency vehicles for ages. Managed to send an email, though. Thank fuck.'

'This is awful,' said Shauna. 'Nobody comes, nobody goes. It's awful.'

'We don't even know what we're waiting for,' said Jim. 'It's weird. We don't know why we're here, and we don't know what we're waiting for.'

'I know what I'm waiting for,' said Shahid.

'For fuck's sake,' said Shauna, 'will you give it a rest about that van?'

Shahid rolled his eyes and fell silent.

Shauna massaged her temples and rotated her dry tongue inside her mouth. What she wouldn't do for a bottle of water!

It was then that she noticed a figure getting out of a silver Golf GTI, several cars back, and walking in their direction. She had not noticed the car before; there was no reason why she should have. But when she caught sight of its driver, she saw the GTI in a new light: as an expression of disguised wealth.

Because the driver could be measured at a glance. Clothes: black gilet, checked shirt, jeans, trainers. Hair: longish. Nose: strong. Forehead: broad. Cheeks: ruddy. Little finger: signet ring. A quiet confidence of bearing, at once chummy and commanding. Assertive in his modesty, haughty in his politeness, impenetrable in his impression of candour. In the gait, a controlled muscularity. In the gaze, a can-do practicality, underpinned by the impression of homely bonhomie. All this her practiced eye took in immediately. Here, at last, was a known quantity.

'Evening,' he said as he drew within range, 'I don't suppose I could ask a massive favour? It's just that the lighter in my car is broken and I'm desperate.' He waved a cigarette like a conductor's baton.

There was a moment of silence as the group, so recently and randomly formed, regarded him suspiciously.

'I've got one in the van,' said Jim at last.

'Oh, that's your van, is it?' said the man.

'It is. And I'm not opening it.'

Jim got to his feet, rubbed his behind, and walked heavily over. It was eleven o'clock now, and he was tired. He'd be in bed by now, easily, on a normal night. When he arrived at the van he looked around and thought he could see a thousand eyes glinting from cars. But what could he do? When he opened the door, he was sorely tempted to lock himself in, try to get some sleep. But he felt that this would somehow be an immoral act; some primordial instinct told him that he needed to stay with the group. Was Shahid right? Was he just a cog in the machine? Being exploited? Had his mind been conditioned to think only inside the framework of oppression? Was he an idiot? He supposed that he was. He retrieved the lighter and sat for a brief moment, gathering his strength to return.

Shauna accepted the hand that was stretched amicably in her direction. It was large, spade-like, rough as sandstone. The man's smile lingered, as did his eyes.

'Popper,' he said. 'Tom Popper. They call me Popper, or Pops. Sometimes Poppy. How do you do?'

'Shauna Williams,' said Shauna, holding his gaze. But etiquette demanded that he turn his attention to the other members of the group.

'Tom Popper.'

'Max King, pleased to meet you.'

'A great pleasure . . . Tom Popper.'

'Shahid Anwar.'

'A pleasure.'

'Yeah.'

Jim lumbered into view, the lighter cupped in his hand. In response to the newcomer's request, he introduced himself; then he struck the flame and offered it. Popper's face was, for an instant, illuminated by a whitish glow as he brought his cigarette to life; then the clouds of darkness passed across it again, punctured by the cigarette's orange tip. Jim sat once again on the motorway barrier, and Popper sucked gratefully on the tobacco.

'Thanks so much,' he said. 'You've absolutely saved my life.'

'Where are you from, Popper?' said Shauna.

'I live in Pimlico,' he replied. 'But my parents live in Oxfordshire. You?'

'Fulham.'

'Ah, yes. Lovely part of the world.'

'Can't compare to Oxfordshire.'

'True. But then if you lived in Oxfordshire you'd have a bugger of a journey to work, I'd have thought.'

'Of course. Sorry. I'm feeling a bit worse for wear. I've just come back from a wedding.'

'Enough said.'

She laughed, and it sounded new in her ears. Popper looked at her strangely for a moment, and she stopped laughing. Then he drew on his cigarette and said, 'This is a really random question, so apologies in advance. But you don't happen to know someone called Hodgy, do you? Harry Hodgkinson?'

Shauna's face went hot, then cold, then hot again. 'Hodgy? Foreign Office?'

'That's the man.'

'Yes. I mean, no. We met at the wedding. Briefly. God, what made you say that?'

'Just that he was at a wedding this weekend as well. I had a hunch.'

'That is a weird coincidence.'

'It is, isn't it? Degrees of separation and all that.'

'This is uncanny.'

They looked at each other as if trying to untangle some obscure conundrum of the universe. Then Shauna noticed something about Popper that she hadn't seen before. A darkness about the eyes, a slight rheuminess, an exhaustion. Not just the tiredness of a late night or a hangover; an existential tiredness, a tiredness of the spirit, as if something was draining him.

'So,' he said, sucking hard on his cigarette, 'anybody know what the bloody hell's going on here?'

'I have no idea,' said Max, with feeling.

'I heard it was something to do with a herd of deer attempting to run across the carriageway,' said Popper.

'That's a new one,' said Jim, a mocking tinge to his voice.

'It was flooding,' volunteered Shahid. 'Or a pile-up. Or both.'

'Well, whatever it is,' said Popper, 'I predict that we're in it for the long haul.'

'What do you mean?' said Shauna.

'You know, the long haul. The night.'

'No. Surely not.'

'Why not?'

'I just can't. I need water. I need paracetamol. I need my bath and I need my bed.'

'Well put,' said Popper. 'You never know, it might move sooner. I tend to have a rather pessimistic outlook.'

'I don't know what we'll do if we're here all night,' said Jim.

'It would be easy if you just opened that fucking van,' said Shahid. 'You're bound to have all sorts in there. It'd make spending the night easy, innit? With all the kit.'

'Who knows what's in there, anyway?' Max interjected. 'Jim's probably at the end of his delivery round, this time of night. The van's probably empty. Isn't it, Jim?'

The hesitation in Jim's response was all that was needed to reveal the truth.

'Well,' said Popper diplomatically, 'at least we know it's there if push comes to shove.'

'It's not there if push comes to nothing,' said Max. 'It's off-limits, OK?'

'Of course, of course,' said Popper. 'I completely agree with you. I think we'd all agree with you there, actually. I was just talking . . . in extremis.'

'In extremis?' said Max.

'Yes,' said Popper. 'I'm sure that in cases of emergency, his employers would permit him to distribute the necessary supplies.'

'I was stuck in the snow once at Golders Green Station,' said Shauna. 'A few years ago. It was late at night, and I'll always remember that the Costa Coffee shop stayed open and gave everybody free drinks.'

There was a pause. Popper extinguished his cigarette butt on the ground. 'Anyway,' he said, 'let's not think about the worst-case scenario. We might all be home within the hour. Two hours, perhaps.'

'The problem is,' mused Jim, 'that if I gave out a couple of things to people in crisis – and kept a record of everything, of course – then everybody else in the traffic jam would see it happen and demand handouts too, like.'

'That is a problem,' said Popper. 'I wonder if a solution might be found? Can you access it from the inside?'

Jim thought for a moment. 'I've never used it,' he said, 'but there is a little hatch thing, like.'

'And people could carry things away . . . subtly.'

'Suppose so.'

'Well, then,' said Popper. 'There we are. Now let's say no more about it.' While the other members of the group gradually digested this game-changer, Popper turned the conversation to other things. 'Funny how groups of people are thrown together at times like these,' he said. 'People who'd never normally mix together.'

'Tell me about it,' said Shauna. 'Did you see the guy who came over here earlier? Nutter. If it wasn't for his friend there might have been trouble.'

'It has been a weird night,' said Max. 'Really weird. We had three students over here just before you guys arrived. They were wasted.'

'Really?' said Shauna. 'Wasted? In a traffic jam like this? That would do your head in.'

'I keep thinking about them,' said Max. 'There was a girl with them, a black girl. Can't remember her name. I got the feeling she was in well over her head.'

'How do you mean?' said Popper.

'Couldn't put my finger on it, really,' said Max. 'Just seemed out of her depth.'

'Wait,' said Shauna suddenly. 'What was that?'

The group looked around them. Out of the orange-washed gloom came a tall figure.

'All right?' he said.

They all nodded warily.

'Popper,' said Popper. 'Tom Popper.'

'I'm Monty,' said Monty, giving his outstretched hand a cursory shake.

Monty, thought Shauna. So that's his name. Monty.

'Know what the hold-up is?' said Popper.

'No idea, mate,' Monty replied. 'Look, I can't stay and chat. I just wondered if I could borrow a fag. We've run out, and Rhys is desperate for one. I thought it would be better . . . well, you know, better if I come over. Rather than him.'

'I have some cigars . . .' said Jim tentatively.

'He's welcome to one of mine,' said Popper. 'I've got lots of duty free in the car.'

'Are you sure?' said Monty.

'No problem. I know what it's like to be desperate.'

'You'd be saving us all a lot of grief.' Monty's gaze fell on Shauna, and as it did so, they both felt something surge within them. 'You all right?' he said.

'Fine, thanks,' said Shauna. 'You?'

He nodded. 'Shame about the circumstances,' he said.

'My car's just down there,' Popper interjected. 'Come with me.' The order was authoritative, as if there could be no other option.

Monty allowed himself to be led off along the line of cars. As they went, Popper turned back and shared a knowing glance with the group; they all understood what he meant. Monty may have been protecting them from Rhys, but Popper was protecting them from Monty.

Hsiao May and Harold

'Well?' said Shauna, as Popper returned and sat on the barrier next to her. 'What did you make of him?'

'Who? That chap there? Monty?'

'Yes, him. Monty.'

'Decent enough.'

'Yes, I thought so.'

'But I'd say he's got his own problems. Debt problems, probably. Or a divorce. With kids.'

'What makes you say that?'

'I don't know. Something in his general outlook, I suppose. His demeanour. You get to know how to read men like those.'

'Do you?'

'Yes. Oh, sorry, I didn't mention. I'm an army officer.'

'So you're in charge of men like that?'

'Known shedloads of them,' said Popper, sliding a cigarette from the packet and placing it between his lips. 'A good sort, really. Seemed like he was thinking of the wider good, you know, the way he came to get some cigarettes for his mate. He'd probably make a good soldier.' He looked her in the eye, and Shauna, certain that he could see into her soul, blushed. And then he had taken a light from Jim and was smoking, and she looked at him again, and once again was struck by the feeling that something deep inside Popper wasn't right. Something in the way he hunched around the cigarette, the way he pulled so aggressively on it and let the smoke leak out in front of his face. Something in his preoccupied eyes. There was a silence.

'Look up there,' said Shauna. 'Do you think anything's watching us?'

'You mean God?'

'No, not God. Not a creator – more of an observer. Not like an astronaut, or an alien, or anything. Something with a completely different perspective, who can see everything and everybody equally. Something that might care enough about us to notice our existence, but not enough to have it eclipse the importance of everybody else. Something who can see us in proportion, in the context of the world at large.'

Popper looked up into the blackness for a while.

'No,' he said. 'Can't say I do.'

Max had all but forgotten about his wife, his daughter, his daughter's friend. So it was with a start that he looked up and saw Ursula sitting up in the passenger seat, rubbing her eyes, and looking bewilderedly around. He got to his feet.

'I'd better go,' he said. 'The wife's woken up again.'

'Bring her over,' said Jim. 'It's not like you've got anything better to do.'

'Thanks, but my daughter's asleep in the car. And that other monstrous child. Anyway, my wife wouldn't . . . she wouldn't get this.' He lumbered off, opened the door and disappeared into his vehicle.

'Good bloke, that,' said Jim.

'I thought he was a bit of a prick,' mumbled Shahid.

'We all have our moments, mate,' said Jim.

'This fucking jam,' said Shahid. 'On and on and on. We've been here for what, four hours? Five? Feels like a fucking week.'

'Yeah,' said Jim. 'I've just about forgotten what normal life is like.'

Just when it seemed like nothing would ever happen again, a man could be seen walking casually along the hard shoulder towards them. He was of late middle age, with a round belly tautening his shirt and a pair of slacks that flapped as he walked. The lower part of his face was covered in a bearish beard; it was perhaps this, combined with his manner of walking, which gave him the impression of a pilgrim.

'Evening,' he called in a light Scottish burr, raising a hand. 'Just thought I'd come and see if anybody knew what's going on.'

'Not a clue, mate,' said Jim, as if to spare him the inconvenience of continuing. 'I don't think anybody knows anything, to be honest.' But the pilgrim went on undeterred, and comfortably entered the circle of the group.

'I have to admit, I'm struggling,' he said. 'I'm gasping for a pint. And I've got a camper van. I don't know how you folks are surviving at all.'

'No way – a camper van?' said Shahid.

'Aye,' said the man, eyeing him levelly. 'A camper van.' He turned and pointed into the distance. 'That greenish one there.'

'I'm not opening the van,' said Jim. 'Let's get that clear from the start, like.'

'Mine?' said the pilgrim.

'No, my one. That one. There.'

'That delivery van?'

'Yes.'

'That's yours? But why . . . oh, I see,' said the pilgrim with a chuckle. 'You're afraid I'm trying to get at the groceries. Times like these do make people predisposed to suspicion.'

'Right,' said Jim. And then, after a pause: 'Sorry.'

'The traffic is horrendous,' said the pilgrim, 'but just look at this wonderful piece of engineering. We never get the opportunity to appreciate it normally. Not up close like this.'

'What do you mean, engineering?' said Jim.

'This. You know. This. Spectacular, isn't it?'

'What?'

'The M25.'

This was met with silence.

Popper, who had been watching the newcomer, got to his

feet. 'Tom Popper,' he said, extending his hand. 'They call me Popper, or Pops. Occasionally Poppy.'

'Harold,' said the pilgrim, shaking his hand vigorously. 'They call me . . . well, Harold.'

'Far more sensible,' said Popper. 'Allow me to introduce Shauna, Jim and Shahid. Those two chaps over there are his friends, but I'm afraid I can't remember their names.'

'Kabir and Mo,' said Shahid sharply.

'Quite.'

'Have you heard anything about the hold-up?' said Shauna.

'Not a sausage,' said Harold. He breathed in deeply, as if savouring the air, and breathed out again. Suddenly he caught sight of something behind them. He craned his neck, nodded, and gave a little wave. 'Well, well,' he said.

A diminutive female figure stood behind a Prius in the middle lane. Only her head and shoulders were visible; they could see that she was Oriental. She threaded her way through the traffic to join them.

'Goodness, I am glad it's you,' said Harold. 'For a moment I thought I was waving at a total stranger.'

'No, it is me,' said the woman, without any trace of an accent. 'And it's you.'

'Aye, it is me,' said Harold.

'And who is me?'

'I'm sorry?'

'Who is me? I mean, I know who I am, but who are you? I'm sorry, but I've forgotten your name,' said the woman.

'Harold Ritchie,' said Harold. 'Professor of history.'

'Do you remember who I am?'

'I have to confess I don't.'

'Ling Hsiao May,' said the woman. 'Entomology.'

'Of course,' said Harold. 'How rude of me.'

'That's your camper van?' she said.

'It is, it is. You're welcome to pop in for a cup of tea. If you get bored, you know. Or if it rains. It's starting to feel like rain.'

'You have a kettle in there?'

'Of course. And a stove, and a wee fridge. The works. You'd be very welcome.'

'So you're colleagues,' said Popper. 'What a coincidence.'

'Indeed we are,' said Harold, 'though our paths have not really crossed, save for the occasional departmental meeting. Nevertheless, it's very nice to see a friendly face.'

'It has been a night of coincidences,' said Popper. 'Shauna and I discovered that we have a mutual friend.'

Shauna coloured, then nodded. She was looking increasingly worse for wear; the dark smudges under her eyes were deepening, and she persisted in massaging her temples.

'How rude of me,' said Popper. 'I haven't introduced us to . . . Ping, was it? Or Ling?'

'Hsiao May,' said Hsiao May.

'Quite.' He proceeded to introduce himself and the other members of the group with eloquence.

'You've got one of them electric cars, innit?' said Shahid, suddenly turning to Hsiao May.

'Me?' said Hsiao May.

'Yeah. It is, isn't it?'

'Yes, it's a Prius.'

'That's the one. A Pious.'

'A pious?'

'That's what my dad calls them.'

'I thought he worked for the *Guardian*,' said Shauna acidly.

'He does,' said Shahid.

There was a pause, which was broken by the sound of running. They turned to see Stevie dashing at full pelt down the hard shoulder, all angular elbows and flailing feet, a foolish smile spread across his face.

'What are you doing, mate?' called Jim.

'Any chance of a Crunchie and shit?' called Stevie, and laughed. Then he ran off, swerving crazily along the tarmac.

Jim shook his head. 'That boy's a right strange one,' he said.

'I don't know why you don't just open that van,' Shahid broke in. 'We might be here all night without food or drink.'

'Will you stop going on about that fucking van,' said Shauna. 'Honestly. Honestly.'

'I just can't understand it,' said Shahid. 'It doesn't make sense, that's all.'

Jim began to form a response, but Shauna stopped him. 'Rise above it, Jim,' she said. 'Rise above it.'

'We should have a game of footy, innit? Pass the time,' said Shahid. 'I've got a ball in the car. Me, Kabir and Mo against the rest.'

'You can count me out, I'm afraid,' said Harold. 'I've got a gammy knee.'

'Girl's blouse,' said Shahid.

'Oh, I rather take that as a compliment,' said Harold.

But before the idea could be further explored, the flow of their conversation was interrupted by a smattering of rain, which increased quickly in intensity until it became a downpour. As one, and with much cursing and covering of heads, the group dispersed, leaving threads of nascent relationships and discussions hanging in the air. And so Jim went back to his van; Shauna went back to her Smart car; Shahid and his friends to his grandfather's old Peugeot; Popper to his Golf; Hsiao May to her Prius; Harold to his camper van. One by one, they threw themselves into their cocoons of metal and plastic, slamming heavy doors on the world. In seconds, no trace was left of their gathering.

The rain was lashing mercilessly across the landscape now, bowing the heads of trees, stippling the flanks of cars, making intricate designs on windows, and washing the tarmac into a sleek river. Like animals in their holes, their nests, their burrows, their caves, the beleaguered inhabitants of the traffic jam had no choice but to give themselves over to solipsism.

Bugs

Dr Ling Hsiao May watched the jagged trails of raindrops making their way down her windscreen, separating, joining, separating again. The vehicle was vibrating slightly around her under the force of the water, and she began to feel afraid. It was getting cold, and she was tired and hungry. Already she had missed dinner with her sister Lulu, a farewell dinner put on especially for her. At this rate Lulu and Ricky would be asleep by the time she arrived, if she arrived this evening at all; and as her plane was leaving early the following morning, she ran the risk of not seeing them at all before she left. Anyway, if the traffic didn't move by the morning, she'd be going nowhere. Did her travel insurance cover eventualities like this? But if she missed the conference, no amount of compensation could change that.

Should she take the invitation from the professor seriously? She never knew if people said these things in earnest or not. Oh, she could do with a cup of tea, and, unusually, felt a need for human company. But dare she go and impose herself like that? Her pulse was quickening just thinking of it. The rain was dreadful now too. Surely it would be foolish to brave such weather as this just for the sake of a cup of tea in the camper van of a colleague? No, she'd wait for the rain to blow itself out. Then she'd see.

She tilted back her seat, testing the possibility of sleep. The voice of her mother was, as ever, loud and clear. So she hit traffic, so what? So it was a particularly bad traffic jam; so it wasn't moving at all; so what? She shouldn't mind waiting. She should be a patient girl; she shouldn't be in hurry. (Since she was a child she always liked to hurry, and it had never done her any good.) She could arrive at Lulu's any time this evening – her flight wasn't leaving until tomorrow, was it? – and she had already written her lecture. The main thing? Make the most of the wait. That was the main thing. She could easily get work done in the front seat of the Prius, which was comfy. After all, she loved her new Prius, didn't she? When she bought it, the first thing she had done was to drive it round to her mother's house and take her on a spin, showing off how it fell silent when idle. Wasn't one of her arguments for buying the new car that she could work more efficiently? So.

Hsiao May reached into the cool bag on the front seat and prised open a Diet Coke, indulging a habit of which her mother was ignorant. Put quite simply, there are times when the correct gesture – like a punctuation mark in the paragraphs of life – was a Diet Coke. Cigarettes? Never. Diet Coke. Feeling, as she always did, a small frisson of rebelliousness, she sipped. The can wasn't as cold as it should be, which cheapened the experience. She turned on the overhead light. The silver cylinder showed no trace of rime. A bad sign. She turned off the overhead light. Trying not to read too much into it, and focusing on the taste, the familiar stinging bubbles, she drank.

When she saw the rows of cars, vans and lorries, all frozen in the act of teeming around her, all resisting the rain with their hard bodies, it was impossible for her not to think about insects. It was experiences like these that made her feel closer to the creatures she studied, and she liked that. She could feel what it meant to be one in hundreds of thousands, and being inside a car was – she imagined – similar, to some extent, to having an exoskeleton. Generally, she spent her life so absorbed in the minute details – the wing construction, the breeding habits, the adrenaline production process, the aggression instincts – that she rarely had the time to consider what attracted her to insects in the first place. But here, in this stationary swarm, she could allow herself to enter their scuttling, teeming, burrowing, feeding world. She could imagine that she was a cricket, or a caterpillar, or a mealworm, or a grasshopper. She was particularly fond of a grasshopper, with that inertia masking the pent-up energy, that dignified, almost statesmanlike bearing, those powerful legs, powerful jaws, beautiful proportions, elegance.

She slipped the can into the holder on the dashboard, taking a little pleasure at the snugness of the fit. The drink had eased her anxiety, but not much: this was a big trip. Finally, an invitation to present a paper at the annual conference of the Entomological Society of America! She had just completed her Ph.D. on the escape behaviour of the Oedipoda caerulescens, a rare blue-winged grasshopper found in the Channel Islands. It had taken her five years. During that time she had built up a body of published work in journals, and had presented papers at various conferences around the world. She was becoming known as an emerging authority on the subject. This was a male-dominated world at the higher echelons, and she, as a Chinese woman, was, ironically enough, at an advantage on account of her disadvantage; departments wanted to demonstrate their ethnic diversity, and a face like hers helped no end. (Relatives called her a 'banana' – yellow on the outside, white on the inside – though she thought that her insides, if they were any colour at all, would be not white but a sort of pale yellow, not custard, but lemon curd perhaps. To be exact, the shade of a Hymenopus coronatus, which she had once seen in its natural habitat during a field trip to the Malaysian rainforests.) Her mother would have said, though not in so many words, that if British discrimination allows certain Chinese people – in certain circumstances – to have a marginal advantage, why not make the most of it?

Hsiao May knew that if she hadn't become a doctor, her mother would quite possibly never have spoken to her again. She was covered in shame as it was. *Thirty-three years old, no married, no children. And bugs? You study bugs? For this you can become doctor? Why not you become a real doctor, one that help people with broken leg? With cancer? Why bug doctor? You crazy?* She had tried at length to explain, and her mother had, in the end, fallen into a sullen silence. A doctor was a doctor, even her mother grudgingly had to admit. But if she were to have studied bugs and *not* become a doctor? It didn't bear thinking about. *Aiyah.*

Hsiao May was not overjoyed, of course, about being thirty-three years old, not married, with no children. But she had her work. Her real passion – and the subject of the paper she was on her way to deliver in New York – was, in her view, one of the most important fields of study around. As much as she loved studying the Oedipoda caerulescens, that was just one tiny piece of the vast puzzle of the universe. The sick would not be healed, the poor would not be elevated, the incarcerated would not be freed, as a result of her studies of a blue-winged grasshopper from the Channel Islands. No, her real interest lay in something bigger, something with profound sociological implications, something that cast her – a slightly built, bespectacled academic from Slough – as a prophetess who would save mankind. Something that could hold the answer to the very biggest questions of the twenty-first century. Something on which the future of the world may very well depend. The name of that something? The word that rang like music in her ears, like a string of waterdrops falling in a well? No, not entomology – *entomophagy*.

On the bidding of her inner mother, she turned on some Mozart – she still practised the piano, even now – reached into the slim briefcase that lay in the footwell, and drew out her lecture notes. They were enclosed in a buff folder, creaseless, perfect. Everything about them was pristine, in both form and content. Though she did not expect to need it, she took out a highlighter pen as well. Then she turned on the overhead light, reclined her seat and sat, papers poised, looking out of the window.

Night was deepening. The vast car-swarm was brooding in the deluge, the fumes from the last few engines coiling into the air like condensing breath. A feeling of unease filled her chest: we are destroying ourselves, she thought. These cars live on the lifeblood of the earth. This electricity is produced from the burning of its carbon. This paper from its trees. This leather from its animals. She snapped herself out of her reverie and returned her focus to her notes. But these she had re-read so many times that she had lost all objectivity, and no detail had been left unconsidered, so there was nothing for her mind to latch on to. It was not long before she was looking out of the window again. The Mozart bubbled around her like a child's laughter, enveloped in the hiss of the rain . . . this, she thought, is an age of destruction.

The title of her lecture was 'Ethnocentrism in Entomophagy: A New Approach'. The audience, she knew, would be refreshing. Unlike many of the people she was used to addressing on her evangelical lecture tours, all would have a solid science background and would already be familiar with the facts she would draw upon to form her argument. They would know that eighty per cent of the world's population eats insects happily. They would understand that with the increased pressure on the world's resources and climate, World War Three would likely be fought over water and food. They would know that insects, being cold-blooded, were four times more efficient at converting feed to meat than cattle, who burned energy needlessly by keeping themselves warm. She would barely have to mention that insects, pound for pound, had the same amount of protein as beef; that fried grasshopper had three times as much; that bugs were rich in micronutrients like iron and zinc; that they were so genetically distant from humans that there was little chance of contracting spillover diseases like bird flu or H1N1. They would understand that insects were natural recyclers, happily living on cardboard, manure, and food by-products. They would know how humane insect husbandry could be, that filthy, overcrowded conditions made bugs happy. Yes. They would know already that it made sense. Her job would be to give them confidence in proselytising. Insects, she would argue, were economical, clean, ecological, sustainable, nutritious, and, importantly, tasty – a gastronomically pleasing answer to the growing food shortages of the world. She would be strong. She would persuade members of the Entomological Society of America that society's instinctive distaste towards ingesting insects was culturally specific and ethnocentric. They must take people by the hand and introduce them to the mushroomy tang of beetle larvae; the rich chewiness of the sarcophagid maggot; the mouthfeel of a lightly fried young *chapulín*.

They would give her a standing ovation.

She drained her Diet Coke and realised that for a long time she had needed a pee. What could she do? Panic began to spread through her. How long would this traffic jam last? Her phone rang. So she had a signal now? It was her sister. She muted the Mozart and pressed *accept*.

'Hello, Lulu,' she said.

'Are you moving yet?'

'No, still stuck.'

'You're joking.'

'No. It's solid. Completely solid.'

'Still on the M25?'

'Still the same.'

'What? Sorry, you're breaking up.'

'Don't need to wait up for me, Lulu. It's really late. God knows how long I'll be.'

Sorry, what? This is a terrible line. Are you OK?'

'I'm fine.'

'This is fucking annoying. I had dinner ready and everything.'

'I'm sorry, OK? I'm sorry. It's not my fault.'

'I know . . . Hello? Hello?'

'I'm here. Can you hear me?'

'I just don't know what we'll do without you for a whole fortnight.'

'You'll manage.'

'The kids are going to miss you. Their favourite auntie.'

'Mama will step in.'

'I wish I could just swan off to the States like that. Just pack in all the housework, leave the kids somewhere and piss off. I can't remember the last time I went on holiday.'

'You went to Malta.'

'Yeah, but I mean by myself. That was with Ricky and the kids. You're lucky. In a way.'

'Thanks.'

'Look, I'm losing you . . . I'd better go.'

'OK.'

'I'll leave the key in the red Wellie. Good luck with the traffic.'

'Thanks.'

'I'll leave my phone on when I go to bed. I . . .'

The phone went dead.

Hsiao May held it glowing in the palm of her hand until the light dimmed and went out. Miracle that she got through with no signal. Miracle. If only people could see the power of the ideas contained in the modest buff folder in her hands! That was the true miracle. She closed her eyes.

In the camper van

Shaking the rain from his hair like a dog, Harold clambered stiffly into the cab of his camper van and heaved the door closed behind him. His knee was giving him gyp, his shoulders and thighs were soaked. Leaving the vehicle hadn't been worth the effort. He had craned his neck until it hurt, had walked – no, limped – up and down the hard shoulder, and still had not been able to find a vantage point from which the obstruction could be seen. It could, he had supposed, be many, many miles away. His fellow travellers, but they had proved too preoccupied to sustain anything but a fragmented conversation. Ah well. Seems like everybody is preoccupied these days. It wasn't until he had reinstalled himself in the van and caught his breath that he began to think about that diminutive Chinese woman – he had forgotten her name already, that was a worry – who had something to do with insects. He couldn't remember with any certainty, but he thought he may once have attended one of her lectures. She intrigued him. Her evangelist's zeal. She was something of a celebrity, really. The wee bug lady. Fancy her being here like this.

He scratched his beard, treated himself to a Mr Kipling's Angel Delight, brushed some crumbs from the dome of his stomach, sighed. The M25 hadn't known traffic this bad for years, and he should know. In the sky he thought he could see the lights of a helicopter, thought he could hear it far off, beneath the noise of the pelting rain. In all probability, a major accident. Major enough to warrant closing both carriageways. Major enough, perhaps, to be included in future accounts of the M25. He shuddered. What was going on as he sat in the safety and comfort of his camper several miles down the road? Twisted metal, burning vehicles, people trapped, people unconscious, people dead? There but for the grace of God, he thought.

Although he was disturbed by the idea of the accident, he was relieved that he seemed not to have become preoccupied by it. Dad had died the year before, and the depression he had subdued twenty years before came crashing back like a ruffian uncle from the war. Once again he found himself in a battle with himself. Back to square zero. In the early months, his mood was on a hair-trigger; the smallest thing could set off one of his old black dogs. He even went into a three-day-long spell of melancholy after watching an advertisement on television for cheap diamond rings. The consumerism. The failed dreams. The bleakness of modernity. The wilful ignorance of mortality it entailed. The loneliness of it all.

But then, in the spring, he had felt better. Memories of his father were accompanied not by an immobilising pain but a dull, bittersweet ache, a sadness that had the right to be there, that felt natural. His favourite memory, and the one to which he returned most often, was of Dad taking him to the zoo, five decades past. It had been one of those charmed, halcyon days. Just him and Dad (his mother had died when he was small). The classic components of childhood happiness were all present: the candyfloss, being swung up onto Dad's shoulders, the feeling of his hand being engulfed in that of his father, the ruffling of his hair, the laughing at the daft monkeys, the swaying elephants, the aloofness of the birds of prey. Most of all, that day showed Dad's taciturnity at its best. He had been a man of few words, had Dad. He was of that generation, the war generation; he had lost a foot at Dunkirk – spent the rest of his life on crutches – and emotion had never been his strongest suit. And although this, as Harold entered his 1960s adolescence, became a source of frustration for him, at times it made things take on a sense of the numinous. In the zoo they had looked at the lions, the zebras, the penguins in silence, and in the absence of any name, and any comment, he was faced with things as they really were; not the wall-frieze animals but the beasts themselves; he saw everything with the clarity and immediacy not available to those who fracture their every experience in the kaleidoscope of language. There was just himself, the solidity of Dad, and the magnificence of the animals, all imbibed with a sacred immanence. That was enough, and Dad, in his wisdom, knew it. Dear old Dad.

When he had started to feel well again, he had taken on the project of renovating Dad's old camper. The one in which they would go on rambling trips in the school holidays to the Scottish Highlands, the Western Isles, the lochs, even – once – to Snowdonia. A 1967 Type 2 Volkswagen Kombi, khaki in colour, with a split windscreen – a 'Splittie' to the enthusiast – it had languished in the garage for many years and was in a state of serious dilapidation. There had even been a brittle bird's nest in the roof-rack. On the first day, after a good three hours of solid work, Harold had managed to get it going, and trundled it out of the garage and onto the driveway in the sun. My goodness, it was in a state. Over the weeks that followed he'd cleaned it thoroughly, both inside and out; dealt with the rust; painted it a slightly lighter shade; half-rebuilt the engine with parts available only from the most obscure corners of the Internet; installed a fold-out bed and kitchenette; fitted it with cheerful orange curtains. And one morning at the end of June, as he stood with his sleeves rolled up, beholding the machine in all its splendour, backlit by a brilliant sky, he was infused from top to toe with a feeling of warmth, an embrace of unmistakable love, as if his father had been with him all this time, as if this task had been one of devotion, as if he had cleaned away the obstacles to the full blessings of heaven and suddenly they were raining down upon him; and he imagined that within the freshly buffed paintwork of the trusty Kombi there lay reflected the face of the old man himself, anthracite and stoical, yet with eyes twinkling as brightly as ever they had.

A cup of tea. Why not? This lot wasn't moving. From the galley of the camper he could easily see the smeary windscreen, so he would know if the jam began to move. Even if he fell asleep, he thought, he'd be OK; the ensuing cacophony of hooting would doubtless be sufficient to wake the dead. Impatient, people, these days. He climbed out of the camper again, puffing with effort, and made his way into the rear galley. Here he had to stoop; he was a tall man, more than six foot, and here the ceiling was low. He sat heavily on the sofa and manoeuvred crablike along it until he was next to the kitchen unit; from there he filled the kettle and put it on to boil. Then he sat back.

This sitting, this silence, was kin to him; it was kin to all Quakers. As he waited for the kettle – it would take some time on that pygmy stove flame – he naturally fell into the state of spiritual openness, of wonderment, that was required at Meetings. The peace came quickly, and he was pleased. I am one cell in the vast body of life, he thought. In this traffic jam alone, which itself is surely but one among countless throughout the world, I could be one of thousands, even tens of thousands. Who could tell? My life, though of great significance to myself and to God, takes its importance principally from its connectedness to every single other creature, past and present, in the entirety of creation. The parts derive significance from the whole; a sense of fellowship with God's universe makes one a good person. He sighed, felt another brief pang of love for his father, and felt the poignancy of God in his heart.

His eyes came to rest on the vase that he had screwed down in the far corner of the galley. It was filled with young lilies, beautiful and in the briefest peak of their existence. He was not a lonely man. Being an only child, his own company had never fazed him; his mother having died before he could remember, self-sufficiency had been instilled in him from an early age. There had been housekeepers, of course, and Nanny, and the ubiquitous figure of Dad. But when a boy grows up without a mother, there is no companion to the most intimate reaches of his soul, and he usually becomes either angry at the world or at himself. In Harold's case, that anger had taken the form of depression. He had been a member of the Anglican Church then, even at one time considering ordination, but the rigidity of the hierarchy had compounded the problem and he had been driven to the brink of madness; after that, his path had led to Quakerism, and this had sustained his soul in a way that he had never thought possible. He had become accepting. A gentle God was now his companion. Not a God of fire and brimstone, but an unprejudiced God, with compassion for all of His creation and without the slightest trace of violence or jealousy. Not a personal God. The presence of ineffable truth and goodness, nothing more. So he had been healed. At least so far as healing was possible in this vale of tears.

The kettle had boiled. Harold turned off the flame and, still sitting, reached into the cupboard and took out his favourite mug, a handsome, rustic affair with no chips. He plucked a teabag from the tin and dropped it into the centre of the mug. Then, listening to the sound it made, he poured the boiled water quietly into the mug until it was two thirds full. After the tea had stewed for two minutes he removed the teabag with a teaspoon and dropped it into the pull-out bin, which he had emptied before setting out that afternoon. A wee thimbleful of milk from the fridge and the tea making was complete.

It was important to Harold to do things like this correctly, in their proper order, with due care paid to the detail. Many years ago he had spent a year in Japan as a visiting lecturer, and had been most impressed by their approach. It had become his belief that the little things in life, the tea making, the house cleaning and eating and grooming, should not be dismissed as insignificant; these were the building blocks of life, which although utterly unremarkable when taken individually, had the capacity to create a larger picture of great beauty if proper attention was given to each. This he had made his life philosophy, and from time to time he sensed that perhaps his way of being made an impression on others. In this modern world, where speed was of the essence, where productivity was held above beauty, functionality above beauty, money above beauty, something important had been lost. This was what he valued: the modest, dignified life. This, after all, was what his father had exemplified in his own time. The quiet elegance of a bygone age.

He took a bottle of Balvenie from the bottom shelf, had a single hot swig, put it back.

The first sip of tea was always the best; he took his time, savoured it. The curtains were drawn, but he knew exactly what lay behind them: the grey motorway barrier dividing the carriageway from the land, a foot-high strip of grey metal waisted in the middle and supported every two metres by metal posts; the grassy ridge beyond, dotted with trees; the sign for the next junction, which would be approaching fairly rapidly had not the motorway ground to a standstill.

He got to his feet and opened the curtains all around the camper. The scene was exactly as he had visualised, with the addition of the ferocious rain and stationary cars. For some reason he hadn't remembered the cars. And lorries, and vans, and so forth. All with lights twinkling, a few still spewing exhaust pointlessly in vertical ropes towards the heavens. This vast mass of creation, how could he have forgotten? Perhaps it was not surprising. If ever his fellow creatures would be eclipsed in his thoughts it would be now, when contemplating the magnificence of the M25. This hellish ring of ordered chaos, this profoundly ugly – there could be nothing uglier – testament to Thatcherite capitalism, this extraordinary gesture of utter disregard for the land and the people living in it; this homage to the machine; this wonderful, polluted, grimy, exhibitionist, offensive, belligerent, self-absorbed, consumerist, dystopian concrete wonderland, this endless strip of highway to nowhere. This beautiful thing. He had made of it his professional life. He knew off-the-cuff all the stats: that it cost a billion pounds to complete, and took eleven years; that it was the biggest city bypass in the world until it was itself bypassed by the Berlin Ring, the A10, which was four miles longer; that the toll on the Dartford Crossing, which was supposed to be scrapped in 2003 once construction costs had been recouped, was still being collected; that Balfour Beatty had constructed both the first stretch of motorway in 1975, and also the last in 1986; that the question most frequently asked of the AA by customers on the Internet is how one can avoid the M25; that it would take an hour and forty minutes to lap the road driving at a continuous seventy; that Sir Horace Cutler, head of the old Greater London Council and a leading lobbyist for the M25, discovered only on the day the route was announced that it would pass through the grounds of his Buckinghamshire home; that its sections to the north follow the route of the Second World War Outer London Defence Ring; that there are only three service stations along the entire route of the motorway. And, perhaps most importantly given the current circumstances, that in the last eighteen months, between Junctions 16 and 23 alone, roadworks caused 118 years of hold-ups.

At some time, he thought, south-east England formed part of an ocean floor. By some violent movement of the earth's surface it was thrust steaming out of the water, except for the valleys which continued to be washed by shallow seas. During this period, before the ocean retreated altogether, sand and gravel was deposited by the massive shovel of nature on top of the other strata. On the North Downs of Junctions 1 to 5, site of the Dartford Crossing, chalk coagulated; thenceforth south to Junction 7, it was hard sand and grey Gault clay, extending from beneath the chalk which continued, cliff-like, to the north; from that point past Reigate to Junction 9, the North Down chalk re-emerged; the miles that followed, culminating in Junction 13, which lay poised just on the north bank of the Thames and beneath the busy umbrella of Heathrow, were comprised mainly of poor soil, interrupted by the silt of the rivers Mole and Wey; the next two junctions around Slough were largely gravel, webbed by an intricate network of half a dozen rivers; beneath the seven junctions thereafter – looking out towards High Wycombe, Watford, St Albans – were clay soils, beneath which in turn, buried deep like some horrid secret repressed, lay more tightly packed chalk; from 22 to 30, from Hertfordshire to Essex, the substance was clay, with gravel panned over the surface as if by some builder god; and from thence southwards, back to Junction 1, that arbitrary point of beginnings, the north bank of the Thames jutted to receive it, an isolated outcrop made once again of that fickle and persistent rogue, chalk.

Taken clockwise, the ancient rivers: Thames, Darenth, Mole, Wey, Thames reprised, Wraysbury, Colne, Chess, Gade, Misbourne, Lea and Roding; the modern canals, Wey, Grand Union, Lea Navigation; the rivers made by man to suit his vanity, Duke of Northumberland, New and Mardyke.

The Romans had built nine roads which crossed the M25. For their part, the Normans had established churches, parishes, parks, forests around its rim. Munificent Elizabethans had built here, on the clean, dry hills but a few hours' ride from the city, retreats for the health, clear springs; later, unannounced travellers along the route would have swiftly and firmly been turned away by gamekeepers, shotguns nestling in their tweedy armpits.

In 1905 a Royal Commission had proposed an orbital road around the capital at a radius of twelve miles, which was to be populated by horses and wagons, lined by water troughs, and patrolled by wheelwrights and farriers in the event of breakdown. Then motorisation. The Great War. Between the wars, a policy was implemented to build 'arterial' roads aided by 'cross routes' passing from one artery to the next, resulting in the construction of an Inner Circular Road tracing a line past the Tower and King's Cross, and a South Circular Road curving in a crooked smile beneath it. In 1939 the *Evening Standard* published a map projecting what they referred to as the 'Great London Road'. Finally, in 1943, embedded within a planning document known as the Abercrombie Report, there appeared a new word, a landmark of a word, imported from America and Germany: the suggestion of the construction of 'a possible inner ring motorway'. A *motorway*. A road for motor traffic only, with access possible only at certain points. On which all stopping would be flatly prohibited. The genie had slipped, belching exhaust, from the bottle, and never would he countenance being stuffed back in.

In 1975 construction started, amid heated clashes between green policy advocates and those of machines and speed. By the time the motorway was opened at the snip of Thatcher's scissors in 1986, thirty-nine Public Inquiries had been held, spanning 700 sitting days – six days of Public Inquiry for every mile of motorway. It had only been when construction was already underway that the road was conceived of as a band, rather than two separate arcs, and given a single, unified name: the M25. Between this christening, made official by the Minister for Transport in the House of Commons in 1975, and the original suggestion, there had passed a full seventy years.

Harold finished his tea. Still the traffic had not moved, and the rain had not abated, and neither showed any sign of so doing. The sense of Godly peace had left his heart, but he had expected that; he had long ago arrived at the understanding that the Holy Spirit would come and go as it pleased, and that it was counterproductive to grasp at it when it came, or grieve for it when it went. He was not a lonely man. He washed out his rustic mug, dried it and replaced it in the cupboard; then he took one more swig of his single malt before clambering back through into the cab and returning to his rightful place behind the steering wheel, to sit quietly and gaze through the rain at the magnificent, stinking ribbon of the motorway.

Shampoo

Dave, shawled in darkness, was gazing through sheets of falling water at the unmoving traffic when through the crackle of the rain came the sound of someone fast approaching; then the back door was wrenched open and Stevie, sodden and chuckling, fell into the driver's seat. He slammed the door; the atmosphere changed; Natalie groaned, changed her position, continued to sleep.

'Been for a run, you dirty mank?' said Dave.

'It's wet out there, dude,' was all that Stevie said. 'It's wet out there.' Then his mirth faded, and his laboured breathing subsided, and he removed his wet T-shirt and pulled on a hoodie; and a thick silence came in around them like the tide.

Dave had smoked more skunk. He let his head fall back like a cannonball into the headrest, tried to close his mouth but found that he couldn't, then found that he didn't care. He jerked his head to move his fringe back into position, then realised that he had only imagined doing so, and that his fringe was still hanging in a limp tangle on his forehead. He didn't care. A snowstorm arose in his mind, and he remained there for who knows how long, thinking of nothing, watching the strange visions that emerged sporadically from its whiteness and disappeared again. Then came a darkness, blacker than anything he had experienced, and the strings of lights which formed multiple lines converging towards a single point in the distance were bright and pure and beautiful. The thought of Stevie and Natalie caused a dark well of energy to build up in his loins. He became one with the sheeting rain.

*

Dave had tried to be open-minded at first when Stevie had started on about the 'piece of meat'. God, he had even, once or twice, joined in. But he had quickly lost his enthusiasm, while Stevie's had only grown. It had seemed so – not sordid as such – so pathetic. It was sad, the way Natalie was simply giving in; it was sad the way they were all quite capable of being part of the festival village, listening to music, drinking, dancing, without ever mentioning what was going on by night in their tent. Stevie couldn't believe his luck – he had blood in his nostrils and was taken by the thrill of the chase. Dave had been meaning to say something to him. But how could he change his tune now, having tacitly condoned his behaviour, even taken part in it? And anyway: why *was* it making him feel uncomfortable? Was he simply being prudish? It wasn't as if Natalie was bothered. Most of the time she was asleep, or pretending to be, and not once did she complain or pull away. If she didn't mind, why should he?

With a start, he realised he was giggling. Which was strange, because nothing had amused him. Apart from, perhaps, the awkwardness of the situation, someone giving himself a hand job with a stoned girl's hand while his mate was sitting in the front. The rocking, the grunting, the long exhalation. The silence and, after a minute or two, the sound of Stevie wiping himself. Dave heard himself giggle again. He opened his eyes. Stevie was sitting beside him in the driver's seat, his hood pulled over his head. Natalie was asleep in the back.

'You're proper biffed, mate,' said Stevie.

Dave cocked the rear-view mirror and looked at Natalie. She was sprawled across the back seat, one arm dangling downwards to the floor, the other resting across her belly. Her large breasts were splayed, only partially covered by her T-shirt; her hair was hanging over her face, and she was breathing deeply. Water was dripping from a rusty crack in the ceiling, falling into her hair. On the floor was a cluster of screwed-up tissues, like so many white roses. Dave returned the mirror to its original position and she slid out of the frame and vanished.

'You should have a go and shit,' said Stevie. 'She's all yours. Ready and waiting.'

'No thanks, mate.'

It had been strange to meet Stevie again at university. They hadn't seen each other for several years – Dave had moved schools just before GCSEs, when his father was posted up north – and although Stevie was recognisable, he had changed. He was still small and skinny, with the same pale skin, the same tightly curling ginger hair, but there was more wiry strength about him, and his eyes had grown shrewd. Doubtless Dave had appeared likewise transformed to Stevie, as the first thing he had done, when they had encountered each other in the student bar, was to stand back and whistle softly.

'Dave Shelton, isn't it?' he had said, without smiling.

'Stevie,' Dave had replied. 'Is that you? What are you doing here?'

'Sociology. You?'

'English. I mean, I'm studying English. English and creative writing.'

'It's been a long time, Dave boy. Eh?' A strange, mocking light had entered Stevie's eyes; a delight, Dave thought later, in seeing the tables turning.

'It . . . it has, Stevie. It has been a very long time.'

They stood there making small talk, with every word over-shadowed by an event from years ago. It had happened at school, after some sports game or other. Swimming perhaps; one of the few sports events in which Stevie took part. He hated laddishness in all its forms, and sport represented every-thing that was a torment to him. This was, however, school, and sports could not be avoided for ever. On the few occa-sions when Stevie could not escape participation, he would try to blend into the background, get rid of the ball as soon as it came to him, and afterwards kept himself to himself in the changing rooms. Dave had noticed this. He had also noticed that Stevie would habitually wait until everybody had finished showering before he towel-wrapped his scrawny frame and slipped into the showers himself. Then he would slink out, dress hurriedly, and make his escape, if he was lucky, without being mocked.

The idea, which he had taken from a prank video, had seemed hilarious, and Dave – who, looking back, was anxious to impress the other boys – put it into action immediately. He waited until Stevie had disappeared into the showers (he almost didn't notice him going in, even though he had been keeping an eye out). Then he beckoned everyone to gather around, and sneaked in after him. Stevie, as always, was facing the wall, head down, water spluttering onto his head and cascading down the channels of his body; his white buttocks were clenched, a thread of soapy water was streaming down between them and onto the shower floor, creating frothy bands around his feet. He had just applied the shampoo, and was rubbing the suds into his hair, rinsing it. He was even humming a tune. Stifling nervous laughter, Dave flipped open the cap of his own shampoo bottle and squeezed a worm of it onto Stevie's head. Stevie didn't notice; he continued to rinse as before. The froth proliferated. Dave leaned over and added another turquoise worm of shampoo. The froth proliferated again, and Stevie continued to rinse. Then another – he was rinsing more agitatedly now – and another. The bubbles and foam were multiplying furiously. After a few moments, Stevie let out a low moan. This shampoo, he mumbled, distressed. It's not going away. Dave added another three loops of shampoo. The bubbles were magnificent. Now Stevie let out a wail: Come and help me. Come and help. This shampoo, I can't get it out. It won't come out. It's not going away. Dave added another reckless spurt of shampoo, the biggest one so far. Stevie began to scratch wildly at his hair as if infested with lice, then raised himself on his toes and thrust his head directly into the showerhead. Tendrils of foam were coiling down his face, his shoulders. He wailed, wailed again: What's happening? I'm going fucking crazy! It's not going! It's not going! Dave looked around. Everyone was laughing, holding their bellies, doubled over. Spurred on by the merriment, he turned back to Stevie and – to his shame – added another generous spiral of shampoo. Stevie, staring at the thick gluts of foam that were slipping down his shoulders and gathering around him like snow, yelled in panic and beat his hands against the tiles. People were laughing at him openly now, but Stevie did not hear them. Suddenly he let out a howl, so loud, so raw, that it killed the laughter. Then he began to beat his head against the wall, against the shower piping, until the white foam became streaked with crimson. Dave sprang forward and pulled him, naked, from the water flow, eyes wild, blood running in tributaries down his face. His mouth, a gaping crescent, was filled with blood and foam and water. It was just a joke, said Dave, just a joke. Calm down. Calm down. At first Stevie was unable to take in his words, kept trying to return to the shower. But when he finally understood what Dave was saying, he stopped perfectly still, the shower hissing behind him. He saw for the first time the press of people in the doorway of the shower, all staring at him. He was naked – white and naked, a prisoner facing execution. His hands slowly moved to cover his penis; the thin lines of blood multiplied across his face, his chest.

'It has been a long time,' Dave repeated uncertainly. 'So. Sociology, eh?'

'Yeah,' said Stevie. 'Took the easy option.'

'You could have taken creative writing,' said Dave, 'that's got to be even easier.'

'I don't know,' said Stevie, 'I've never been the creative type. I don't really feel I've got anything to say.'

There was a pause.

'Do you . . . want a drink?' said Dave.

'Sure,' Stevie replied. 'If you're buying I wouldn't say no.

Packet of crisps, too, please. Prawn cocktail. Actually, you know what? Two packets.'

'Two?'

'Yeah. Didn't have any lunch. Thanks, Dave.'

The rain was still falling. They had been there for a long time, and Dave's trip was wearing off. Stevie had pulled out his phone and was scrolling through something, his face under-lit by a pale blue glow. Like Gollum, thought Dave. He rotated the mirror and looked at Natalie again. She hadn't moved. Same as before. He carefully watched her chest, and ascertained that she was still breathing. He moved the mirror back into position.

'Hey,' said Stevie suddenly, 'I didn't show you my new fail compilation.'

'No,' said Dave, 'I don't think you did. This is a new one?'

'Yeah, new for this month. It's hilarious.'

He propped the phone up on the dashboard. The compilation was thirteen minutes long, fail after fail after fail. It began with grainy CCTV footage of a man slumped against an automatic door, asleep – when the door opened, he cartwheeled onto the floor and lay there groaning. There followed a clip of a cat trying to leap from a branch to a wall, missing, and plummeting out of frame; then several shots of teenagers messing up skateboard jumps, and ending writhing in agony on the ground. There were also a couple of car crashes; a man attempting a wheelie on a green racing motorbike, then falling off while the machine shot into the distance; a few skiing accidents; a woman attempting to bounce from a trampoline into a swimming pool, and landing face down on the concrete; a BMX biker jumping from a low roof onto the pavement, his bike buckling under him, howling in pain. All the way through, Stevie laughed his manic laugh as if this was the first time he'd seen it. Dave laughed too, sometimes spontaneously – he was still stoned, after all – and sometimes out of a sense of obligation. They continued in this way until the video had run its course, and the screen of the phone went black. The car was quiet again. Still Natalie in the back seat hadn't moved.

'I'm bored,' said Stevie. 'Fucking bored. This fucking traffic jam.'

'It isn't the most exciting way to spend a Sunday evening,' Dave conceded.

'Why doesn't somebody just sort it out? How hard can it be? We pay our taxes, don't we? And I'm starving. Plus I've got the munchies real bad.'

'Actually, we don't. We're students.'

'Have the munchies?'

'Pay taxes, dick.'

'Yeah, but our parents do.'

'I just wish something would happen. Anything. You know?'

'Telling me,' said Stevie.

Dave sat up and looked groggily around. 'Hang on,' he said. 'I think it's stopped raining. When did it stop raining?'

Stevie squinted through the window for a moment. 'Yeah,' he said. 'It's stopped.'

'Fuck me,' said Dave. 'Fuck me.'

'Let's go find the Asian dudes,' said Stevie in an American accent. 'Have a game on the motorway. We should go out and challenge them to a game.'

'What are you on about?' said Dave, hearing himself giggle. 'You hate football. You hate all sports.'

'Correction, I used to,' said Stevie. 'I'm a new man now, don't forget. I'm getting quite into football.'

'We've got a Frisbee in the back.'

'Don't be a pussy. Look, I'll prove it. I'll prove it to you, I'll prove it to them. Come on.' He opened the car door, and a wedge of cold air slid in.

'I can't,' said Dave, 'I swear. I fucking can't.'

'Why not?'

'Still lean, aren't I? Still fucking biffed.' He laughed, and Stevie laughed too. 'OK,' said Stevie. 'Let's let you recover. Then

123

we'll challenge those cunts to a game and shit. Or play Frisbee, or whatever. I don't fucking care.'

Involuntarily, Dave grinned. 'Fine by me,' he said. 'Fucking anything for something to do.'

Cider

Now that they had eaten their fill, the three men in the white van – Rhys, Chris and Monty – sat in silence, staring out at the night; and when the rain descended, none of them commented, or even noticed, for a long time. The smell of burgers and chips lingered in the cab, that familiar smell that implied that the world was on pause and all was well. And it had been perfect: pulling cold slugs of Coke through straws, feeling the dull knock-knocking of ice-cubes against oversized cardboard cups, hearing the familiar squeak of straws adjusting in the X-shaped holes in the lids. The burgers had been moist and warm and comforting, like a childhood snog; they always disappeared too soon, that was part of it. And the fries had been stringy and salty and moist, to be gathered in little bundles to scoop up slicks of ketchup. Then they had licked their fingers, and stuffed the packaging into a brown paper bag, and finished their Cokes, and laughed, and the recent tension was all but forgotten.

'It's raining,' said Monty at last. He looked across at the brothers: Chris had fallen asleep, his chin cushioned by the collar of fat around his neck, his lips lolling loosely; Rhys was sitting upright, staring straight ahead. Yet he didn't appear to have heard him. In his eyes was the reflection of the windscreen, and within that the car-studded road; and across the glassy lens danced millions upon millions of raindrops.

'What do you reckon he's got under that hoodie?' said Monty.

Rhys emerged from his reverie. 'What?' he said. 'Who?'

'Your brother. Look, under his hoodie. He's got something.'

'What, under there? Nah, mate, he's just fat.' Rhys leaned over and plucked the hoodie away, revealing a blue plastic bag. Chris let out a loud and irritated snore and sat up, laying his hands over it. His eyes opened; he rubbed them, gathering the bundle to his chest.

'What's that?' said Rhys.

'What's what?'

'That. That bag. There.'

'What, here?' Chris looked surprised at what he was holding in his arms. 'Oh, nothing.'

'Bollocks. Let's see.' Rhys leaned over and made a grab. Chris was groggy but managed to keep hold of it. Then, smiling, he opened it voluntarily.

'Booze!' Rhys exclaimed. 'Chris, you fucking wanker. Give it here.'

Chris passed him a fat bottle of cider. He opened it – the bubbles foamed and bubbled – and took a long draught. 'I don't believe it,' Rhys said, wiping his mouth. 'Why the fuck didn't you say anything?'

'Emergency supplies, innit?' said Chris. 'Saving it for when the time's right.'

'The time's been right for a long time, bruv. Fucking dick.' Rhys took another long swig before handing it to Monty, who raised it to his lips and allowed himself a few mouthfuls – he was driving, in theory at least. Then he handed it back to Chris.

Rhys lit a cigarette, and his smoke rose in double helixes towards the ceiling. He dug out the takeaway cups from the brown bags of rubbish, tipped out the ice, and filled them with cider; by the time he had finished, most of the bottle was gone. He handed them out and whooped, loud and long, into the rain-filled silence: 'To our fucking English streets.'

The brothers laughed as if they were already drunk, and took big gulps. Some splashed onto Chris's chest as he drank. Then they let out almost simultaneous burps, replaced their cigarettes and laughed again.

Monty took a small sip and turned away, gazing out the window at the people in the Chrysler. It wasn't such an idyllic scene this time. The woman was turning away, rubbing her forehead, and the black man was staring straight ahead, chin jutting. He looked away. The inertia, the rain, was oppressing him, and being in a confined space with Rhys and Chris made him feel like a caged animal. He leaned over and put on the radio, turning it up a couple of notches too loud. Then he pulled out his own cigarettes, took one out with his teeth and lit it with the van's stubby lighter. Rhys was speaking to him.

'So what I want to know, mate,' said Rhys, raising his voice over the noise of the music, 'is how I can get into this drugs game of yours.'

'What?' said Monty.

'It's all right for you, mate.'

'What?'

'Don't be a cock. This drugs game you're playing. You're flush all the time, innit? Got fucking cash coming out your arse. I ain't got a job, innit? I want to, I dunno, I want to be your apprentice.'

Chris guffawed. 'Me too. Fucking cool,' he said, drawing out the 'cool' and tailing it off into a melody. 'Alan Sugar, innit?'

'You know I can't talk about any of that stuff,' said Monty. 'For your sake as well as mine.'

'What a hard bastard,' said Rhys, 'what a fucking hard bastard.' He took another gulp of cider.

The sound of sirens cut through the air, through the music, like lasers, and flashing lights appeared in the mirror. Rhys and Chris instinctively held their ciders down low, and turned their faces from the window as the vehicles raced past on the hard shoulder.

'Look,' said Chris. 'The pigs rush by with all guns blazing and old Monty don't even flinch.'

'You got to act completely normal,' said Monty. 'Anything else and they'll pick it up.'

'Anything else and they'll pick it up,' Rhys repeated girlishly.

'Look,' said Monty, his temper rising within him, 'if you got something to say, just fucking say it. Be a man. Don't just poof around, say it. I can't be dealing with your shit all the time. You're giving me shit all the time.'

'I am the man-boob man,' Chris interrupted, trying to defuse the tension.

'Fine,' said Rhys, licking his lips. 'I think you're a bit of a fucking poser, all right? A fucking posh poser. Happy now?'

'What?'

'All this hard man stuff. All this fucking money. All this swanning around the fucking world. All this big fucking talk. Some of us ain't got no money, Monty. Some of us got a shit flat, and a shit fucking car, and not a pot to piss in.'

'What you on about? I'm a labourer like you. That money stuff, it's all for the sake of the boys, innit?'

'Bollocks it is. You might fool Gaz like that, but you can't fool me. I know what you're in it for, mate. Your own big fucking ego. It's all about being the big man with you. You don't really believe in nothing.'

'You take that back.'

'Bollocks I will. I'll say what I think. What we all think. You don't believe in what we believe in. You ain't the same as us. For you it's all just one big crack.'

'You're jealous, Rhys.'

'You know it's true. You know it's fucking true.'

'You know what's true?' said Monty. 'You hate it that I'm the one that Gaz trusts. You hate it that I do all the shit in Europe. That I get to travel, meet the big boys, make the big decisions. And you don't.'

'Look at you,' said Rhys. 'There's nothing to you, is there? All words, words, words. It's people like me that are going to do this fucking thing. People who have the balls to stand up and be counted, to get our hands dirty. To get out on the fucking streets, week after week, with no fucking money behind us. My mum's still on the waiting list for a council flat while all those fucking Muslims jump the queue. I'm the heart and soul of the boys, mate. Not you.'

'I'm not going to waste my time doing this now, Rhys. I've already stopped you making a dick of yourself once tonight.'

'What have you given up, mate? What have you sacrificed? Fuck all. You've bought your way to the top. Like a fucking banker wanker. Fucking tosser. But you can't buy respect, Monty. You got to earn it.'

'I've earned it, Rhys,' said Monty. 'You know I have.'

'Bollocks you have. You didn't even have the balls to get some fucking food from that van. We could of done with that, innit? Food, fucking posh toothpaste, all sorts. We're going to be here all night, and it's going to be shit. Because with Monty, all the fight is in his head. No red-blooded English guts.'

Monty began to say something, then stopped himself. 'I'm going for a piss.' Pulling the keys from the ignition, he swung down on to the road and slammed the door behind him. All at once, the brothers felt far away. The night air was crisp, shocking; the rain had abated, and the world left behind was more vivid than before. He dropped his half-smoked cigarette onto the tarmac and stomped it out aggressively with his heel. He looked around. Cars, lorries, in every direction, and on the other side of the barrier nothing. So many people in the world! So many different lives! And here he was living in this trap. With people like Rhys giving him shit, after everything he'd done for the boys. Load of shit.

He vaulted over the barrier and walked up the grassy embankment. The wet grass enfolded his trainers, dampened the cuffs of his jeans. He groped for his anger, but strangely it had deserted him; instead he was filled with a feeling of dread, dark as the night. He looked over his shoulder: nobody. At the crest of the embankment he opened his flies. The piss took some time to come, but when it did it was good, fulsome and flowing, a pale line pattering in the darkness. It was cathartic and he felt strengthened. How pathetic to feel strengthened by a piss.

He could not recall the moment when his commitment to his job eclipsed his concern for the rest of his life. With each promotion he had become focused on the next step; and when the opportunity had come up to go undercover, he had jumped at it. He had not understood at the time what this kind of work could do to a man, how it could swallow up years of your life. The guy in the Chrysler. What did he have to put up with at work? Office politics, longish hours, perhaps a bit of RSI. He didn't have to put up with . . . well, he didn't have to put up with Rhys.

And he didn't have to put up with enforced celibacy. These days it was out of the question. Getting involved with someone while on the job was a sackable offence, yet there was barely a time when he was not on the job. And he needed a woman, he needed one. It was a basic human need. He believed in what he was doing – the job satisfaction, he often told himself, was its own reward – but the successes were disproportionate to the long years of deprivation. Tonight was proving it: he had been unable to pursue a conversation with the woman by the super-market van, as his obligations had been with Rhys. That woman. He had not even learned her name. It would probably have come to nothing. But maybe, on the other hand, a single conver-sation would have revealed a path to a different future. But he had not been able to allow himself to find out. And for what? For what? For what?

Something moved nearby. He looked down at the van. Both of the doors were closed; he could see the outline of Chris's shoulders, hunched over his mobile; he could see the white glow of his screen. He peered into the darkness. There – a shape that didn't fit. A human figure, crouching in the shrubbery. He sidestepped into the shadow of a tree and crouched down himself for a better view. Now there was a noise that didn't fit; a whispering, of water perhaps, or someone's fingers in the leaves. Then it stopped. The silhouette moved, fumbled, got to its feet. It took a step, then another, and emerged. A woman, facing away from him, stumbling down towards the motorway. By some sixth sense she turned, looked back. An Oriental woman, slim, bespectacled. She hurried down the embankment and disappeared.

Monty squared his shoulders and closed his eyes. He knew that in a moment he would have to go back down to the van and face Rhys. He balled his fists and opened them, balled them and opened them, then flung some punches into the air. He had no choice, he knew that. He would have to try to make peace.

Hubster

Shauna Williams raised her head from the steering wheel at the sound of sirens, watched the lights streak out of the world and pass away into it like something out of *Star Trek* or something. Knowing that it would be no use at all, she tried her phone once again, and once again it was dead as before. Rain was battering the outside of her car; the air was cold, but she didn't want to start her engine. So she drew the soft folds of her jumper tighter around her body, up around her cheeks, and for some time visualised Hubster with his arms around her, warming her.

She was still horribly thirsty, and still her head was pounding. It was as if the end of the world had arrived. A numbness crept over her brain and much time passed. Nothing moved but the rain.

Inevitably, her thoughts turned back to the wedding. In the weeks preceding the ceremony, her anxiety had shown itself in disturbed sleeping and eating patterns, which were the dual indicators of mental unease, according to her therapist at least – the therapist she hadn't seen for over a year. (Who had turned out to be far too balanced and successful to make her clients feel anything other than inadequate; her with her big fucking house in Primrose Hill, her thriller-writer husband, her picture-book children and Labradoodles. Her boutique boho style. Her perfect garden.)

At work Shauna had been stressed, and in the evenings she had gone out, night after night, and got drunk, a clichéd drunk drinking to forget. She had refused to give herself time to trawl through her memories of Seedie and what he had meant to her, what he still, if she was honest, meant. For this reason it wasn't until the day of the wedding itself, when midway through the ceremony the sky behind the boiled-sweet-stained glass darkened and the buttery church light suddenly turned chill and grey, that she was reminded of the curse that she had invoked so many years ago. It had been contained, she remembered, in a letter she had sent to Seedie; it had been couched in playful terms, if unmistakably bitter in tone. Dear Seedie (she recalled with a start as she sat there nauseated in the darkening church in her turquoise and her fuchsia, avoiding the eye of his mother, looking up at him in his grandiose morning tails and Chloe in her exquisite off-the-shoulder ivory wedding gown, with that simple rollover neckline and Mikado mermaid silhouette), I do understand that sometimes people, like cruise ships, have to move on to new horizons. Well done you. I do also understand that Chloe is as decent a new horizon as any, given that you've made your mind up to leave Port Shauna. For your own reasons. Whatever they may be. So I wouldn't dream of telling you that if you ever get married, you and Chloe, I hope it rains on your fucking wedding day. I wouldn't dream of saying that I hope the inevitable poncey garden party in Hampshire is a washout, and everybody's hats get ruined. Because that would be incredibly rude. Wouldn't it. With very best wishes, S.

So the curse had been cast. And it was before the end of the ceremony that the rain, utterly unforecast, began to fall. As Seedie's lips drew to Chloe's at the crowning moment of the thing, Shauna fancied she heard a thunderclap, as if the day had been choreographed by the *Wizard of Oz*.

The morning having been spotlessly clear and bright, little provision had been made for the downpour. An umbrella was somehow found for the bride and groom, and they left the church amid a half-hearted shower of soggy confetti, which fell from the air in woebegone clumps. Everybody put a brave face on it, tried to frame it as romantic, as a sign of grace, as a novelty that would give people something to remember (in which lay the tacit acknowledgment that until that point the wedding had been unremarkable in every way).

Shauna, trying to stifle her superstition, and attempting – unsuccessfully – to brush it off, left the church even more anxiously than she had entered it. She got through the inevitable handshake with the mother, the father, the kiss on the cheek of Seedie himself, and of Chloe, without incident. She had sailed through numbly, thinking of nothing, 'Raspberry Beret' still playing relentlessly in her ear, allowing herself to channel polite convention as a witch doctor channels the spirits.

Then came the champagne. With strawberries bobbing in it, bejewelled with golden bubbles. With waiters subtly offering refills when the glass was only half-empty – a ploy, Shauna was convinced, to get the guests trolleyed. In her case certainly it worked. The reception was held in the house itself instead of the garden, while the staff scurried around outside collecting umbrellas, moving buckets of champagne to shelter, sealing the marquee like a submarine. It stretched on and on, that reception in the house, while the sky framed in the old windows glowered more angrily than ever, and began hurling down great twisting sheets of water that exploded relentlessly across the county. Elemental. The rain was complicating things for the staff; there was so much more to be done. Still the champagne flowed. Shauna found herself in a corner of the drawing room, sitting side-saddle in the window seat, talking to a man with very high cheekbones and big pink hands, who went by the name of Hodgy and was busy learning Arabic for the Foreign Office. They had started their conversation as parts of a group, but somehow this and that had come up and people went this way and that, and then it was just him and her fixed by the window, and she shunted up to make room beside her on the seat while the rain sprayed like gravel handfuls on the glass behind them. Their legs touching from thigh to knee, their arms elbow to shoulder as well. Hubster? In her excitement and growing drunkenness she mistakenly called him

Podgy, and he flushed a shepherd's delight, and in the ensuing laughter she nuzzled her head into his chest like a foal. Thereafter a lone waiter entered with more bubble-beaded champagne; they accepted almost without noticing, but both refused the strawberries. Hodgy was a big man, strapping, with a laugh that resounded in her gut. He was also, she reluctantly detected, rather boring, and possibly a bit of a wanker. But the quantity of bubbly was such that these imperfections were smudged out in the roseate haze of alcohol. And then they were called for dinner.

The humiliation of it. The humiliation of it. She was drunk, he was drunk, they were both as drunk as bishops. She had dashed to her car to grab a pashmina and he had accompanied her with a folding brolly (where had he got that from?). On the way back they found themselves shortcutting through a flower-bed, lost, effectively, in the grounds, and one of the heels of her Manolos became hopelessly embedded in the mud, and, as the wedding music mewed somewhere in the background, they found themselves alone and laughing crazily in the bushes, and before she knew it they were lip-to-lip, and tongue-to-tongue – such was their desperation and intoxication – and he was muttering something about a quickie, his words slurred as his mouth was pushed to the side against her cheek, and her hands were inside his shirt against his body in the rain, and with some surprise she saw that her breasts were out and scooped in his large pink palms, and then, beneath a waterfalling tree, she dropped to her knees in the mud, and in a drunken swirl in which the world rolled around her like Plasticine, she took his weight in her mouth and sucked him off.

Afterwards, sobered by the act, they cleaned themselves off as best they could. Shauna felt foolish and ashamed. Still 'Raspberry Beret' played on. Hodgy begged her not to tell anyone, and that made it all the worse; he had a girlfriend, he told her now, and if she were to breathe a word of this to anybody she could single-handedly ruin the lives of so many people. Muddied and sullied, they made their way to the marquee separately and sneaked in on opposite sides of the tent. But somebody somehow had spied them, and the gossip had already – already! – circulated. Everybody knew. And did that stop her? Did it make her bow out, cut her losses, slink off home? Did it fuck.

This can't go on, thought Shauna. This abominable thirst, this headache. This hangover, this life. She could be at home by now, drinking sparkling water and lime, popping paracetamol, running a bath. She could be drinking a peppermint tea. Damn it, so she should be. She shouldn't be here. More sirens, more lights, whipping past on the hard shoulder, premonitions embodied. She tilted her seat backwards a little, as if that would ease the pain. If this went on much longer she'd have to get out, hope for the best, find somewhere she could buy some pills, some water. Take a piss. She raised herself onto her elbows and could see no sign of civilisation. It was chucking it down, anyway. She would wait it out, or try to. This jam simply couldn't go on for too much longer. Somebody somewhere must be doing something to sort it, to clear – whatever it was. She shuddered to think. Was that a helicopter? It was so difficult to tell with the noise of the rain. She passed her dry tongue across her dry lips, swallowed with some effort, pinched her eyes tight. She knew then, huddled by herself in the darkness and shadows in the middle lane of a frozen Orbital, cradled in the impersonal embrace of an indifferent universe, that she hadn't put that curse on Seedie and Chloe all those years ago. She had put it on herself.

She slept, and when she came to her senses the rain had stopped. Her bladder was fit to burst, and she was cold. She stepped out into the fresh air and slammed the door behind her. The squall had moved on. She slipped between bumpers, through the lanes of traffic, and across the hard shoulder to the barrier; there she crossed paths with Hsiao May, and for reasons largely physiological – on Shauna's part at least – they shared just a comradely nod. Then, concentrating on keeping her bladder clenched, she made her way up the hill towards the copse.

She was so focused on reaching her goal that she didn't notice the figure standing in the shadows of the trees until she had almost bumped into it. A movement of the hand alerted her to its presence; she jumped, almost overbalanced, let out a yelp.

'Don't be scared,' came a voice. 'Sorry. Sorry. It's just me.'

She cast her eyes into the shadows, and at the same time Monty stepped out. He looked tired, dishevelled, and had a slightly otherworldly expression, like somebody awoken freshly from a dream.

'Monty?' she said.

'Yes.'

'What . . . what are you doing here?'

'How shall I put it? How shall I put it?'

'Call of nature?'

'Yes.'

'Me too.'

'Not exactly glamorous,' said Monty. 'Anyway, I don't think I even know your name.'

'Shauna. Do you want to know my last name?'

'Why would I want to know that?'

'I don't know. You might want to send me a letter or something.'

'A letter? Who sends letters any more?'

'I don't know. Look me up on Facebook, then.'

'I'm not on Facebook.'

'Nor am I. Lawyer, you know.'

'You're a lawyer?'

'For my sins.'

'At least you're not a banker.'

'No. More's the pity.'

'Oh?'

'They earn a darn sight more than people like me.'

'True.'

'Sorry,' said Shauna, 'this is great but I'm desperate for the loo. That is, loo in the most general sense.'

Monty flushed. 'Don't let me stop you.'

'You're lucky being a bloke. Women need more coverage. And tissues and things.'

'Well, avoid that spot just over there. Three trees back.'

'Why . . . oh.'

He laughed, awkwardly. Shauna made her way into the copse, and found an appropriate spot. Here and there she could see movement in the trees, figures moving furtively in the shadows, but she was not afraid. This was the loo of the motorway, she thought. And anyway, Monty was there.

But when she emerged from the copse, he was nowhere to be seen.

The beautiful game

It was an hour after midnight. People were snuggling up as best they could. A light, cloudlike drizzle passed without becoming rain, and the motorway was shimmering again. Ursula, having woken briefly, had returned to her sleep, her coat bunched against her cheek; beside her, Max sat in silence. Jim, in the cab of his van, now lay sprawled across the seats, his forearm over his eyes. Popper lay in the reclined front seat of his Golf, looking up at the constellations of stars that could vaguely be seen beyond the orange lights, beyond the clouds. Chris was sound asleep and snoring like a child; Rhys was looking idly out of the window, wondering where Monty had got to, beginning to feel a little tired now. Shauna's car sat empty. Hsiao May and Harold, in their separate vehicles, were reading by the overhead lights. In the battered Ford estate, Dave, Stevie and Natalie slouched in various states of consciousness, too stoned to make the effort to contrive a pillow or a blanket.

All were contending with the cold, which seemed to grow around them like a living thing. Some huddled into jumpers and coats, some turned on the engine to get a blast of heat, and some mused on the urban myth that it would be best to have a candle, because candles give disproportionate amounts of heat in an enclosed space.

And with that distinctive sharp thunk, a football struck the tarmac of no-man's-land, the deserted southbound carriageway of the M25.

Cushioning the ball expertly on the bridge of his foot as it came down and commencing a fluid dribble across the lanes,

Shahid wondered whether this could be the first ever time the motorway had been graced by the magic of a football. Probably. He dragged the ball around his body, spun, continued, a seamless emulation of Ronaldinho. When he reached the other side he executed a step-over dummy and stopped, foot atop the ball; he wasn't even slightly out of breath. He looked back over his shoulder. Kabir was crabstepping wide with his hand up, as if preparing to receive a high ball. Mo – typical Mo – was warming up, alternating between stretching his calf muscles and jogging on the spot, his eyes fixed on the ball as if it was the only thing of interest in the world. They both looked tiny, backdropped by the columns of traffic, the dim hills behind, the black night overhead. Shahid scanned the line of cars, and for a moment could not locate his own. Or rather, his grandfather's. But then he saw it, nestling humbly, inconspicuously, amid newer and shinier models, a beaten-up, ancient Peugeot estate, not eccentric enough to be interesting, not new enough to be decent. Like his grandfather himself. Shahid was ashamed to be driving it. That car which still smelled of goat and spice, underpinned by the pungent scent of the ornament on the rear-view mirror, which was engraved with the names of Allah and filled with perfumed Othr. Shahid's father had left the world of his own father behind, gone up to Oxford, and from there to the *Guardian*. Shahid himself was even further removed. But the car remained, an echo of a former time, an ancestor that refused to die.

But Shahid was no longer in the car. He was on the M25, a football at his feet, his two best friends jogging out before him like Redskin scouts, and despite the shittiness of his life he felt at peace. Suddenly pumped with exhilaration after the stress of the day, which had been compounded by sitting in this ridiculous traffic, Shahid threw his head back and laughed.

They threw down hoodies for goalposts and began a kickaround. Shahid started off in goal. From his spot between the posts he could allow his eyes to wander all along the great phalanx of traffic, and everywhere he saw pale, pale faces watching. A sour taste crept into his mouth. Fuck you, knobheads, he thought. He could challenge them all to a game, he could take them all on. He picked up the ball and booted it high into the air; it had bounced twice before either of his friends could bring it under control. He turned his head and spat, and for a moment saw a ghostly face in the front seat of the white van – that psycho who had come for the crisps. Fuck him, he thought. Fuck him.

Today had all been his fault. To begin with, it was a dream come true. When the scout came down to watch London APSA train several weeks ago, when he offered Shahid his card and asked him to come up for a trial, he had not been able to believe it. Chelsea? Chelsea? You're lying, brah. Serious. This is bare lies. But it hadn't been. It had been the truth.

Excited, and without properly thinking it through, he told his parents.

'Dad, Mum,' he said, standing in the doorway to the kitchen, beaming as if he was about to break news of his engagement. They both looked up: his father was tamping down espresso coffee into the wand of his coffee machine; his mother was writing something on the magnetic calendar on the fridge. The late afternoon light was casting them in partial silhouette, creating halos around their heads. His mother lowered her pen. His father raised his eyebrows and ran a hand through his mane of hair.

Shahid took a breath. 'I've been offered a trial at Chelsea.'

'Chelsea?' said his father.

'Yes, Chelsea. The Blues.'

'A trial?' said his mother.

'Yes, Mum, yes. Chelsea.'

'Well, that's wonderful,' she said.

Then his father's eyebrows knitted low and he walked purposefully, once, around the table, coming to rest with steepled fingers in the exact spot he had previously vacated, in front of the coffee machine. He took his iPhone out of his pocket, began polishing the screen. His mother slipped the end of the pen into her mouth, pondered, carried on writing.

'Don't get me wrong,' said his father, 'this is brilliant news. Brilliant news. You must be over the moon.'

'Yes, Dad, I am. Just got to give it my best shot.'

'You know we'll stand behind you, whatever you do.'

'I know.'

'So.' He put his iPhone back in his pocket, and with all eight of his fingers he scratched his trim beard. Then he returned them to their steepled position.

'Yes, we're right behind you,' said his mother softly, still writing on the calendar. 'But you've got to listen to us as well.'

'I am listening.'

'We don't want you to give up on university for this.'

'Mum . . .'

'We're all for you giving it a go, a proper go, but we don't want you to close down your options.'

'It's football, Mum. You can't do it by halves.'

'You're still young, Shahid. We can't have you giving up on your life before it's even started.'

'Everyone knows I'm the best player on our team.'

'The London All Peoples' Sports Association.'

'London APSA, Mum. London APSA.'

'All-Asian.'

'But I'm good enough to play mainstream. I'm good enough for the Premiership. At least, I will be one day. They scouted me.'

'It's an amazing achievement, and I'm so proud. Like I said, we're all for you pursuing your dreams. But a lot of people are scouted.'

'No, they're not. Barely anyone is. This is Chelsea. It means I'm bloody good.' Shahid felt stupid saying all of these things that should never be said so plainly, and he flushed.

'And if you don't make it?'

'I will.'

'I believe in you. But if you get injured, say?'

'I don't know. I'll do something else.'

'What something else will you do? Without a university degree?'

'I'm not going to fail, Mum.'

'But if you do?'

'I won't.'

'You might.'

'I won't.'

'You'll at least need something to fall back on.'

She pressed the pen into a bolus of Blu-Tak on the fridge, and exchanged a glance with her husband.

'You're a clever boy,' he said. Somehow he had walked back around the table without Shahid noticing, and was now sitting with elbows askance, hands folded. The light danced on his grey-flecked hair. 'The world is at your feet, and not only the world of football. You're on track for some sterling A-level grades. You could go to any university you choose. Oxford might be an option. Everyone was very impressed when you did work experience at the *Guardian*. Your mother and I . . . we just want what's best for you. If you get off the racetrack now, there'd be no knowing whether you can get back on again.'

'A chance like this doesn't come along very often, Dad.'

'I know. You're doing brilliantly. But you still need something to fall back on. Like Mum said, you might get injured.'

'Dad, I'm not going to fail.'

'Football is one of the most unstable professions around. I'm not trying to be pessimistic, just realistic.'

'It's difficult to get in to the *Guardian*, Dad. But you made it, didn't you?'

'Sure. But I got my degree. If it hadn't worked out, I could have done something else. Look, you're a lucky boy, Shahid. We're offering to pay your tuition fees with no questions asked. You don't share many of the worries and pressures that a lot of young people face today. The world is at your feet.'

Shahid said nothing. All his life, his parents had been pushing him. On principle he had been sent to the local comprehensive, but his education had been supplemented by countless private lessons. His father in particular had been constantly on his back for as long as he could remember, trying to instil in him the ambition to succeed in a different kind of world. Out of nowhere, he felt a hand on his shoulder, looked up into his father's glasses, saw himself lensed upside-down within them. Behind him, his mother was rooting around in the fridge.

'If I don't give it my all, I might as well not bother,' he said.

'Take it from me, Shahid,' his father replied. 'Don't throw away your studies. Don't throw away your life. You can still play football as much as you like when you are at university. That would be the best way. Do it for the love of it.'

'So you're saying I shouldn't go to the trial?'

'Of course I'm not. You can't pass up on something like that. I'm just talking about university.'

'What about Zesh Rehman?' said Shahid. 'He's played at the highest level.'

'I know,' said his father. He drew a breath, exhaled, dropped his arm from the shoulder of his son.

Kabir aimed a playful, looping shot from his position on the deserted southbound fast lane. Shahid stepped to the left and caught it, then spun and tossed it neatly to Mo's feet. Mo, from the far side of the middle lane, screwed in a low drive, but again Shahid was too quick; he trapped it dead beneath the sole of his trainer, flicked it into the air, and booted a high ball back out to Kabir. He tried to bring it down on his chest but muffed it, and the ball caromed away across the tarmac. He shrugged, turned and jogged after it. Shahid, both feet on the boundary with the hard shoulder, jogged on the spot and grinned.

It was good to be out in the open, after sitting in the traffic jam, after the long and tortuous car journey, after the hellish

Chelsea trial. Shahid secretly suspected that his parents' lack of enthusiasm had jinxed it. That's how it had felt at the training ground in Cobham – as if he had been cursed. A disaster. But fuck, he had thought about it enough, they had talked about it enough, and now he just wanted a kick-around. Let off some steam. Try to take his mind off this nasty weight, this dull ache that sat inside him like a parasite. The ball flew towards him from Mo's trainer, and Shahid trapped it without difficulty. Aggressively, he booted it into the heavens. It hung there for a moment, a circle of starless sky.

People

Hsiao May was hungry. Her supplies were limited, but the time had come. She reached over into her cool bag and brought out a brown paper packet. It was weighty and springy, a wrapped chunk of flesh in her cupped palm. A crackle of excitement ran through her at the capacity of the contents to change the world for ever, as well as its unavoidable taboo. Already she could hear her mother's voice, and she hadn't even opened the bag. *What you doing, Hsiao May? What you got in there? What? You come here home and let me make food for you. I have rice cooking now, and chicken leg. You don't need to go so low as eating those things.*

She sat with the packet in her lap and started slowly, with the very tips of her fingers, to unfurl its scrolled mouth. Then, before slipping her hand inside, she glanced over at the camper van. In the light of an overhead lamp, Harold was reading something balanced on the steering wheel, from time to time passing his hand across his bearded cheek. He glanced up, briefly, the sort of look one might give someone making too much noise in a library, and returned to his reading. Then he raised a mug to his lips and drank, gingerly, from something hot. The steam misted his glasses; patiently, he perched the mug on the dashboard, removed his glasses, wiped the lenses individually on his jumper, replaced them. Then he carried on reading. Come on, she thought. Don't stalk.

But as she weighed the paper bag in her hands, she knew that she wanted somebody to share it with. If truth be told, she wanted someone to share her life with, someone other than Mama, Baba, Lulu, Lulu's kids. People, it was all about the people. Here she was, the answer to the biggest question of our times wrapped in paper in her hands, and she, the bearer of the knowledge, was alone and obscure in the world. She had her work, she had her passion, but without people to share it with she was like a woman without a reflection. She was dead space, a statue whose face had been worn smooth by the elements. She looked up at the man in the camper van again. She couldn't very well knock on his window and demand that Harold share her life. But if she offered him a snack? That would be a test of his open-mindedness, his intellectual curiosity, his ability to carry out rational analysis regardless of his culturally constructed preconceptions. It would be a meaningful topic of conversation, one which usually she could not introduce. But with him – potentially a fellow independent-minded academic – it might be possible. If he clicked, they could be friends, and if not, perhaps acquaintances. Either way, it would be a start. But dare she?

What was she thinking? She could not. She had noticed Harold once at an inter-faculty meeting, he had spoken with some passion and bravery against the commercialisation of higher education: against the rise in tuition fees, and against the university's policy of recruiting Chinese students indiscriminately in pursuit of their parents' wallets. He had also argued eloquently against positive discrimination, reasoning that a quota for state school children was nothing but a fig leaf for the failings of state education. She had been impressed at the time, she remembered. She saw his eyes flick up, scan the motorway for a moment, then return to his papers. She turned off the light above her head, put her paper bag away. She closed her eyes.

She just wasn't very good with people. What was the phrase? She wasn't a people person. And truly it is all down to people. The whole swarming edifice of human endeavour serves but one aim, that of the happiness, freedom, and fulfilment of people. The obstacles are produced by people. The solutions, where they exist, are made by people. But now there are so many people, and year by year so many more, that without radical thinking, humanity will buckle and collapse.

She traced with her fingers the contours of the buff folder on the passenger seat. She did not need it to be open. She could draw on it as she pleased; using only her mind, she could surround herself with the landscape of the world's problems as they are today, coupled with a vision of how these problems could be solved tomorrow. It is imperative, she thought, that people – all people – began to share her vision.

Ten thousand years ago, she thought, there were maybe five million people walking the earth. Each, if truth be told, probably harboured concerns and desires which in the final analysis were not that far removed from our own. Certainly they desired sex. By the time of the First Dynasty in Egypt, the global population had trebled in size; and by the time Christ's birth established, albeit in a retrospective sense, our Common Era, as many as two hundred million people were daily drawing breath. From five million to two hundred million in eight thousand years.

People continued to fall in love, to have sex, to have children, to have more. At the cusp of the nineteenth century, when the inhabitants of the world numbered – for the first time – one billion, the economist Thomas Malthus argued in his famous *Essay on the Principle of Population* that human proliferation would be self-regulated by plague, by famine, by war. This marked, at least in Hsiao May's mind – which, though she was a scientist, was drawn to glimmers of poetic irony – the moment things really took off. People everywhere, meeting, loving, fucking, breeding. Fighting, starving, dying from the plague. Meeting, loving, fucking, breeding. By the nineteen twenties, the population had doubled. Two billion. And it only took forty years for the next billion to arrive. Eight years later, when the German Nobel laureate Paul Ehrlich announced that the books would surely soon be balanced by the starvation of hundreds of millions, there were three-and-a-half billion people on the earth. From then until now, a billion newborn eyes have peeled open every twelve or so years.

On 12 October 1999, the world's six-billionth person, Adnan Mević, was born in Sarajevo. (His birth was celebrated with a visit from the UN Secretary General, Kofi Annan, who forgot to bring a present.) On Halloween 2011, the world welcomed its seven-billionth person: Danica May Camacho from Manila in the Philippines. The UN, realising that something had to be done, revised its previous forecast that the global population would plateau in 2050 at a level of nine billion. Instead, it suggested that by 2100 there would be ten billion people on earth. And this was by no means definitive. The more people there were, the more impact small inaccuracies would have; if families on average were to have, say, an extra 0.5 of a child, by 2100 the global population would be sixteen billion.

At this point in her discourse, Hsiao May would quote the American myrmecologist Edward Osborne Wilson, who said that the pattern of population growth in the twentieth century was 'more bacterial than primate'. According to most estimates, in about a decade there would be eight billion souls on this earth, with the brunt of the growth occurring in the poorest regions. India would overtake China as the most populous nation on earth. And here she would come to the point: shortages would be rife.

There were no two ways about it. This plundered planet, its water supply desiccated by rising temperatures, its verdancy and munificence faltering, would be unable to provide the oil, water, arable land, crops and livestock to feed such a massive quantity of humans, all vying for their sustenance, their lives. Bill Gates argued that if humanity is to survive, a second 'green revolution' would desperately be needed. The first, which occurred between 1950 and 1990, had increased global grain yields by eighty per cent through the widespread introduction of phosphorus-rich fertilisers. Even this had become unsustainable: phosphorus supplies were now being exhausted, which had been called 'the gravest natural resource shortage you've never heard of'.

This was the question, the biggest question of our times . . . and the answer lay in rethinking the human food chain.

But now her mind was buzzing again. She leaned over and replaced her notes in her briefcase. Then she looked out once again at the road. Most engines were off; most car lights were out. The occasional car door was open, the occasional figure was leaning against a vehicle, drinking, smoking, stretching as if getting out of bed. On the other side of the motorway, people were even playing football; this had given her a little thrill of delight at first, before it too became familiar, unremarkable.

This was no longer a traffic jam. The cars had shed their attribute of mobility, their function as methods of transport. They had become temporary homes. Individual bases of existence, units in an accidental society. Seen in a certain light, there was something almost utopian about this vehicle village, she thought. This autopolis. All divisions of race, class, and wealth had been done away with by the hand of randomness; fate had netted several thousand people and bunched them together, without the slightest concern for their social instincts. How else would a species collect so randomly, with no ordering principle?

Out of nowhere, a pale face appeared framed in her car window, followed by a torso. It floated there like a glow-worm while her eyes focused. A stocky, rough-looking man, wearing a T-shirt with a faded soft drink logo on the chest; a face that looked roughly hewn from a block of lard. He was motioning for her to wind down the window. After a moment of consideration, she did so.

'Sorry to disturb, Miss. I just wondered if you have any information?'

'Information?'

'Information.'

'What sort of information?'

'You know. About hold-up.'

'No idea.'

'Right, right.'

His accent, though she could not place it exactly, was certainly Eastern European.

'It's just that I am on job right now. That is my lorry there.'

'I see.'

This was the point at which he would have been expected to thank her and be on his way; but he just stood there, half bending over, peering in through her window awkwardly.

'Was there something else?' she said at last.

'From what I hear, there's been massive pile-up three miles down road,' he replied. 'Maybe two. Two lorries. Or one lorry. One lorry and van. One lorry and large van.' He glanced around nervously, then looked back at Hsiao May.

'That's . . . sad,' she said. 'Well, I hope they get it cleared quickly, whatever it is.'

To her surprise, the man straightened up. 'I'll carry on down line,' he said. 'And keep you posted.'

'Thanks,' said Hsiao May, uncertainly. The man nodded and, at last, moved on. She wound the window back up and made sure that the doors were locked. Then she sat back for a few minutes, eyes closed, until her emotions settled. Anything could happen out here, anything. Hush. I could be killed or raped or kidnapped. Hush. Kidnapped? How would they make their getaway? Hush. Finally, once she had composed herself once more and her mind had quietened, she opened her eyes again. The world had returned to normality. It was a traffic jam, that was all.

But now it was raining again. Not hard, slanting rain like before, but a wet, cloudlike mist that settled on everything like cobwebs. Involuntarily she shivered. Would this night never end?

A movement caught her eye. On the hard shoulder a police car was approaching, with flashing lights but no siren, and at a reasonable speed. It slowed, then came to a stop by the emergency phone. The door opened; out stepped a burly policeman, protected against the elements by a tent-like yellow jacket. The collar was raised around his chin, and a cap in a plastic cover sat low over his eyes. He was recognisable as human by form alone; barely any skin could be seen.

She got out of the car and hurried over to the policeman through the rain. By the time she arrived at the hard shoulder, she was soaked. The policeman, who had opened the emergency telephone box and was fiddling with something inside, did not appear to notice her approach. She plucked at his slippery sleeve and he looked at her over his shoulder.

'What's going on?' she said, shielding her eyes from the rain. 'We've been here for hours and hours.'

'There's been an incident, Miss,' he said and returned to the phone box.

'What kind of incident? Do you know what's going on? I mean, can you tell me?'

'An incident of an emergency nature,' he said over his shoulder, 'involving a number of individuals further along the motorway. The emergency services are attending the scene.'

'Can't you tell me anything more?' she said, shaking the rain from her hair. 'Anything? It's awful being stuck like this, not knowing.'

The policeman concluded his task in the phone box and slammed it shut. As he turned to face her, a layer of rainwater slid from the peak of his cap. 'Sorry, Miss,' he said. 'We can't release any further details of the incident at the present time.' He strode back to his car, Hsiao May trailing in his wake.

Then, through the shimmering moisture came Max, charging like a bull. His shoulders were hunched, and he wore no coat. 'Officer! Hello, officer!' he called. 'Any idea what the hold-up is?'

The policemen regarded him perfunctorily, his hand resting on the door handle. 'An incident, sir,' he said, 'involving a number of individuals.'

'What's that supposed to mean?'

'Sorry, sir. It's part of an ongoing investigation.'

'Ongoing investigation? Into what?'

'Sorry, sir.'

'Christ almighty. Can't you at least give us an idea of how long we're going to be here?'

'Anyone's guess, sir, I'm afraid.'

'What about supplies? Where can we get water, food? I have a young daughter in the car, and she's starting to run a fever.'

'If you're in urgent need of assistance, sir, call the emergency services.'

'But you are the emergency services.'

'Sorry, sir. I'm from traffic.'

'You mean you're the wrong sort of policeman?'

'Sir, the best thing would be for you to return to your vehicle now. Just calm down and return to your vehicle.'

'But I am calm,' said Max. 'I'm . . . perfectly . . . calm.'

'Then return to your vehicle, sir.' He lowered himself into his car and drove away.

Max and Hsiao May exchanged a glance. 'Fucking unbelievable,' said Max venomously. Hsiao May didn't have the words to reply, and could only watch as he slunk away into the darkness. She felt on the verge of tears. As she returned to her car, the mist billowing around her, she thought again of Harold.

Evading Tomasz

Shauna's hangover, which by rights should have been dissipating by now, was deepening. Her head was throbbing to some satanic rhythm, her brain pulsating in its bony case. She had relieved herself of the discomfort of a full bladder, but this had merely allowed her to become aware again of the potency of her hangover. It hadn't seemed so bad earlier, when she was speaking to the people by the Waitrose van. But now that she was alone once again, and sitting in her stuffy car, it had reached truly epic proportions.

The problem was that when she had sat down at the table for the wedding breakfast, and sensed immediately that people were treating her oddly, she had hit the bottle with a vengeance. This, come to think of it, was typical; whenever she felt intimidated, or knew she was making a fool of herself, she would react by talking more, courting attention more insistently, yes, drinking more, all the time dying inside. By the time pudding had been served, and the speeches had commenced, she was so drunk – so drunk – that the scene was set for what was to happen next. And the hangover was inevitable too.

She sat in a zombified state for several minutes while a fine rain fell. As soon as it relented, she swung her feet out of the car and into the wall of chill night air. Action had to be taken. Her head swam and she had to pause before standing up. The sky was murky and solid, yet at the same time seething, different islands and continents of cloud overlapping and obscuring one another. The acrid taste of wine was still in her mouth, unholy fumes rising from a dark heat within her. She got to her feet, felt a pang of nausea, let it pass. Now that she was out of the car, standing with her feet planted firmly on the tarmac, it struck her how dwarfed the human being was by his own creation. Here were thousands of stationary vehicles, tens of thousands, each one of them stronger than fifty men, and here was their highway, their temple. Here was her hangover, imposed upon her by a culture more powerful than she was, using a poison more powerful than she was. What was left?

These were the sorts of thoughts she would have from time to time, after particularly heavy sessions. (At uni she had written a book entitled *Heavy Sessions*, a compilation of drunken stories of herself and her friends.)

She turned slowly through 360 degrees, trying to discern where the nearest outpost of civilisation might be. She had no idea where she was exactly, at what position on the M25, though she thought she could recall passing the Dartford Crossing not all that long ago. Perhaps it didn't matter where she was, since this road was circular. God, she was shit at this kind of thing. Why couldn't everything just work as it was supposed to? Then she would be at home in her bath by now. She knew what her father would say. He would say: Nam Sibyllam quidem Cumis ego ipse oculis meis vidi in ampulla pendere, et cum illi pueri dicerent: Σίβυλλα τί θέλεις; respondebat illa: ἀποθανεῖν θέλω. This was his set piece, the only passage of Latin (and Greek) he was able to remember. Did she know what it meant? She did not, regardless of the fact that she got a C at Latin, and regardless of the fact that her father had explained it to her many times. She vaguely knew it was taken from *The Waste Land*; she vaguely knew it had something to do with a goddess in a bottle living out some bleak and awful existence; she vaguely knew it had to do with wanting to be dead.

A man up ahead was windmilling his arms in the air. At first she thought he was in some kind of trouble, but then he gave a final stretch and disappeared back into his car. Everybody was contained within their little pods, unable to look beyond the tiny fragments of their lives. She had thought that Londoners would step up in times like these, start banding together and sharing resources. That was what was supposed to happen, wasn't it? Like when there's a power cut or a flood or a strike. Had the human spark been finally obliterated? The spirit of the Blitz? Was all that was left an endless system of machines and concrete, populated by bodies, not people? Either way, she knew that shortly after the camaraderie came the time when people would start eating each other. She was growing maudlin, she knew that, and she knew it was the hangover. She was a fool. Still, she wished that someone would dash off and get her supplies, her paracetamol and water, and perhaps a nice box of chocolates, and come back and make her feel as if everything was going to be all right. They would stay in touch, fall in love, build a life; they would have babies, and together, eventually, grow old.

The strongest possibility, she thought to herself at length, is that the low hill beside the road, bobbled with tufty trees, hid behind it some village or hamlet; and that within that village or hamlet lay an all-night pharmacy, or something similar, that sold paracetamol and water. And perhaps some prawn crackers. Failing that, some prawn cocktail crisps. Or a bacon roll. Or olives – still she was craving olives. Yes, there was a faint glow behind the ridge that suggested some inhabitancy or other. But how could she get up there and over the other side? There was no visible path, and she wasn't confident that she was able to ascend at such an incline in her current state. And, ultimately, would it be worth the effort? Or would it simply be a facsimile of the sort of experience she had doing cross-country at school, where there would always be one more hill behind the one she had hoped would be the last? If that were to happen – if she were to haul her sorry arse up that steep slope, through the mud and the puddles (inevitably there would be puddles) in her inappropriate shoes, which would almost certainly be ruined beyond repair, only to find that all her efforts had been wholly in vain, well, she would literally sit down and die.

It was while Shauna was looking up at the ridge, weighing her options, that she got the feeling that she was not alone. She turned to see a man in a faded T-shirt approaching along the line of traffic, between the middle and fast lanes. Before she knew it she had caught his eye, and he smiled and raised his hand as if he knew her; automatically she raised hers in return. She waited awkwardly as he got closer, and then he was standing before her, smiling.

'Nice evening,' the man said, in, Shauna guessed, a Polish accent.

'Glad you think so,' Shauna replied guardedly. 'We'll never get home the way things are going. Or rather, not going. Ha.'

'Any idea what hold-up is?' said the man.

'How would I know that?' said Shauna.

'Don't know. People know things.'

'Sorry, I don't know anything.'

'Strange things could have happened. Fog.'

'Whatever it is, it's bound to be something horrid.'

There was a pause. How could she get rid of him? She couldn't think straight.

The man squinted. 'What's your name?' he said abruptly.

'Jane,' said Shauna. 'You?'

'I am Tomasz,' he said. 'Pleased to meet you.'

'Likewise,' said Shauna, searching for inspiration. 'Well,' she said at last, 'I'll let you go.'

Her words rang flatly in the darkness. She nodded, smiled, bolstering their impact. Still Tomasz did not move. Blitz spirit, she thought. Fuck.

As if in answer to her prayers, she saw a familiar figure moving amongst the cars.

'Popper!' called Shauna. 'Over here, Popper! Popper?'

Popper finally located her and waved. At the sight of this intruder, Tomasz withdrew into himself and moved towards Shauna, triangulating her as if they were on intimate terms. Shauna shuffled backwards towards the car, clipping herself in with the car door.

'What's up?' said Popper.

'I just ... I just thought I'd say hello,' Shauna replied pleadingly.

'Who's this?' said Popper.

'I am Tomasz,' said Tomasz. 'I was just speaking with Jane.'

At this Popper looked quizzically at Shauna, then a look of understanding came into his eyes.

'Where you from, mate?' he said convivially; only Shauna picked up that Popper's tone of voice had become adversarial.

'I am lorry driver.'

'Oh, right. What are you carrying?'

'Supplies for supermarket.'

'I see,' said Popper. 'Any idea what's going on?'

'I have heard some rumours,' said Tomasz, brightening up. 'Maybe attack.'

'A duck?'

'No, attack. Attack.'

'Oh, I see. Attack. Sorry, it's the accent.'

'Terrorists.'

A cloud passed across Popper's face, followed immediately by an expression of good humour. 'Not sure if there wouldn't be more sirens and so on for a terrorist attack. Not sure if there wouldn't be rather more fuss. What do you think?'

'Yes,' said Tomasz. 'There would be more police. And army.'

There was a pause.

'To tell you the truth,' said Popper, 'I am actually in search of a light. I don't suppose ...'

'I've got one,' said Shauna. 'I don't smoke, but I do have a lighter in the car. For special occasions.'

Popper laughed loudly. 'The ceremonial lighter,' he said. 'This is very good of you. Sorry to put you out. I wouldn't dream of asking normally, it's just that I'm desperate. Mine's on the blink.'

Shauna leaned into her car, the tilt making the taste of alcohol rise in her throat, and located the lighter. It seemed to be in working order. Then she was in the night air again. Popper lit his cigarette, head cocked to the side, eyes slitted. Then he gave a cigarette to Tomasz and puffed, scanning the country like a landowner surveying his estate.

'Nasty business this,' he said, 'that's for sure.' He looked at Shauna and gave her a tiny nod, as if to suggest that he'd sort this out now. 'Where are you parked, mate?' he said to Tomasz.

'Down that way,' said Tomasz. 'You can see my lorry from here, just about.'

'That big black one?'

'Is blue. In daylight, is blue.'

'How long did it take you to walk all the way over here?'

'About five minutes.'

'Five minutes? You're a bit of a mover, aren't you?'

'Yes,' said Tomasz.

'Don't think you'd get stranded, do you?' said Popper.

'Stranded?'

'You know, if this traffic began to move.'

'Will be fine. The traffic is not going to move, man. Never.'

'Why did you walk down here, anyway?'

'I'm gathering information,' said Tomasz.

'The terrorist attack theory?'

'That and other things.'

'It would be good to know the truth. The only way to do it is to make your way to the obstruction and see it with your own eyes, I suppose.' Popper sucked his cigarette. 'But the question is, how far do you go? Beyond a certain point you run the risk of being stranded.'

'I think . . . perhaps I should get back.'

'Oh, I wasn't suggesting that,' said Popper. 'Just that if I were you I'd make a choice. Either head for the obstruction, or head for your lorry. Either way, stick at it. Keep going till you get there. Otherwise you'll get caught with your pants down. So to speak.'

Tomasz furrowed his brow. Then he said a cursory farewell and disappeared along the line of cars.

'God, thanks so much,' said Shauna when he was gone. 'I'd been trying to get rid of that man for ages. Bloody creep.'

'Ah, he was all right. Struck me as something of a lost soul.'

'I haven't much time for lost souls these days.'

'Why not?'

'Had enough of them.'

Popper cleared his throat. 'What are you going to do now?' he said.

'Now? Oh, I was about to go for a walk.'

'I'll come with you if you like.'

'Thanks, but . . . I'm fine. I need a bit of space after that.'

'Of course you do, of course you do,' said Popper. 'Anyway, it's getting rather nippy out here. Can I just light one more ciggy before I go? To take to the car?'

Shauna obliged. He thanked her courteously, then bid her goodbye. She was alone.

She tried to gather her thoughts. Why on earth had she rejected Popper? On paper he would certainly be a potential Hubster, and the story of their meeting like this, quite by chance in the midst of a hellish jam on the equally hellish M25, would make the perfect wedding speech. Yet she had felt not one iota of attraction stir within her. It was as if she was in a bell jar, at a remove from the world. What was happening to her?

Decisively, she locked the car. Then she stepped awkwardly over the barrier and picked her way through the longish grass towards the hill. For a moment she wavered; then, driven by thirst, she went on. The wet grass clutched at her ankles. What a night. Behind her, a door slammed. She turned, and at first could see nothing. Then a figure appeared from behind a white van, heading in her direction. As he came closer, she took a breath. Him again!

The test

Monty was pacing though the shadows around the copse, speaking on his phone. 'Fine,' he said. 'But I'm not happy about the way this is going. It's a fucking farce. I'm going to get myself killed. I just wanted to tell you that.' He ended the call with a thumb-hook, deleted the number from his history and slipped his phone back into his pocket. A fine, misty rain was descending; this, he thought, was a sign that he could put off his return to the van no longer. He took a deep breath and approached it quietly, from an oblique angle. It was past one in the morning now.

When Monty reached the door he felt certain that Rhys and Chris hadn't detected his approach. He lowered his ear gently against the elephantine flank of the vehicle, hoping to overhear them talking about him, but there was no sound. For a moment he wondered if they had sloped off somewhere. They wouldn't have, would they? But then there was a loud burp. He waited a while longer, the breeze skating around the van and over him, and gripped the cool, curved handle. Then he counted to three – don't rise to the bait – opened the door and hoisted himself up and in.

The air was thick with cigarette smoke and the stuffiness of two men breathing. He climbed into his seat, slammed the door and was once again part of their world. Rhys, who had been asleep, looked up groggily. At first, nobody spoke.

'Thought you'd fucked off,' said Rhys at last.

'I had.'

'And then?'

'Then I thought about the boys.'

'What did you think about them?'

Monty took a breath. 'Rhys, this ain't no good, all this shit,' he said.

'Yeah?'

'Yeah. All this shit between us. It ain't good for the boys.'

'But you are?'

'What?'

'Good for the boys?'

'Look, Rhys. Everything I do pisses you off, and that's just the way it is. I can't do nothing about that. But if the boys are going to be strong, this shit's got to stop.'

'I agree, bruv.'

'You agree?'

'Yeah. This shit has got to stop. It'll stop when you do.'

'Come on, Rhys. You know I make the boys stronger.'

'No, mate, no. I don't know that. Monty, mate, your heart ain't right. You ain't right. I saw you with them fucking Pakis out there. There was no real hatred in you, mate. I can smell proper hatred, and it ain't in you.'

There was a pause. Chris was rubbing his eyes, befuddled. Don't rise to the bait, Monty thought. Just don't.

'Look,' he said, 'what would it take to convince you? I work my arse off for the boys. I bankroll half the movement. Without me, we'd be nothing. And still that's not enough for you. So what the fuck can I do?'

'What would it take?' said Rhys. 'You serious, bruv? Well, you can help me storm that fucking van for one thing. Get us some proper food and stuff. Booze.'

'That's not what the boys are about, mate, you know that. The van driver's one of us. Even if he wasn't, it would just be stupid. We'd get arrested and all. We can't escape in this traffic. Gaz would have a fucking fit.'

'All right,' said Rhys quietly. 'I'll think of something else.'

Monty looked up sharply. Rhys' face was half hidden by

darkness, and he couldn't see his eyes. Beside him Chris picked up an almost empty packet of M&Ms, plucked it taut and tipped the final cluster into his mouth. His jaw moved with bovine regularity.

Rhys shook a cigarette from the packet, took it in his teeth and lit up. Then he tossed the packet onto the dashboard. Chris reached forward to retrieve it and lit a cigarette for himself. Neither of them offered one to Monty.

'Way I see it,' said Rhys through the smoke, 'you're all fucking talk, innit? Always giving it that.'

'I know the way you see it,' said Monty. 'And I know how fucking paranoid you are. I know what a fuck-up you are.'

Rhys smiled as if he had heard something sad. 'What I want to see,' he said, 'is you taking a hit for what you believe in. Chris wants to see it too. Innit, Chris?'

His brother nodded, uncertainly.

'I take hits every fucking day,' said Monty.

'That right?'

'All the money, for one thing.'

'Money don't mean the same thing for you as it do for us, Monty. For you it don't mean fuck-all. There's always more where that came from.'

'That's bollocks.'

'Like I said before, you can't buy respect. You got to earn it. Innit, Chris?'

His brother said nothing.

'What about me having to go all the way round the fucking world at the drop of a hat?' said Monty. 'France? Sweden? Germany? You think that's fucking fun? What with a job on top of it and all?'

'Makes you feel like a right big man, dunnit?'

'Fuck's sake. This is what I mean, Rhys. I just can't win with you.'

'Ain't my fault.'

'All right, what hits have you taken, then?' said Monty.

167

Rhys pushed up his sleeve to reveal several deep scars, healed but livid, mapping the back of his hand, his wrist, his forearm.

'They'd have killed you if it weren't for me,' said Monty quietly.

'Yeah, yeah. The big fucking man.'

'I should have let them gut you. Like a fish.'

'I'll gut you like a fucking fish, mate, if you don't shut the fuck up.'

There was a moment's silence.

'So, like I said,' Rhys continued, 'you ain't never taken no proper hit.' He inhaled deeply from his cigarette and held it up as if admiring the glowing beauty of the tip.

'Whatever,' said Monty.

'No, mate,' said Rhys. 'Not whatever. Not fucking whatever. We can put it to the test.'

He took a final pull on his cigarette, then offered it to Monty. 'Go on, big man,' he said. 'Prove it.'

'Prove what?'

'Ain't no big fucking deal, is it? One in the arm for the boys.'

'One in the arm?'

'Yeah. One in the arm.'

Monty watched his own hand gliding up to meet Rhys's, taking the cigarette, rotating it slightly, the smoke forming a thin column, like that from a crematorium on a windless day. He looked at Rhys. A snakish smile was playing about his lips.

'Go on then, mate,' said Rhys softly. 'You're a proper one of the boys, like me. Like Chrissie. So prove it.'

Monty raised the cigarette and took a long drag. The smoke grated on his lungs. Only half was left.

'Finish it if you want,' said Rhys, 'There's more where that came from. And Chris got a packet too, innit, Chris?'

Monty took another drag. Amid all the adrenaline, an insanity was growing in him, a wild recklessness. 'Fine,' he said. He rolled up his sleeve. 'Pass me the cider.'

'Dutch courage, eh?'

'Give it here. One drink and I'll do it.'

'Not so bothered about drink fucking driving now, then?'

'I'll just have the one. Just one swig, that's all I want. Then I'll do it. Anyway, there's not much driving going on is there?'

Rhys brought the bottle up from the footwell and tumbled it in his hands. 'You're out of luck,' he said, 'it's gone.'

'Bollocks.'

'Fraid so, mate. You'll just have to stop being gay and fucking do it.'

'There might be some in the back,' said Chris suddenly.

'Just fucking do it, you poof,' said Rhys. 'It's almost burned down.'

Monty looked at the object between his fingers. It was smouldering like a fuse in the half-light. Would it smell?

'If you ain't got the balls to do it,' said Rhys slyly, 'I can always do it for you. Wouldn't say no, innit?' He laughed.

'I'm going to do it.'

'Go on then. Fucking big man Monty. Go on. Go on.'

'I need a drink.'

And suddenly he was in the night air again, on the black tarmac where no feet but his own had trodden, the van door slamming behind him, his arms, the backs of his hands intact. He strode round to the back of the van, crushing his keys in his fist, feeling the pain. The back door was closed but not locked. He pulled it open. There were his tools: the baseball bats, the chains, the cans of mace. But no alcohol. No alcohol. He slammed the door shut and, as if partitioning some bad memory to an obscure corner of his mind, pushed his key into the lock and turned it. Then, without giving himself time to think, he walked round the front and shouted at the window, without opening the door: 'I'm going to get some booze.'

'You what?' said Rhys, winding down the window.

'Booze. To see us through the night.'

'I'll get you some, mate. From that van and all.'

'Look, I've said I'll do it and I will. I just want a drink first, that's all. You should fucking thank me. You look like you need a drink.'

'Where you going to find an offy, anyway? This time of night?'

'Over there. On the other side of that hill. Past the trees.'

'How do you know that?'

'Saw it before, didn't I? Lights from a village or something.'

'You're desperate, Monty my son. Fucking desperate. You're just shitting yourself, aren't you? You're shitting yourself good and fucking proper.'

He stepped away from the van, trying to ignore the peals of laughter that rang out inside the vehicle. His face was burning. A primal fear that he had not experienced since childhood was coursing throughout his body, making him feel nauseous and enfeebled and humiliated.

Half walking, half running, he reached the barrier and struggled over. It was as his feet nested into the long grass on the other side, the mud giving way with gentle reluctance, that he looked up.

There, to his surprise, was Shauna, making her way laboriously up the hill. Monty took a deep, wavering breath and began to clamber up the groove she had trodden in the grass.

And she looked back, and saw him, and took a breath.

Monty and Shauna

Shauna was clearly struggling in the long grass; she wasn't dressed for walking, and didn't seem comfortable outdoors. The silhouette of the hill hunched darkly up against the sky, the faint glow behind making it look flat, like a stage prop. The place on Monty's arm that had escaped a branding was tingling, as if something physical had actually occurred, rather than been avoided. As he trudged through the grass, he cradled his forearm as if its wholeness was the result of a recent healing, as if he suddenly appreciated how vulnerable this body can be. I'm not cut out for this, he thought.

The girl reached the summit; she turned, saw him, made an ambiguous gesture, and then appeared to diminish in height as she disappeared over the other side. Why wasn't she waiting for him? Had he been misreading the signals all along? This was typical of his life, he thought. But he was determined to break the cycle.

When Monty bridged the peak of the hill, Shauna was leaning heavily on a fence. Trying to tame the turbulence of his emotions, he approached.

'Jesus Christ,' she said.

'Have you been drinking?'

'No. I mean, yes. Last night though. I've still got a raging hangover.'

A blonde female (though it was dark and there was not much in the way of colour to rely on); five feet six; rather underweight; professional; fairly well-off; functioning alcoholic, perhaps. Mental health problems, question mark? She was beautiful.

'What are you trying to do?' he said, hearing his accent change to match hers.

'Get over this fucking fence. Who would put a fucking fence here? What's the point? Who would even do that?'

'I don't know.'

'Tell me about it.' She stopped, rested against the fencepost more heavily, feet splayed, as if going into labour.

'Are you all right?'

'Yes, fine, fine. Just feeling a bit queasy. It'll pass.'

'Just try to relax. Maybe you should go back to your car.'

'Maybe. Fuck, I think I'm going to chunder.'

'Do you want to sit down?'

'Don't worry, it'll pass, it'll pass.'

'Take deep breaths.'

She did not answer this time, just continued puffing, slowly, rhythmically. She closed her eyes, looked faint. Monty stepped closer and put a hand gently on her shoulder.

'Are you . . .'

'I've told you, I'm all right,' she snapped. 'It's the altitude.'

'Altitude? We're only on a little hill.'

'Shut up.'

'Look, you don't seem well,' Monty said. 'If you've taken any illegal substances, you need to tell me now.'

'It's just a fucking hangover, Christ's sake. Have you never had a fucking hangover?'

The exertion of this line proved to be the final straw. She just had time to turn away before the vomit came; she retched into the grass, holding her hair away from her face. Monty put his hand on her back, supporting her. It went on, great grey plumes splattering into the grass, until there was nothing left to come, and even then she continued to gag, making reptilian croaking sounds. The smell was fetid and sour. Finally, she sat down in the grass. Monty gave her a tissue.

'I'm sorry,' she gasped. 'What an utter tit.'

'Have you taken any drugs?' he said.

'I keep telling you. I haven't taken drugs, I'm not drunk, I'm not suffering from AIDS or fucking myxomatosis. I'm just hung over. All right? Hungover.'

'OK, sorry.'

'What are you, anyway? Drugs squad or something?'

Monty flushed. 'Me?' he said. 'God, no.' He turned towards the fence and contemplated scaling it. Not a difficult task, he thought. About five feet high, obvious footholds, almost as if it had been designed to be climbed. Moisture-soaked wood. No barbed wire or rusty nails that he could see. And beyond it, unmistakably, the few late-night lights of a village. He turned back to Shauna. 'You came all the way up here just to be sick?'

'Jesus,' she said, scrambling to her feet. 'I'm trying to get down to the village, get some water, some paracetamol, you know. This has been a really shitty weekend, and an even more shitty night. I should be tucked up in bed right now. I had the evening all planned out. A nice bath, soaking in essential oils with a glass of Bordeaux . . . aren't you heading there too?'

'To the village?'

'No, to Bordeaux. Yes, to the village.'

'I suppose so.'

'Well, then.'

'Are you feeling better now?'

'Yes. Throwing up usually does that, don't you find? God, what a total tit. I'm sorry, Monty.'

'Don't worry. Seen it all before.'

'Yeah, but it's not exactly dignified, is it?'

He smiled. 'I'm sorry I haven't got any water.'

'If you wouldn't mind giving me a hand over the fence, that would be fab,' she replied.

He linked his fingers to form a stirrup. She pushed her foot into it and he tried to boost her up, but her leg did not have sufficient strength, and she did not have sufficient coordination, and she almost lost her balance.

'Christ,' she said, 'this is hopeless.'

'It's probably better if you just climb over by yourself,' he said. 'I'll tell you where to put your feet. Look, sort of stick your foot here . . .'

Slowly, falteringly, without elegance or panache, Shauna dragged herself up the fence, rolled over the top, and dropped heavily to the other side, where she lay sprawling in the grass. One of her shoes had come off.

'You haven't sprained anything?' said Monty.

'No, I'm fine. I'm fine. Just having a breather.'

He climbed the fence in one fluid movement, brushed himself down and helped her to her feet.

'Look,' said Shauna, 'shall we walk down together? If you don't want to, just say. I haven't exactly made a fabulous impression.'

'No, no, not at all. I know how it is. I've been there.'

'How I'm going to get back up that fence I don't know. I think I'm losing it.'

'Maybe there's some way you could go round.'

'You're not a crazy guy, are you?'

'What? No. I'm not a crazy guy.'

'Good. Because I just couldn't deal with that right now.'

'No. And why should you?'

'Though if you were a crazy guy, would you tell me?'

'Of course I would.'

'That proves you're not.'

They began to scramble slowly, side-by-side, down the steep, bumpy hill toward the village.

As it turned out, they could have simply accessed the village by following a half-hidden path that carved a shallow groove around the hill and led directly to the High Street. When they got there, they could see it signposted. The shops were closed and a timeless slumber lay across everything. The place was deserted. A helicopter passed overhead, its bulbous nose tilted towards the earth; they speculated as to whether that meant that the traffic would soon be moving. They both worried about what would become of them if that happened before they got back, she to her Smart car, he to his van, with his two passengers in it; but they had been sitting in traffic for so long, and both, for their different reasons, felt so alienated from their vehicles, from their lives, from themselves, that they preferred to suffer the worry than return to the queue of traffic, in Shauna's case, without water, food and paracetamol; in Monty's case, without protection from Rhys. But a garage, thankfully, was open. Can't do much business, Monty thought, considering it's not a service station, considering it's not signposted from the road. The man behind the counter was nonplussed. Shauna bought a packet of paracetamol and a large bottle of cold water; Monty bought a large packet of Doritos and some Maltesers, knotting himself with anxiety over whether or not to pay for Shauna's purchases. Either way, she wouldn't have it. They took their booty to a small bench on a patch of drab-looking grass opposite the garage and shared their spoils. Both felt dreamlike; their evenings had taken such strange turns. They began to talk in a way that was both abstract and personal about their lives. Shauna described in a rather abridged fashion how she had humiliated herself at the wedding of an ex, and talked obliquely about her fears for her future. The conversation steadied her nerves, made it easier to accommodate the stress of not knowing when the traffic would move, whether her car would end up marooned in the middle of the motorway. Monty described in general terms how he was in a bad place, in over his head, in a situation he had never signed up to; how he felt trapped; how he just wanted to go back to having a normal life again, like any other normal person. Shauna said she knew what he meant. Then she asked him what exactly he meant, and he shook his head and said sorry, I can't really tell you. Which should have made her feel rejected, but in the event far from it, as she could tell that he was being more open with her than he would ever normally be with anybody. She could tell, somehow, that he wanted to tell her everything. And so strangers became friends, in the space of half an hour.

It was true: talking comfortably to strangers was familiar to them both. Shauna did it all the time when she was out, and at work quite a lot, albeit not usually with somebody like Monty. And Monty, for his part, had become accustomed to making connections with people he had only recently met, bringing them into his confidence, insinuating himself into theirs. But this, now, for both of them, was different. They each felt as if they already knew the other very well. There was something uncontrived about the way Monty was communicating with Shauna. And something uncontrived about the way she was communicating with him.

Skybirds

Popper paused with his hand on the handle of his car, looking up at the sky. The longer he stared, the more stars appeared. As a child, he used to imagine that they were tiny windows into heaven. He took a drag on his cigarette, opened the door of his car, folded himself into the front seat.

He reclined the driver's seat of his Golf and angled the rearview mirror downwards. Now he could see himself, this man he used to know, half hooded in shadow. Were others able to discern the change in him? Had the person he used to be gone forever? These were questions he had never seriously needed to ask himself before. He had always known exactly who he was, where he was going. There had been a sense of inevitability about his course through life, the one stage following the next, the one achievement after the other, building alongside his contemporaries towards a peak of stability, accomplishment, wealth and a family of his own. But now it was falling apart.

Who was this man that he used to be? He used to listen to Kings of Leon, that was one thing, that was definite. He reached forward and turned on the car stereo: there they were now, an echo of a lost world. He used to like Cheese, too, to dance to, but would never have had it playing in his car. So far so good. What else?

He used to wear Asics trainers. In the dark footwell, there they were still, two pale fish. Asics trainers, jeans, a body warmer; a North Face body warmer, a little American but top quality. He used to understand the value of good gear. Gore-Tex.

What else? His parents lived in Oxfordshire and he himself lived in London. Pimlico, near St James' Barracks. His father had worked as a private banker for Lazard, and had married his mother before they both went out to Hong Kong; they had returned to the UK when he was starting prep school. Now his father was retired, but still did the occasional bit of private consulting for trusted clients. He was a compassionate Tory, Popper's father, concerned by Britain's reduced standing on the world stage. They used to enjoy long, boozy lunches at White's, during which they would discuss Europe at length, and after which, if sufficiently sober, or perhaps sufficiently drunk, they would leaf through the leather-bound book to find prospective Members, and add their signature to the ones of whom they approved. Popper's father was anxious about his son's choice of career, the danger of it, yet he was proud of him all the same. He could never say so, of course, being a man of his generation. Nonetheless he was confident that his son knew of his pride. Mother and father would come and see him from time to time in London. They wanted him above all to find a good girl to marry.

He used to love skiing, walking, cycling, not surfing. The occasional game of touch rugby. He had been a decent flanker at school, but not the star player – always there clearing up, always a quiet authority, offering the team a sense of equilibrium when the others were losing their heads. He used to harbour bitter memories of losing to Harrow having outplayed them man to man. If truth be told, latterly he used to play touch rugby mainly to show he could still do it. Come to think of it, he had been a ringer for the City Sevens.

He had had one long-term relationship at university, and no others since. He had been no womaniser. Though at the same time, he wouldn't have resisted if the opportunity had presented itself. He had gained a reputation as a very good usher. A solid bloke. A good lad. His friends had worked in hedge funds, in private equity. From the King's Road it used to be only a short way home, by taxi, by bus. He used to like ales, he could hold his drink. He was tall – not ripped as such, but wiry and muscular. He had always been good with his hands.

Yes, he had liked school. It had been a privilege, and he had appreciated it as much as it is possible for a boy of that age, in that circumstance. He had excelled in physics and mathematics, had shown flair for building things. He had been a House Prefect. He had been a House Captain. He had been everyone's mate. Five years living in a school with a whole range of different people had taught him, like the others, to be always charming. And he had been presidential, able to take command without being dictatorial. Leadership, that was it.

He had graduated from Sheffield with a 2:1 in engineering, then gone straight to Sandhurst. His parents had come to visit one year, just before Christmas, for dinner with the officers; they both had got rather drunk but neither had been in any way embarrassing. Although his friends didn't understand it – they all signed up for the Infantry, the Cavalry – he had joined the Engineers. Not as sexy, not as glorious, but he loved building things, and without the Engineers the Army would be sunk.

Why don't you join the Scots Guards? They fought in the Falklands. Or the Queens Royal Lancers? Coldstream Guards? As an Engineer you'll be commanding chicks, you know. Spending your time digging holes. Yes, he had doubted his decision, but had never wavered. He used to be good at his job. He had been well loved by his men, who felt they could go to him with anything: marriage problems, financial problems, emotional problems. His first tour, of Iraq, had been effective and, in a strange way, the happiest time of his life. After that he had worked in Afghanistan.

Popper reached over and turned the music up, as if this would silence his mind. He found himself thinking about that woman. What was her name? Shauna. She was attractive, undeniably; he could see she had a hot body even under that jumper. And she was funny too, in an odd sort of way. Yet she had made him feel so tired. He knew her sort, had met count-less women like her in his time. It was inevitable they would share a mutual friend; inevitable, in a way, that it would be Hodgy, ladies' man that he was. He wouldn't be surprised if Hodgy had tried it on with her at that wedding.

Formerly, he would have enjoyed having a laugh with a random girl, flirting a little, talking about this and that. There was nothing else to do, after all. But he couldn't take people seriously any more. Especially not people like her. His energy had gone.

For he was a man who had been forced face-to-face with death, and this was a concern of his, this dying. Nothing but a shroud-scrap lay between a man and the darkness; he had been awakened to that fact, and in the process the person he used to be had died. What was left? Nothing. Numbness.

He reclined his seat as far as it would go and tried to make himself comfortable. He heard the sound of sirens, the whup of a helicopter overhead. The image that came into his mind was a thing of transcendent beauty and purity. It was towards the end of May, in the early morning. The sun had just risen above the slouching silhouettes of the Hesco blast barriers – massive, sand-filled, soft-edged canvas cuboids – that rimmed the Shawqat Forward Operating Base. Or rather what would later become the Shawqat Forward Operating Base if he and his platoon managed to complete it without getting killed. They had been at it for several weeks already, and they still felt no closer to completion; there were twenty of them there, only twenty, and they lived every moment with the knowledge that if the Taliban saw through their illusion of strength and mounted a coordinated attack, the Engineers would be over-run. They would have their genitals cut off, the women would be raped; they would be beheaded with religious relish.

The sun was a borehole in the blue. Dust swirled in great plumes across the wasteland, coming close to taking form but each time refusing. He was standing in the lookout station at the westernmost corner of the FOB, his radio crackling in his hand, looking up at the sky. Two American A-10s swooped across the face of the sun. These were no F-18s; they were balletic, graceful visions of poise and elegance as they cut through the sky laden with enough armaments to end the world. They released a volley of crescent flares, a show of force. His eye was drawn vertically downwards, following the perpendicular line of smoke that seemed, for an instant, to connect the jets to the earth. There, almost hidden by the landscape, lay the smoking remains of the Viking that had been carrying two of his men, on his orders, to Bastion for some R&R. The jets made another pass. Then they banked and flew away, skybirds returning to the sky.

The football

It was weird playing in the orange glow of these tall, tall lights. Like playing under floodlights, but with a crowd all sitting in their cars. A drive-thru footy game, Shahid thought dryly. Watching the Pakis. Knobheads.

It was two in the morning, and they had been playing on and off for a while. When the rain returned, they had scurried back to their car; when it passed they came out again, kicked it around for a while, then gave up when a man emerged from his van and told them that some people were trying to sleep. But as time went on, and sleep evaded them, and still there was no sign of the traffic jam moving, their listlessness stoked their bravado, and they headed out onto the tarmac again.

Compulsively, as he received the ball, dribbled it, juggled it on the wet hardtop of the London Orbital, Shahid's mind returned to the trial, running through the events again and again as if revisiting them would exorcise the demon. He, Kabir and Mo had planned it all carefully, and it had all gone smoothly at first. They had borrowed Baba's car, driven round the M25 to the Blues' training ground in Cobham several hours early, sat outside in the car listening to the radio, saying little. The windows were open so that the smell of the car wouldn't stick to their clothes. Chelsea! This was beyond all of their wildest dreams. Professional football invariably began as the stuff of fantasy, and for the vast majority of boys it never progressed beyond it; most British men had somewhere locked away their personal dream of playing for club and country, of scoring spectacular goals. For some the fantasy was elaborate, worked out to the finest detail; for others it was confined to snapshot moments of glory. And for the talented and ambitious minority – of which Shahid was one – the dream existed as a signpost indicating how his present reality should be lived. He was the sort of person who believed that the world, if challenged enough, would eventually have no choice but to yield up its fullest fruits. The reward, in his eyes, had always been his destiny. Now he needed to make it happen.

Half an hour before the allotted time, the three of them entered the reception area, the sun at their backs. Shahid was wearing the black Adidas tracksuit he had bought for the occasion, and was humping on his shoulder his sports bag. The other two were in jeans and trainers; Mo held a ball under his arm. Shahid felt springy on his feet, jittery, a champion boxer approaching the ring. Hearts fluttering, they approached the desk.

The man who greeted them was like nobody they had ever seen before. He was bright-eyed, tanned and svelte, and dressed in a Chelsea tracksuit; there was something in his manner that exuded affluence and ease.

'Here for the trial?' he said.

'That's right,' said Shahid.

'You're a bit early, mate.'

'Yeah. Sorry.'

'Welcome.' He took Shahid's hand in a hammy grip, then picked up a clipboard.

'Nervous?'

'Not too bad.'

'Just relax and be yourself, OK? Now, is it all three of you?'

'No. Just me.'

'Just you.'

'Yeah.'

'Name?'

'Shahid Anwar.'

He consulted his clipboard. 'Ah, that's the one. Great stuff. And these two are?'

'They're my mates. Team-mates as well. London APSA.'
Shahid felt himself flush.

'But they're not booked in for a trial.'

'No. They've just come with me. Like, for support. We do stuff together. They didn't want to miss it.'

The man looked doubtful. 'Did you let us know you'd be bringing your mates?'

'No. Is that a problem?'

'Bear with me.'

With another flashing smile he turned and disappeared through a door, pulling out his mobile as he went. The three friends sat in dark blue plastic chairs, and marvelled at everything around them. The Chelsea crest was everywhere, and everything was in the Chelsea colours; on the walls were framed pictures of famous players, photographs of their crowning achievements. The opulence of the place was beyond what they had imagined, what they had been capable of imagining. The cream tiled floor, the deep-pile carpet beyond, the oak-panelled walls, the sliver of emerald grass just visible through the windows on the far side. It seemed more like a luxury hotel.

At one point, a cleaner, also in a Chelsea tracksuit, passed through and mopped the floor. He didn't make eye contact and cleaned around their feet. He paid special attention to an ingrained smudge of mud on one of the tiles by the door; within a few minutes, it was as sparkling as the rest. Then he steered his cleaning trolley around the desk and disappeared through the same door as the man who had initially received them.

Slowly but surely, other lads began to arrive. They strode past without a second glance, talking and laughing among themselves, and clustered around the reception desk. None of them looked awestruck, or even impressed. A woman in a Chelsea tracksuit came out and registered them, shaking them each by the hand, and one by one they were waved through and down a corridor. Several seemed to know each other already. They were tall, broad and confident, these athletic boys, and many were silent and deadly-looking; they had cobra-like bodies.

When eventually the man came back, it was with a dazzling grin of apology. The three friends hurried to their feet and approached the desk. Shahid became aware that neither Mo nor Kabir had said a word since entering the ground. It was as if the whole thing wasn't happening.

'OK,' said the man, 'it's been cleared. Your friends can come in and watch. They can go in the family stand. But they can't come down to the pitch.'

Shahid nodded, sighed with relief; but when he glanced at Mo and Kabir, he saw that their eyes were downcast.

'We're going to try and make you extra welcome,' said the man confidentially. 'We understand how hard it is.'

'How's it hard?' said Shahid.

The man was scrolling through something on his phone. 'Now, straight down there, third on the right is the changing room. Go and get your kit on, then go straight ahead down to the pitch. The geezer'll be arriving in a minute.'

In the changing room, Shahid felt very young and alone. Around him on the benches were the kitbags of the other lads, all shining in the bright light, all spotless and professional and slick. The trainers lined up beneath – a sports shop. Shahid added his inadequate bag to the line, his inadequate shoes. He took a long time putting on his shin pads. The place was strangely quiet, and there was a barely audible hum that he could not ignore now that he'd noticed it. He wanted to get out there; he didn't want to get out there. They had probably started already. He needed to move. The thought of that emerald pitch – was he cut out for this? Kabir and Mo were probably in the stands right now, looking down at the pitch, looking for him. He needed to move. He opened his bag and pulled out a banana, peeled it, began to eat. It was important for the sake of the blood sugar, he knew that much. In one of the other bags, somewhere around him, someone's mobile went off, buzzing insistently. He finished his banana. The door opened, and a tall, redheaded boy jogged in, his white boots – twin fangs – clicking loudly on the tiles.

'Fuck,' he said, 'you gave me a shock.' He laughed, unzipped a bag at a stroke, dug into it. 'You ain't here for the trial, are you?'

'Yeah,' said Shahid.

'Nice,' said the boy. 'Where'd you play?'

'Up front.'

'Me too.'

A pause, and they avoided each other's eyes.

'Well, good luck, mate,' said the boy, rezipping his bag with a flourish. 'See you out there, yeah?' And he was gone.

Shahid got slowly to his feet, feeling sick to his stomach; he tilted his head one way, then the other. Exhaled violently. And again. He clenched his fists, brought them up over his head, brought them quickly down to his sides. Snap out of it. This was his chance. He was not going to let it slip through his fingers. He shook his head, bared his teeth, blew out his cheeks. He had to get out there. He began to stretch his hamstrings.

Preceded by a chain of footsteps, the man entered, smiling that summery smile. 'Everything all right, Shahid?' he said. 'Got your boots on? Good stuff. We want to give you the best possible chance, right?'

Shahid nodded.

'Come on then,' said the man, 'get yourself out there. We're about to get cracking, OK?'

Shahid went back in goal. After saving more than a few shots he let one in. It was Mo who had struck it, drilled with his left low to the right-hand side, and Shahid was out of position. The ball ricocheted off the tarmac and clipped the top of the motorway barrier, which sent it shooting up almost vertically into the blackness. Shahid vaulted the barrier and, scrambling ten yards down the grubby bank, managed to catch the ball before it hit the ground. He skidded to a halt, picked his way back onto the road and jogged out into the middle lane, the football at his feet. 'You go in goal now,' he said to Mo. 'You scored, innit?' And he slipped a peach of a ball into the path of Kabir, who had been steaming in as if for a massive shot. He wound up to strike; Mo, now in goal, cringed; and at the last minute Kabir reigned in his swing and trapped the ball instead. 'Cunt,' said Mo. Laughing, Kabir backheeled it into the path of Shahid, who he knew would be running around in a crescent behind him. Shahid received it with the toe of his trainer, where it remained for a moment as if glued, then slalomed around three imaginary opponents before turning tightly and unleashing a shot on goal. It was from the finest of angles; Mo palmed it stingingly away and it rolled out to Kabir. But the shot had been on target. That's more like it, thought Shahid, my touch is proper back. Typical that I should be on form with my mates on an empty motorway, and two left feet at Chelsea. Typical.

It had started off OK. He had pranced out on to the emerald sward, blinking in the brightness, trying to appear composed and confident, and managed to hold his own during the warm-ups. But they were tougher than he was used to; within minutes he had a stitch. In the back of his mind, a suspicion was surfacing like a snake from a swamp. What if the Essex Senior League was piss-easy? The other boys ate up the ground as they sprinted; when they took a strike on goal the contact was crisp, and the ball fizzed through the air like a dart. The keeper, too: he seemed to fill the goal, saving ball after ball in his thudding gloves. After the warm-ups, while the teams were putting on bibs, Shahid took a shot. The keeper met it with his body, gripped it comfortably, rolled it back out. The next one Shahid, overcompensating, blasted high and wide into the stands. The keeper impassively picked up another ball and threw it out to another boy; it was returned on the volley with some pace, and this time, although the keeper dived full-length, the ball ballooned in the snowy net. Then it was time for the game.

Ah, his two left feet. Under normal circumstances, Shahid would enter another plane of existence, one in which his unconscious instincts were king. When this happened, he was unstoppable, like a fish reading perfectly, instinctively, the currents. But this time he was thinking too much.

The first ball that came to him squeezed under his boot and out of play. The second he trapped fine, but the pass he released went straight to one of theirs. Frustration was building inside him. Why couldn't he play? He made a good interception, one that provoked a few handclaps from the touchline, but then attempted a long ball to the opposite wing and again it fell to one of theirs. Why was he throwing this away? The ball fell to him again, out on the flank, in a position that he knew he could shine. But he tried too hard, was clumsy in the dribble, lost control of the ball, pushed it too far in front of him, and the centre back – who had the build of a wrestler and the blondest of hair – nicked it easily and turned him inside out. This time the handclaps were for the defender. Someone yelled at him to release it sooner. In his fury at having been dispossessed, Shahid went in hard on the next tackle and brought the lad down from behind. They rotated as they fell and the boy landed hard on top of Shahid. It was as if a fire had been ignited; he had caught a knee in the balls. He rolled over and over, unable to stem the whining that spilled out of his mouth like vomit. Somebody kicked the ball to touch and a few of the players gathered round.

For some minutes the pain was blinding. He lay on the floor like a miscarried foetus, in an ocean of the brightest green, and all he wanted was to be back on the muddy field for London APSA, weaving past defenders as he used to. He raised his eyes and caught sight of Kabir and Mo shouting encouragement, and this pricked his sense of pride. He wasn't going to allow it to end here, like this. This could still be his moment. He was going to fight. Feeling the rush of the playground scrap, he struggled to his feet and heard polite handclaps at his bravery. Then, just as he was steeling himself for the resumption of play, somebody said just two words: man's game. What? Nothing, came the reply. Nothing.

And he had seen red.

Afterwards, in his grandfather's car on the way back to London, Kabir and Mo described what had happened. He had bore down on the other boy – the big defender – shouting shut up, you fucking cunt. Want to feel what a knee in the balls feels like, brah? Before he reached him he was seized by many hands, and he struggled, ripping his top. On the touchline there was much shaking of heads, drinking from water bottles. Finally he had strode off the pitch, chucked his shirt into the stands and run off down the tunnel. Kabir and Mo had found him waiting in his grandfather's car with the windows up, still in his kit, his boots, his bag and trainers on the back seat behind him. Come on, he had said. This was one big fucking mistake. It's not my time, I'm not ready. It's not my time, I'm not ready. Let's get the fuck out of here. And they had.

Now Kabir went in goal. Mo clipped the ball across the tarmac and Shahid met it perfectly, struck it clean and true; the ball sailed, curling slightly, through the night air, blocking out a moving circle of stars; it soared smartly into the goal, smacked off the barrier and bounced back onto the motorway. Kabir hadn't had a chance of saving it; it had been one of those shots so perfect that you don't feel the impact of the ball on your boot. Shahid trotted off to retrieve the ball and found it nestling against the wheel of a white van. He looked up; for an instant his eyes met those of a man a little older than him, turning an empty bottle of cider in his hands. It took him a moment to recognise him as the one who had stolen those crisps.

When he returned to his friends, Shahid was surprised to see a pair of gauche-looking white boys with them. One was hold-ing a Frisbee, twirling it like a plate on his finger.

'They want a game,' called Kabir. 'What do you reckon?'

'What, Frisbee or footy?'

'Whatever you like,' said the shorter lad, tossing a long fringe over one eye.

'Football,' said the taller one.

'All right with me, brah,' said Shahid, dropping the ball and cushioning it with his instep. 'But we can't play three-on-two.'

'I'll be goalie to start with,' said Mo. 'We can play two-on-two, with one goal.'

The white boys nodded their agreement. Both were smiling broadly. Cunts, thought Shahid. Fucking cunts.

Initiative

Ursula had been slumped in the front seat of the Chrysler for a long time, in the whale's belly of sleep. This was not unusual; once a month, her body would tend to shut down almost without warning, she would sink into a blackness so profound that it was like a pre-birth state.

As she slept, Max, in a variety of forms, had faded in and out of view, sometimes as a forest, sometimes as an oppressive weight, sometimes as a malevolent child that she both loved and hated, sometimes as a cloud, sometimes as the razor-like tooth of an alligator hanging limply on a cord; sometimes as a theatre, sometimes smothering pillows, sometimes the rush of heat that comes from a hot oven when it is opened. And also he appeared in a more recognisable, humanoid form – though sometimes monstrously huge, or monstrously small, or with distorted limbs and head, a distended belly, wings, or the leathery skin of a walrus. Frantically she found herself trying to close windows on an Internet browser, but the more she closed the more there were, and they were multiplying all around: all of this was Max. And when these dreams deserted her, and, bereft and alone, she swam to the surface and emerged, gasping, into the stuffy air of the Chrysler cockpit, she had no idea where she was.

'Max?' she said. 'What time is it?'

'Two,' came the reply. He was sitting upright in his seat, wiping his face and head with his T-shirt.

'What's going on?'

'Traffic jam, that's what.'

'And we're still stuck?'

'Still stuck. And it's raining outside. I'm soaked.'

'Christ.' She struggled upright, rubbing her eyes, then looked back at the children. 'Are they OK?'

'Carly was tossing and turning, so I felt her head and I think she has a temperature. But I got a bottle of Calpol. For when she wakes up.'

'What? Calpol? Where from?'

'It's a long story.'

Ursula leaned into the back and felt her daughter's brow. 'She's fine, Max,' she said. 'You must have just been panicking.'

'Maybe the fever's subsided.'

'Fevers don't come and go like that, Max.'

'Well, I've got the Calpol. So that's all right. And if either of them wake up and won't go back to sleep, we can give them a double dose.'

'Don't be ridiculous, Max. Even you wouldn't do that.'

He didn't reply.

'Did you get anything else from the shop?' said Ursula. 'Water or anything?'

'Which shop?'

'Where you got the Calpol.'

'I didn't go to a shop.'

'Where did it come from, then?'

'I told you, it's a long story.'

'What, did you hijack some woman's buggy or something?'

'Don't be stupid.'

'Where did you get it from, then?'

'If you must know, the Waitrose van. There.'

'What, that one there?'

'Yes, there.'

'How did you manage that?'

'I got chatting to the driver. He wouldn't give me anything else, mind. And I had to write out an IOU.'

'An IOU?'

'Yes.'

'Max, that's just bizarre.'

'Why?'

'Well, for one thing, how did you just fall into conversation with a delivery man? That's not your style.'

'If you must know, I went and asked him if I could borrow his phone. To call James and Becky. Which was your idea.'

'And what did they say?'

Suddenly Max had a sinking feeling, a premonition of doom. 'I . . . Jim didn't have a signal either.'

'Jim?'

'The Waitrose bloke.'

'Whose phone did you use, then?'

'Look, Ursula, it's not as easy as that, OK? Nobody had a signal. Either that or they wouldn't let me use their phones. It was fucking humiliating.'

'Don't tell me.'

'Don't tell you what?'

'Max, tell me you've spoken to James and Becky. Tell me you've spoken to James and Becky, Max.'

'There was no signal anywhere.'

'Max! They'll be going absolutely spare!'

'Calm down. I sent them an email.'

'And we know how well that went last time.'

'No, I sent it properly. I went back to the 3G spot, brought up the email, and sent it with my own hands. I'm telling you. I checked.'

'Let me see.'

'What?'

'Let me see your phone. I want to see it in Sent with my own eyes.'

'I'm not having you check up on me like a child.'

'Max, after your performance earlier on you can't very well complain.'

Reluctantly he handed over his phone, hoping that it was clean of messages from Nicole. There was a tense silence while Ursula scrolled through.

'There's no email in the sent items, Max.'

'What? There must be.'

'There isn't. Have a look for yourself.'

'Must be because it hasn't been able to download it. Check the outbox. I promise you it won't be in there.'

There was a tense pause. Then Ursula blew out a stream of air, tossed the phone on to Max's lap and sunk back into her seat, her hands over her face. He looked at the phone. There was the outbox. And there, still unsent, was the email to James and Becky.

'I don't . . . I don't get it,' he said. 'I just don't fucking get it. Ursula, it . . . maybe it sent a duplicate.'

'Max,' said Ursula, her voice strained and repressed, 'Max . . .'

'It's not my fault.'

'Whose fault is it, then, Max? Whose fucking fault is it?'

'There's so little signal . . .'

'Can't you apologise? Can't you at least fucking apologise? Do you always have to be right about everything?'

'Look, I'm sorry, OK?'

'They'll have called the police! They'll be frantic! Are you out of your fucking mind?'

'Calm down. They'll have heard about it on the radio or something.'

'For crying out loud. You're taking the piss. I give you one thing to do and you couldn't be bothered to do it.'

'It wasn't that I couldn't be bothered. I told you, there was no bloody signal.'

'Well, *use your fucking initiative!*' said Ursula. She turned suddenly away to the window, not wanting her husband to see her tears. From the back seat came the sound of toddlers stirring.

'Right,' said Ursula suddenly, groping for her bag. 'I'll go and find a signal myself.'

'Don't be stupid,' said Max, 'it's the middle of the night. James and Becky will be asleep.'

'They bloody won't. Not with their daughter missing, Max. They're not like you.'

'You're just using this as an excuse to have a go at me.'

'Max! You just don't get it, do you? You just don't fucking get it. I don't know if you're stupid, or insensitive, or arrogant, or just a fucking man.'

'Maybe all at the same time.'

'Yes,' said Ursula. 'That's the first sensible thing I've heard you say.'

'Look,' said Max, 'I'm not letting you go out into the dark by yourself.'

'What do you fucking care? Where's my phone? Where's my fucking phone?'

'The kids are waking up, anyway.'

'So, you deal with it, Max! You deal with it. I don't know why it's always got to be me who does all the fucking childcare.'

Max flung open the door and got out.

'Oh, no, no, no,' said Ursula. 'You're not going anywhere, my friend.'

'I'm going to find a signal,' said Max. 'I'll walk to the top of that hill.' He slammed the door and jogged off out of sight.

A fog had descended, thickening all around, clinging in a great translucent blanket to the earth. His head was spinning, his upper back hurt as if it had been clenched in a vice, and his wet clothes were cold against his skin. I need to damage something, he thought, I need to do some serious damage. That's the only thing that will help me now.

He felt as if his mouth was filling with unspoken words, the secrets he had been keeping from Ursula, the darkness that was gradually corroding his marriage. His life. Despairingly, he checked his phone again: still no signal, and the battery was starting to run low. Out of the mist, a man in a faded T-shirt appeared like some Arctic explorer, making his way carefully along the line of cars. He didn't see Max watching him, and vanished in the swirls of white fog. Max turned up his collar, clenched his fists, and strode off in the direction of the escarpment.

Good sport

For a while neither of the brothers spoke. Rhys kept smoking cigarettes, and every time he lit one, Chris did the same; he noticed that and it annoyed him. After the cider he was buzzing, not yet drunk, and his mind was fixing vividly on one old memory. Something he had not recalled for years and years, decades even. From before his dad moved out, one of the final days. How old must he have been? Fourteen perhaps? And Chris, then, would have been twelve. Something like that. It was late at night, and he had been awoken by some ruckus downstairs. Chris, in the bunk below, was still asleep, making not a single sound. Rhys, in his pyjama trousers, crept out of his room. He remembered the long shadows stretching up the wall. At the end of the hall he squatted down, not daring to go any further. Something was going on in the kitchen, now his father roaring drunkenly, now his mother talking, also drunkenly. He couldn't move. He could hear them lurching around, colliding with things, the sound, he thought, of the table scraping across the lino. He waited, for he could do nothing else; he couldn't move, it was as if his body no longer belonged to him. And then there they were, lurching like stage wrestlers down the hall. Now all he could see was their four legs, some pantomime horse, tottering back and forth, the occasional jolt as blows were struck; the sounds were incoherent now, two interweaving notes from either end of a scale. His father pivoted, leaning back, dragged his mother in a swerving crescent until her head hit the wall. Rhys could see her face lolling to one side. He ran silently back to bed.

*

'You going to make him do it, then?' said Chris.

'Who?'

'Monty. When he gets back.'

'If he fucking gets back.'

'You reckon he won't come back?'

'Would you?'

'Like fuck I would. But Monty's hard, innit?'

'He ain't hard. He's a posh fucking poof.'

'He'll be back.'

'We'll see. Probably come back pissed. Won't do it even then, I reckon. Fucking poof.'

'I reckon he'll do it.'

'Are you his fucking boyfriend or what?'

'Just saying.'

'Well, just don't. OK?'

They returned to their silence. Rhys was getting thirsty, but there was not a drop of Coke in the van. All these cigarettes were burning the back of his throat, yet still he could not stop. At this rate he would run out of fags in another ten minutes. Without knowing why, he felt a broad smile spread across his face and he began to laugh.

'What?' said Chris.

'Nothing. Nothing.'

'What's so funny?'

'Nothing. I'm telling you, bruv, nothing.'

Coming all at once to a decision, he opened the van door and stepped out, thigh-deep into the fog.

'Where you off to?' said Chris.

'Just going for a slash, mate,' said Rhys.

He walked across the hard shoulder, hurdled the barrier, tested the wind with his hand and relieved himself luxuriantly into the grass, watching the urine penetrate the fog like a spear. For what felt like a long time he watched the blades of glass bending under the force of his flow. Then he was spent. One shake, two shakes, three; he zipped himself up and made his way back.

On a whim, he took a detour to the Waitrose van and peered through the window. The driver was stretched out in the shadows with his arm over his face. Rhys tapped softly on the window. No response. He tried the handle: locked. He tapped again, a little harder this time, and the man propped himself up on an elbow. When he saw Rhys's face, his mouth worked like a fish.

Rhys made the gesture of a window rolling down. The man hesitated, then reached over and lowered it by just two inches.

'You all right, bruv?' said Rhys. 'Having a nice traffic jam?'

'What are you after, mate?'

'What's your name?' said Rhys.

'What does it matter?'

'Just being friendly, mate, that's all.'

'Jim.'

'Right. Jim, I'm Rhys. Now, I want to ask you something, yeah?'

'OK.'

'But you can't say no, right? You can't just say, like, no, Rhys, fuck off. Nothing like that, yeah?'

'Just tell me.'

'Look, I want two things from you, Jim. Booze and fags. I know you got them in the back. I can smell them, bruv. That's what I want.'

'I can't do it, mate. I just can't. More than my job's worth, like.'

'You don't get me, Jim. I said you can't say no, innit?'

'If it was up to me, mate, I'd give you whatever you want. But it's not mine to give.'

'Jim,' said Rhys, 'you got a choice. Either you give me some booze and fags, or I come in there and take them. And if you make me come in there, I'll be taking a lot more than that and all.'

'But it's not my stuff,' said Jim. 'I can't give you something that's not mine.'

Rhys rattled the handle and booted the door with his foot.

'How much do you want?' said Jim.

'I dunno, bruv. Three packets of fags. Bottle of vodka. Something like that.'

Jim cupped his hand over his forehead and moved it slowly back and forth. At long last, he spoke. 'I don't suppose I could get you to give me some money?' he said. 'I can use my staff discount. It'll be cheap. Or sign an IOU?'

'I don't fucking owe you nothing, bruv,' said Rhys. He gave the door another shake. 'Come on. Before I lose my fucking rag.'

'Look mate,' said Jim. 'We're both working men, right? My dad was a brickie. My mum was a dinner lady. We're both in the same boat. If you do this to me, I'll lose my job. Jobs ain't easy to some by these days, like. Have a heart, eh?'

Rhys, without a word, walked away from the window. Jim waited five, ten seconds, then slumped back into his seat. Thank God for that. Thank God. He held his hands up in front of his face: they were shaking. Then something caught his eye outside the other window. There, with all the whiteness of an apparition, stood Rhys, a half-smile playing across his lips.

'Get me my fucking stuff,' said Rhys, 'now.' He began to shake and kick the door. This time, Jim knew he had lost. He struggled to his feet and opened the hatch that allowed him to access the groceries. He knelt on the seat and reached deep inside. For a moment Rhys suspected that this was part of some elaborate escape plan. But then a pale hand snaked out and dropped the cigarettes, followed by a bottle of brandy, on the passenger seat. Then he opened the window and passed them out, apologising for the substitution of vodka for brandy. Rhys snatched the goods and left without a word, bubbles of triumph rising through him.

'Ever had brandy before, Chrissie boy?' said Rhys as he jumped into the van and slammed the door.

'What?' said Chris.

'And I got us some fags.'

'No snacks?'

'No, Chris. No fucking snacks. I'm playing it clever, innit? Enough to keep us going, not enough for him to call the fucking pigs. And I can go back and get a bit of fucking grub later. Softly, softly, catchee monkey, bruv.'

They both took a swig of brandy.

'Tastes like chocolate,' said Chris.

'Bollocks it does,' said Rhys, lighting a cigarette. 'More like . . . I dunno . . . orange peel. Fag?'

Something moved outside. Rhys shifted in his seat and peered out. The fog was obscuring his vision. He squinted. There, on the other side of the M25, where not a single car could be seen, three – no, five – figures were moving about, breaking into the occasional sprint, weaving, jostling.

'Look at that, mate. They're playing footy, innit?'

'What?'

'There, mate, there. They're playing footy. Been doing it for ages. On our fucking English streets.'

'Not all Pakis, innit,' said Chris.

'Nah. Three of them. Fuck knows who the other lot are. UAF probably.'

'Reckon they've come from the demo?'

'Reckon so.'

The two men drank their brandy and watched. The figures drifted away, almost disappeared in the slow moving mist; then they could be seen again.

'In the back of the van,' Rhys said.

'What?'

'We got our toys in there, innit? What we didn't get the chance to use today.'

'Yeah.'

Chris stubbed out his cigarette. He had been smoking too much; his throat felt like sandpaper. But he had to match Rhys fag-for-fag; it had always been that way, ever since they were at school. Not to match him fag-for-fag would be to arouse Rhys's disrespect; he wouldn't show it, but Chris knew it was true. He needed to keep up. Otherwise he might as well give up.

He was hungry. There was not a single snack left in the car, he knew that. Out of the corner of his eye, he saw Rhys reaching for the packet of fags. Inwardly he groaned; but his brother simply tapped it on his knee, revolving it from end to end, rhythmically, methodically, leaving it closed. Despite himself, Chris let out an audible sigh of relief; his brother glared at him, then turned to look out the window. Chris pulled out his mobile again.

He was sick of Angry Birds. He had completed the game the day after he had downloaded it, and had gone through Angry Birds Seasons, Angry Birds Rio, Angry Birds Space and Angry Birds Star Wars in a similar length of time. Then he had gone back and done them all again, focusing on getting three gold stars on each level; this had taken a little longer, and sometimes he had been stuck on the same level for days. But he never resorted to the Mighty Eagle or other cheats, as he knew it would take the fun out of the game. If it were there, he wouldn't be able to stop using it, and then where would it end? Might as well just Mighty Eagle the entire game; there wouldn't be any point any more.

On a whim, he tapped the icon for the game 'Little Wings'. He hadn't played this as much as Angry Birds, but recently had been getting into it as a secondary option. It was a simple concept; you were in control of a small, round, flightless bird – why always birds? – and you had to scoot over hilly terrain as quickly as possible in a limited amount of time. So far he had completed six islands. He thought he had come close to completing the seventh, but who could tell? Maybe it was designed to be impossible. He could just be wasting his time.

The game began. After several false starts – time was of the essence, so if you made a big mistake at the beginning, you might as well start again – he was on the second island and making better progress than he ever had before.

'You ever read the Koran?' said Rhys suddenly.

'What?'

'The Koran, bruv. Ever read it?'

'Never read a book in my life, mate. You know that.'

'Well, you should.'

'What? Why?'

'Know thy enemy, innit? And you'll get to know how evil those fuckers are.'

Chris did not respond. He was craning his neck towards the little screen, and in his eyes two little birds were reflected.

'I've had enough of sitting on my arse,' said Rhys. 'I'm going to stretch me legs. Hear me, Chrissy boy? I'm going to stretch the old legs.'

'Yeah, yeah. I'll come with you, innit. Soon as I've finished this.'

'Come on, you sad cunt.'

Chris sighed, thumped his head against the headrest, and put his mobile away. Then he followed his brother out of the van.

The football players were playing nearby now; Rhys could hear their calls, the bounce and skid of the ball, the sweet thunk of a cleanly struck shot. He could see them hazily in the mist. Ghost players. He took a swig of brandy and passed the bottle to Chris.

'What do you think of this shit?' he said.

'Does the job,' said Chris. 'But give me a pint any day.'

'Better get some down you,' said Rhys. 'Dutch courage, they call it.'

Now you see me

Ursula looked at her watch: 3 a.m. She dried her eyes, her face, on a tissue, and pressed it into the mass grave in the compartment at the bottom of the car door. The DVD was still playing in the back of the headrests. On the driver's seat, the imprint of Max's behind could still be seen.

Tentatively, she stole a glance at the two girls. Both of them had fallen asleep again, their faces changing from white to green to red to blue as the scenes changed on the television. She had given them both a double dose of Calpol, and this seemed to be working wonders. Now there was just the sound of the TV to deal with.

Dare she? Ursula slipped her hand to the volume control and tentatively, by increments, reduced it by half. The promise of silence grew in the car. Just as she was about to lower the volume further, however, Bonnie stirred and let out a moan. Ursula froze; the girl shifted in her seat and went back to sleep. It was now or never. In a single bold move, Ursula brought the volume down to zero. She turned off both the screens, and darkness joined the silence in the Chrysler. The girls remained asleep.

But the darkness, the silence, brought no solace. Out of the window she could see fog accumulating, piling layer upon layer within itself. Her mind was whirring, replaying the exchanges with Max, trying to determine the innocent and guilty parties, constructing a powerful case that would lay the blame at Max's door. She knew this way of thinking would only drive her crazy, but she was powerless to stop it, and anyway she didn't want to. The problem, she thought, was that Max's door was also her door. Or it would be so long as they remained married.

Why didn't he need her more? He didn't appreciate her, never paid her a compliment, didn't even seem to notice her some days. When she bought sexy underwear, he didn't notice; when she tried to get him to come to bed early, he didn't notice, sat on his computer into the small hours. She was just the person who kept his house running, looked after his daughter and was useful for a shag every few months. If she had a casual affair with someone, he probably wouldn't even care. Could she have a casual affair with someone? Could she?

She shook her head. It was stupid to think this way, stupid to visualise the future as it might be without Max, just her and Carly. What benefit could come from going back to the single life? She had lived out her twenties, her early thirties, as a single-ton, had lived it until she had grown tired. She had fallen pregnant with Carly at the right time, just as she was feeling the hollowness of a life without family, just as her friends were beginning to have children, and the spectre of a barren life had started to haunt her darker moments. She had spent years creating a family home, such as it was. Surely it wasn't all for nothing?

It was stuffy, so stuffy in here. Without making any decisions, she found herself standing on the road, closing the car door behind her, weighing the keys in her hand, glancing at the two sleeping babes through the window, their little chests rising and falling like an expression of the rhythm of the world; and the night was expansive and cold, made mysterious by the writhing of the fog; and she could see, and hear, people playing football on the other side of the road. Imagine that! She found herself wanting a cigarette. Despite everything, this brought a smile to her face. It was so surreal. This whole evening had been surreal. This orange light transforming everything into a Seventies sci-fi flick.

She looked around. Most people seemed to be asleep, but she imagined eyes everywhere, watching the children. She pressed a button on the moulded plastic rectangle from which the sabre of the key protruded, and the doors locked with a mechanical clunk. She was a gaoler. Or a prisoner locking the doors as she escaped.

This desire for a fag was too much. Where on earth had it come from? She hadn't smoked for at least ten years, ever since she met Max; he had fundamentally disapproved, made her feel wretched; she had been proud as a child when she quit. How pathetic. Why shouldn't she have a quick fag now? Just the one. Max would smell it on her but what difference would it make? But she didn't have any cigarettes.

Her eyes fell on a tiny orange point of light lying low inside a silver Golf GTI. It brightened, moved to the side, then looped out of sight like a sparkler. She looked down and saw that her feet were moving automatically. For a moment she thought that the spell would be broken and she would trip, but they carried on, these feet, one after the other after the other. And then she had reached the car.

The person lying on the seat, which had been reclined almost to a horizontal position, hadn't noticed her approaching. Music could be heard coming from within, a song she vaguely recognised. She looked back at her car – yes, if the children woke up, she would see them moving – then knocked on the window.

There was a sudden movement in the darkness of the vehicle and the music came to an abrupt halt. Then the seat was cranked slowly upwards and a man arced into the orange light, cigarette clamped in his mouth, eyes haunted by fatigue. Struck by the ridiculousness of the thing – this man rising up like some stage prop, his quizzical expression, the bizarreness of playing out one's story on the motorway – she smiled.

He lowered the window, regarded her, said nothing.

'Sorry to bother you,' she said.

'Is something funny?'

'No, not at all. What could be funny?'

'But you're laughing.'

'Oh God, sorry. I'm not laughing at you. I mean, oh God, I

mean, it wasn't you. It was just quite funny how you rose up like that.'

'Rose up?'

'Yeah. You know.' She laughed again, blushing unbearably.

He looked uncertain, then smiled. 'I'm Tom,' he said. 'Tom Popper. They call me Popper, or Pops. Occasionally Poppy.'

'Ursula. Ursula King.'

They shook hands, formally, through the window. Posh, she thought. Really posh.

'What can I do for you?' he said.

'What? Oh, yes. Right. I – I couldn't help noticing the cigarette.'

He rummaged in the glove compartment, ignoring things that fell to the floor. 'Please,' he said, and then he was holding a packet of cigarettes, already flipped open with a cigarette protruding. She slid one from the pack. The little papery pencil tugged on her lip.

He held his own cigarette, now almost a butt, out to her. 'I haven't got a lighter myself, and the car one's broken. So I got a light from someone down that way earlier and I've been chain-smoking ever since.'

'There's a lesson in there somewhere,' said Ursula.

'Yes: get a lighter.'

She lowered her face to the window, her mouth close to his fingers, and lit her cigarette from his; for an instant she saw herself from the outside, and thought she must look like a whore.

'All right?' said Popper.

'Fine,' she said quickly, and took a drag. 'Just a bit chilly. Still, that's the smoker's lot, isn't it?'

There was the slightest pause.

'How rude of me,' said Popper. 'You're welcome to finish it in here. Sorry.'

'I couldn't.'

'You're welcome.'

'It would be rude of me.'

'Nonsense. It was rude of me not to offer, and it would be rude of you to refuse.'

Rule number one: never get into a strange man's car. Could she . . . yes, she could see the children from here. And she could see the fog-shrouded hill where Max had gone; when he eventually came down, he would be able to see her. There she was, in Popper's Golf, shutting the door behind her.

There was an awkward silence as the car adjusted to the presence of a stranger.

'So what do you do?' said Ursula.

'That's rather direct.'

'Sorry.'

'I'm in the army.'

'Oh, right. Navy? Air force?'

'No. Army.'

'Right.'

'What about you?'

'I'm a publicist.'

'Very showbiz.'

'A publishing publicist. But I don't say that because of the alliteration.'

'Oh, I see. Fiction? Non-fiction?'

'Non-fiction. Niche stuff, as Max puts it.'

'Max, Max. Not the black guy? Tall? I think I bumped into him earlier. He was trying to borrow a phone or something. I have a good memory for names and faces.'

Ursula sighed. 'That would be him.'

'Seemed like a decent bloke.'

'God, this cigarette's good. Really, really good. I haven't had a smoke since . . . for years.'

'I haven't started you smoking again, have I?'

'Don't worry about it.'

'Now I feel guilty.'

'Don't. It's good. It's really good.' She took her iPhone out of her pocket. Of course. No signal.

'Everything all right?' said Popper.

'Oh, yes. Just checking for a sign of him.'

'Who?'

'Max.'

'Where's he gone?'

'Up there. Over the hill, so to speak. To get a phone signal.'

'Why don't you give him a ring?'

'I haven't got a signal either.'

'Same here.'

There was a pause while Ursula peered into the blackness, trying to catch a glimpse of her husband.

'Do you have kids?' she said, without looking at Popper.

'Never been blessed.'

'Married?'

'Nope.'

'God. You know, when Carly, my daughter, was born, Max was out of town on business. No skin-to-skin contact or anything. I think that makes a difference, don't you?'

'I . . . I wouldn't really know.'

Ursula stubbed out her cigarette and sighed. The fog was building outside the window, as if the motorway was lifting into the clouds.

'Anyway, enough about me,' said Ursula. 'What brings you to this traffic jam?'

'Just been to see my father. He's poorly.'

'Flu?'

'Rather more serious than that, I'm afraid.'

'Oh God, sorry.'

'Don't worry. Not your fault. Sorry.'

'Is he . . . I mean, it isn't . . .'

'Well, you know.'

'I'm sorry.'

'No, don't be.'

Popper's cigarette had gone out. The woman's face was lined, her hair desiccated and without lustre, and the backs of her hands looked to him to have the merest hint of ageing. She was behaving rather oddly, too, distracted and jittery. Come on, he thought. She was human, just like him. She – like him – like everybody – would come to death in the end.

Ursula thought she saw movement on the hill. On impulse, she seized Popper's hand.

'Um . . . Ursula?'

'What?'

'You're . . . er . . .'

'Sorry,' she said, and removed her hand, still peering out of the windscreen. 'I thought I saw Max coming down. But it wasn't him.' She caught Popper's eye, and realised how her words sounded. 'Not that . . . I mean . . . look, I'm sorry. It's been a stressful night.'

'That's all right,' said Popper. 'I understand.' He placed his hand on hers. Did all hands feel like this? Like a bird in its final moments of life? Like a mechanical thing, barely living? Like the hand of his father? To her, he thought, his own hand must seem like some matted and bloodstained paw.

He released his grasp. Simultaneously, and in opposite directions, they both looked out the window into the night.

Max's moment

Max strode across the blacktop, through the fog, and leaped the fence to the rough grass beyond, where the ground began to climb. It was a relief to put step after step between himself and the Chrysler.

When he reached the edge of the copse, he stopped, caught his breath, rested his back against the trunk of a tree, looked back. His car had become one among many, each as individually compelling to its owner as his own was to him. Was it possible, he thought, for the human mind to accommodate the idea that every corner of the world was important to someone? Every car was linked to a person for whom the smell, the feel, the hue, the texture, was utterly unique and representative of a particular space and time. Was it possible for the human mind to allow for this? To break down a great column of traffic into so-and-so many vehicles, so-and-so many lives? For him, at least, it was not. For him the Chrysler, which he could from this distance make out, despite the fog, eclipsed all other cars. It was the locus of what made him himself.

He pulled out his phone and turned it on. It glowed, displayed a succession of logos, progress bars and slogans, then ordered its thoughts and began searching for a signal. He waited. One bar; two bars; the word 'Vodafone'; then 'E'; then, finally, the crowning glory, that magnificent pairing of letter and of digit, '3G'. Four whole bars of signal! Should he prepare what he was going to say to Bonnie's parents? Fuck it, he thought.

This time, the phone was answered after only two rings. 'Hello?'

'Becky. This is Max.' The phone was vibrating in his hand as the messages that had arrived during the blackout finally made their way through.

'Max! Max!' came Becky's distinctive South African twang. 'James, it's Max! Is everything OK? Where are you? Christ, it's three o'clock.'

'It's the traffic. On the blasted M25.'

'The M25? You're still on the M25? James, he's still on the M25. What? How long have you been there? How's Bonnie? Is she OK?'

'She's fine. We're all fine. She's sound asleep.'

'We've been going crazy, Max, absolutely crazy. James, call the police and tell them we've found her. You're sure she's there, Max? You're sure she's OK?'

'She's fine. She's absolutely fine. She's asleep.'

'Why didn't you call us before?'

'It's a long story, Becky. The signal's terrible out here.'

'You couldn't find a landline? You must have been sitting there for hours and hours.'

'I know – I sent you an email, but it didn't send. Twice, actually.'

'Max, thank fuck you're all OK. But I can't believe you left it until three to call. What's up with that?'

'Sorry, Becky, I thought the email had gone hours ago.'

'I've got to sit down . . . wait . . . there. Wow. Christ almighty. Wow.'

'Did you really call the police?'

'Where's Bonnie? Can I speak to her? Can I hear her voice?'

'She's asleep, Becky. I'm telling you, she's fine.'

'Did you give her something to eat? Has she done a wee? Has she been worried? Has she been crying?'

Max passed his hand over his face. *So this is my penance.* 'Becky, she's fine. Ursula's got it all under control.'

'Yes, of course, Ursula's there. Ursula's there. Has she done a poo?'

'Who, Bonnie?

'Yes, of course. Bonnie.'

'I don't think she's needed to.'

'Max, I'm glad you called, but why didn't you call before? My God. It's just been such a fucking stress. So why the massive hold-up? What is it, an accident?'

'No idea.'

'Have you broken down?'

'No, no, we haven't broken down or anything. It's just traffic.'

'Just traffic? Nobody's told you what the hold-up is? James, look it up online. There's got to be something about it online. Would you like James to come and pick you up, Max?'

'There's no way he could get through the traffic. We've just got to sit it out. But the kids are fine, that's the main thing.'

'I'm so glad you rang. We were going spare. We left you umpteen messages.'

'I can hear them dropping in now. Sorry, I had no signal. I've had to walk up a hill to call you.'

'You couldn't walk up a hill before now? Is she behaving herself?'

'She's being a little angel.'

'Really?'

'Absolutely.' Max ground the heel of his shoe into the mud.

'Christ, what a nightmare.'

'You're telling me.'

'Is there anything we can do? Order you a pizza or something? I've heard you can do that.'

'You can't. It's a traffic jam.'

'Yes, but they use those little motorbikes.'

'We're fine. We're all fine. Thank you, though.'

'Keep us updated, won't you?'

'Of course. I can't get a signal unless I'm up here, though, so if you can't get hold of us, don't panic.'

'I won't. I won't. God, thank fuck she's safe. You're sure she's safe? You're sure?'

'Anyway, I'd better get back to the car.'

'You're sure about the pizza?'

'Becky. You can't order a pizza for a car in a traffic jam.'

'You can actually. James's brother did it once. Didn't he, James? Andy did it once. Ordered a pizza when he was in traffic. What? Oh god, James, you are hopeless. His memory's going, you know. I swear you can.'

'I'd better go,' said Max. 'Just go to bed. Everything's all right.'

'Christ, Max, I couldn't go to bed now. We'll wait until you get back. At least I will, don't know about James. Well, let me know about the pizza. Give Bonnie lots of kisses for me.'

'I will. Bye, Becky.'

'Take care.'

'Bye. Take care. Bye.'

'Bye.'

Max turned and looked out across the traffic again; then he looked across the hill towards the village. The job was done, but he wasn't ready to go back to the car yet. Not with his head in this state. Not with so much left festering. For a moment he was struck by the notion that all of his problems were actually rooted in the physical. Perhaps his body was out of alignment somehow, which was contaminating his emotions, which was making the world appear distorted. Should he exert himself physically? Try to flush it out, whatever it was? Should he just dash up the hill, sprint up the hill, until his blood boiled and his heart burst, and then thrash around in the grass, hollering and gnashing his teeth, until he had purged the stagnant energy and was fresh and clean, a newborn baby? Until the world was right again? He faced up the slope, took a single step in the direction of the brow, went no further. Then he threaded his way between the trees and came across a stump. He sat down, put his phone in his pocket, cupped his head in his hands. He stayed like this for a long time.

This had to be figured out, and figured out now. The confusion had gone on long enough; he would not leave this copse, he decided, until he had it all straight in his mind. Right. What was required to make sense of all this was cool-headed reason. That, he thought, was where he had been going wrong; his emotions had been clouding his judgement. Proceeding, then, with the basic facts. First: the male homo sapiens is evolutionarily predisposed to have multiple partners. This seemed to him to be self-evidently true. Although he could recall a time when he had eyes only for Ursula, that was when they had been in the very first flush of love, when they had been worlds unto one another. This phenomenon could be explained, he was certain, scientifically; something to do with the amygdala or dopamine, something to do with the evolutionary need to commit to a single partner long enough to mate. And before long the infatuation wore off, as it always did – as it was designed to – and his male instincts took over. The whiff of pheromone, the flash of a cleavage, the curve of a woman's hips, stole his mind and pricked his desire. So far as he could tell, it was the same for all men. It was the power of the basic urge to reproduce, to spread one's seed as widely as possible to ensure healthy fertilisation, healthy progeny. To chase down and conquer a sexual quarry; to dominate her; to impregnate her; to chase down and dominate another. This was his incontrovertible nature, and to restrict it, even with the very best of intentions, was to fight the tide.

Second: the female homo sapiens is biologically predisposed to attract a mate for life. Again, this seemed to him self-evident. Women did have affairs, of course, and sexually could be as profligate as their male counterparts, yet he had a strong sense that beneath it all, their essential nature was to make the home, to feather the nest, to nurture the children, and because a man was an essential precursor to all of this, and a very handy – if not, strictly speaking, essential – addition, it followed that within the feminine nature was inscribed the need to find a man and keep hold of him. He supposed that in terms of evolution, it was beneficial for a woman to be attractive to a wide range of men, for if her principal mate proved unable to deliver the goods, so to speak, she would need the ability to attract a replacement. She needed to make men of all sorts wish to chase her down, dominate her, penetrate her, impregnate her. This explained her preoccupation with maintaining her attractiveness, which was instinctive even in old age. Essentially, however, she demanded only one partner, only one, to have and to hold. Which, obviously, was at odds with the nature of the male.

Third: his duty was no longer to Ursula alone. It was also to Carly, and whatever actions he took now would impact on her to the extent that they defined the entire future direction of her life. This was his responsibility.

This, he thought, was what it meant to be a man.

It was then that the breakthrough occurred. He could feel a thought rising like a bubble from the mystery of his unconscious, and he held his body very still to allow it to fully develop. Love and duty. How closely intertwined these were! He had thought, for a time, that they were polar opposites. He had thought that the love between Ursula and himself had faded, and that duty was all that bound them now; that meanwhile, a new love was blooming between himself and Nicole. Now, however, he realised that the driving emotion that turned his mind daily to Nicole – a woman he barely knew – was the primordial lust. The bonds that connected him to Ursula – of devotion, of nurturing, of fondness, of duty – were not animal. They were of a purely human order, a civilising, compassionate force. If all members of a society were dominated by their lust, how would it survive? And if an individual allowed himself to be dominated by his lust, how could his personal harmony remain intact? It was obvious.

The conclusion, when he arrived at it, was stunning. That companionship, that stability, that affection? That quiet, unremarkable, special thing? That willingness to endure the difficult times? The arguments? That, in fact, was love. He'd had it back-to-front all along, and he was on the brink of ruining everything.

He raised his head from his hands and looked through the trees towards the road. His eyes were swollen, and he felt at once profoundly tired and ready to take on the world.

He reached into his pocket for his phone. It nestled in his palm, a pat of butter, a pebble. He awoke it, scrolled to the number, paused, got to his feet. The signal was strong here. He took a deep breath, exhaled slowly. Then he dialled the number. It rang for a long time; he was almost certainly waking her up, and he didn't care.

'Hello?'

'Max?'

'Yes, it's me.'

'Do you know what time it is?'

'About three, I'm told.'

'Is something . . . wait a moment.'

At the sound of her voice his heart quickened, he was starting to feel intoxicated; they got to speak so rarely. Was this really only lust? Was it not something more, something celebrated in the poetry of the greats? He heard her walking up some stairs, entering a room, closing a door.

'OK, I can speak now,' she said. 'Is something wrong?'

'Nothing's wrong,' said Max. 'I just had to speak to you.'

'You shouldn't call out of the blue like this,' she said softly. 'Especially in the middle of the night. We agreed. Text first.'

'I know. Sorry. I just . . . I had to speak to you.'

'OK. I think Mark's still asleep. Go on, then.'

Her voice was warm, lilting downwards, like champagne being poured into an empty flute. He had woken her up, yet still she was completely devoted to him, not angry at all. He knew her now. He knew what she was expecting: a proposal for another encounter. The words stuck in his throat, and he screwed shut his eyes. A moment ago, it had been so clear. But now? Emotions were strangling his logic. Perhaps it was a mistake to eliminate emotion. Perhaps it should be reason that bowed in the face of genuine, overwhelming love . . .

'Max? What is it?'

'I . . .'

'I miss you, Max. I've been thinking about you.'

'I've been thinking about you too.'

'When can we see each other properly?'

They had fallen so quickly into the familiar pattern. Her voice was so low, so charged with sex, that it seemed to slip down from the phone and caress his groin. The fog that surrounded him felt like an expression of his mind. He knew what he was supposed to say. He was supposed to suggest a place, a time. He opened his mouth.

But then, in the middle of all this, two synapses in his brain fired, and his capacity for clear thinking returned momentarily to him. He did not think he was a brave man. But he knew that he was a man.

'We can't,' he said awkwardly. 'I'm worried that . . . we're both putting our families on the roulette wheel.'

'I know,' she sighed. 'I know exactly what you mean. I feel like such a fraud.'

'I'm just really worried that someone will see us. I'm . . . I don't think any man deserves this much happiness. It's all the deception, I can't live with all this deception.'

'Has something happened? You've got me worried.'

'No, no. God, no. At least, I don't think so.'

'You don't think so?'

'No.'

'You haven't said anything to anybody?'

'Christ, no.'

'Ursula hasn't raised any suspicions?'

'No, no. I'd tell you if that were the case.'

'What then?'

'I'm just worried that something bad is going to happen.

There are only two ways this is going to end. Either we're going to end it, or we're going to be discovered. There can't be another way.'

'I know,' she said, with sudden, unexpected decisiveness. 'I don't think we can ever see each other again.'

Something within him howled. 'We could be friends,' he said, 'don't you think?'

'We can't,' said Nicole, 'not after this. We've started something. Either we manage it or we cut it off.'

'Manage it?'

'Sorry. That doesn't sound very romantic.' She paused. 'I miss you.'

'Perhaps you're right,' he said. 'Cold turkey is the only way.'

There was a pause.

'You're sure about this? There'll be no going back.'

'I . . . there just isn't any other way.'

'This is so sad.'

'I'm sorry.'

'Don't be sorry. You didn't do anything wrong. In fact, you did too much that was right.'

'I'm sorry it has to end like this,' said Max. 'It feels so unnatural. It's so cruel how love singled us out like this. It just feels so . . . right. But it's not. It's wrong. Or is it? Oh God, I don't know. I'm sorry.'

'Don't apologise,' she said. 'It's just . . . this is the way the universe is.'

'You're right,' said Max. 'I think you're right.' Another pause. 'Well, goodbye, then,' he said, his voice sounding, he thought, like the voice of a child.

The line went dead.

Max stood still for a moment, then sat heavily on a tree stump. He pressed his fists to his eyes. What had he done? What had he done? This had been the most beautiful thing that had happened to him. And now he had ended it? Just as it was entering its prime? For the sake of what – duty? Some vow he had made years ago, on the basis of a relic of a relationship? Was this what it meant to be alive? To deny oneself happiness for the sake of an echo of a promise, that was made in such a different time? Did he not owe it to himself, to Ursula, to be honest and acknowledge that happiness lay elsewhere? That they were millstones round each other's necks?

Why had he been so narrow in his thinking? Were there not so many other possibilities? That he was in love with both women, but in different ways? That the force of lust actually belied a deeper truth of love? That for a man to be fully satisfied with his wife, he must also have the indulgence of a mistress? That for a wife to be fully attended to by her husband, he must have the indulgence of a mistress? The possibility of leaving Ursula for Nicole? The chance that this encounter with Nicole had represented a forking path; that if he were to part ways with Ursula, although profoundly painful and traumatic, they would both end up with better lives in the end?

But what about Carly?

At the touch of his thick thumb, the phone lit up. He scrolled down to Nicole's number. In his mind's eye he could see a vision of an ocean-going boat moving slowly away from the shore; the gap was narrow enough to be leaped, but it was widening all the time. His thumb hovered above the call button. It lowered towards it, but did not make contact. Then, just as he was screwing up his courage, and his eyes, and readying himself to throw caution to the winds, to try to reclaim what he had lost, his phone buzzed in his hand. A text message. He opened it. From Nicole. No text, just a picture; her in her underwear, a half-smile playing across her lips, hair tousled sexily from sleep, sitting on the side of a bath. And he knew.

Methodically, he deleted first her picture; then her messages; then her contact number (which he had saved under 'Nick'). At the press of a button, the phone went dark.

He closed his eyes, turned his face into the breeze. For a long time he sat like this, as the ocean-going ship moved off into the waters, further, further. Almost out of sight. Out of sight. My heart is down, my head is turning around, I had to leave a little girl in Kingston town. Now there was only himself; his body; the feeling of the breeze on his skin; the trees around him like sarcophagi; the night. How simple life really was, and how complicated desire made it. He felt, suddenly, like a boy again, as if the gift of innocence had been returned to him. For the first time in a long time, he wanted to buy Ursula some extravagant present, to take her away for a long weekend to the most expensive hotel he could find. He wanted to be near her. He wanted to take her in his arms, whisper how much he really loved her, make love to her. He got to his feet, vertiginous at the narrowness of his escape. The future rose up before him.

When Max emerged from the copse, he saw that the fog had cleared. Below him the traffic jam stretched, coiled, vanished. He could see people running about on the opposite side of the road. He could see lorries, vans, a bewildering variety of cars. His eyes, however, came to rest on one vehicle. Unremarkable to most, remarkable to him. I am a lucky man, he thought.

The visitor

Harold, at the wheel of his camper van, had lost his concentration again. He had already abandoned his reading, changed into his pyjamas and attempted to sleep on the sofa in the back; but he couldn't sleep, not like this. So he had put on his dressing gown and gone back to the driver's seat to resume his study, but it was three o'clock, he was tired and couldn't concentrate. What else to do? Both sleep and study were closed to him. Frustrated, he ballooned his bearded cheeks. There was a quotation, he thought, wasn't there? (There usually was.) Something about how discipline is nothing more than remembering what you want. He had a head like a sieve these days, particularly when it came to little bits of trivia like this. That was the ageing process, he supposed; it robbed one of one's capacities, beginning from the outer reaches and creeping gradually to the core, but offered in exchange the gift of contentment (albeit which usually preceded, in one's ultimate dotage, silliness. If not something worse). Young people, he thought, had no access to true contentment, for in that fiery period of one's life, which lasts perhaps until the age of forty, it is necessary to strive after various goals. Thereafter, whatever the levels of one's achievement, one begins to take one's foot off the accelerator and enjoy what one has. And one has other things to deal with at that time, anyway. The paying back of mortgages. The breakdown of relationships. The old age and death of parents. (That final, horrible event drives home the fact that the family tree is being gradually pollarded, and that oneself is now ripe for the plucking at the top. Is it possible to be termed accurately an orphan at the age of sixty-three?)

But now, lacking discipline, he had nodded off again. He awoke and looked, bewilderedly, about him. The camper van. Ah yes, the traffic jam. Still hasn't moved! His paper was lying curled in the shadows of the footwell. He took a minute to allow his consciousness to right itself. Waking up, he had often thought, should be like getting out of the bath. It should be done slowly and gradually so as not to shock the system. His body felt profoundly limp, as if only part of him had awoken. He moved his arms, made a few gentle attempts to brush some stray crumbs of Mr Kipling's cake from his stomach. For a moment he felt lighter than air. Then the old solidity seeped back. This wasn't just about three o'clock in the morning. These days he could never tell when he was going to nod off.

It was then that Harold noticed a ghostly figure outside the window. He gave a start, peered closer. It had one hand raised in greeting, like the drawings that Man sent into space for the benefit of aliens in the Seventies. But this was no man. It was clear, even in this light – and even with the fog's misty tentacles at the van window – that this was a woman.

With some effort he wound the window down, rubbing his eyes.

'Sorry,' said Hsiao May from the cold, from the darkness. 'I saw you were still up and I thought, well, you know. If we both can't sleep.'

'Aye, right enough,' said Harold, blinking with recognition. 'Come in. I'm so glad, I'm so glad. Let's have a cup of tea. Round the back. I'll let you in.'

She hoisted her cool bag over her shoulder and made her way round the old-fashioned lozenge of goodness. So far, so good, she thought; she was feeling tired, and rather tense, and was finding eye contact awkward, but that was only to be expected, and on the scale of things her anxiety levels were negligible. Once she got into the vehicle, she thought, she'd be OK. This camper van seemed to speak to her of everything that was wholesome in life. Hers was an existence in which affairs of the intellect overshadowed this world and all its pleasures. So, when she came across something like this – something so impractical, so joyful, whose sole purpose was to create a little simple happiness – she was charmed.

Through the back windows she could see Harold silhouetted against the desolate motorway, listing awkwardly as he clambered between the seats and neatened his dressing gown. She smiled. He sat heavily on one of the sofas and shunted along sideways, puffing like a steam train, stimulating in her an overwhelming affection for him, this man she knew only in passing. The fact that he would put himself in the position of such interminable awkwardness, such downright impracticality, for the sake of pootling around the country at fifty miles per hour in a charming old, clanking old, cramped old machine! Straining, he reached over and opened the door.

Inside, the atmosphere was highly private and personal; everything was laid out precisely, everything was in its place. And, Hsiao May noticed, a great deal of thought had been put in to ensuring that nothing would fall over when the camper van went round corners. She put her cool bag carefully on the sofa and sat down. It was bobbled, springy, spongy. Harold busied himself with the preparations for tea, glancing back at her occasionally, holding his head at an angle as if it were horribly stiff, talking over his shoulder.

'What's in the bag?' he asked. 'Did you come bearing gifts?'

'Diet Coke mainly,' Hsiao May replied. 'But there are some snacks as well, yes.'

'Oh goody. What've you got?'

'Let's have some tea first. Then we'll see.'

'It all sounds very mysterious.'

'It is very mysterious. But it will be worth the wait.'

'My dear, I . . . I'm so ashamed to admit this, but I'm finding this happening more and more these days. Would you mind just reminding me of your name?'

'Please don't worry. Happens to me all the time. It's Hsiao May.'

'Of course, of course. I'm getting so scatty these days. It doesn't really happen at your age, does it?'

'It's so amazing that you can make tea in here. It's the perfect traffic jam vehicle.'

'Aye, the old girl's not bad. Not bad at all.'

'Can you cook? Is there a stove? A fridge?'

'Oh yes. One could live one's entire life in this tin can.'

'Is there a bed?'

'Of course. One couldn't live without a bed.'

'Do you ever sleep in here?'

'All the time. But don't worry, it's very tidy. The bed folds away. It's in character as a sofa at the moment.'

'Sorry, I'm just really fascinated by . . . I've never been in a camper van before. It's just so wonderfully practical.'

'That's a matter of opinion. But it's certainly fun.'

'Don't those flowers fall over?'

'No, they're screwed down.'

'Screwed down?'

'Yes. Don't worry, I've done it very subtly. At least, as subtly as I possibly could.'

The sound of water gushing into the kettle gave them both an opportunity to collect their thoughts. How peaceful it was in this van, thought Hsiao May. The littlest sounds compliment-ing the quietude so perfectly. It reminded her of something from her childhood, something she could not quite pin down.

'So,' said Harold as they waited for the tea to boil. 'What brings you to this neck of the woods?'

'I'm going to stay with my sister,' Hsiao May replied. 'I'm flying to America tomorrow.'

'Really? How exciting. Business or pleasure?'

'Business. Pleasure. Well, both actually. I'm attending a conference.'

'I like that. Let me guess. Insects?'

'Good guess.'

'It was elementary, my dear Watson.'

'What about you?'

'Me? I've just been for a wee bumble down to Cornwall and back. Taking a circuitous route, you know, for the long weekend. I find it therapeutic.'

'I think that's lovely.'

'It is. Very soothing.'

'And you're English?'

'English? I'm sorry?'

'Your discipline.'

'Oh no, I'm a historian.'

'Which period?'

'Modern history. Britain and Europe mainly.'

'I study grasshoppers.'

That was an awkward segue, she thought.

'Is that so?' he said. 'How fascinating.'

'Do you think so?'

'Absolutely I do. I've always, ever since I was a boy, found insects utterly fascinating.'

Her heart warmed. 'Me too,' she said. 'I think all children are fascinated by insects. Digging them up, creating farms and colonies, pulling the wings off, eating them. But somewhere along the line we get conditioned out of it. Like drawing.'

'There's not enough wonder in the world any more, is there?'

'There is. But not enough people are interested in it.'

'Aye, you're right there.'

The kettle started to boil.

'Odd, isn't it?' said Harold. 'Making tea at three in the morning on the M25.'

'Yes, very odd. It's quite eerie too. All these cars. I'm very glad of the company.'

'Me too.'

The kettle whistled now, and Harold allowed it get good and loud before removing it from the flame. Then, slowly, deliberately, he went through the process: mugs, teabags, brew, brew, teaspoon, squeeze and hoist, dump, milk, unscrew, little dash, little dash, lid back on, stir, stir.

'Sugar?'

'Thank you, no.'

'You're sure?'

'No thanks.'

Stir again, a piece of kitchen roll – rip – mop up the drops, align the handles, steam, a little smile.

'There,' he said, 'we're ready.'

He handed a mug carefully to Hsiao May.

'That was very . . . focused.'

'What was?'

'The tea-making.'

'Ah, you noticed. Well, I think it's important. It brings together a couple of my philosophies. Sorry, that sounded horribly pretentious. My philosophies! I mean, well, my attitudes to living.'

'What are they?'

'Goodness, you're putting me on the spot now.' He sat down, and the sofa bowed under his weight. They were opposite each other, illuminated dimly by the glowing honey-coloured lights, cupping their hands around their mugs, as if in a bomb shelter waiting for the All Clear.

'I suppose the first is,' continued Harold, 'to try to beautify the little things in life. To instill order where before there was chaos, loveliness where before there was ruination, and so on.'

'Like when you make tea?'

'Making tea has the potential to be a very ugly affair. Don't you think?'

'I suppose.'

'It's an extension of respect for all of humanity. That of God in every man and so on. Curating the world for the benefit of humanity, so that when I pass on, the fruits will still be there for others to enjoy.'

'I agree,' said Hsiao May emphatically. 'That resonates with me. With one of my principal ideas.'

'Oh?'

'Yes. But first tell me about your second philosophy.'

'Mmmm? Oh, it's not anywhere near as grand as a philosophy. It's more an affinity, really. For the East.'

'The East?'

'More specifically, Japan. You're Chinese, aren't you?'

'Ethnically, yes. But I've lived all my life in Britain.'

'Han?'

'Yes, Han.'

'Well, I'm ashamed to say that I've never been to China.'

'Don't be. I've only been a handful of times.'

'But Japan . . . now, Japan's another story.'

'Do you speak Japanese?'

'Hai, sukoshi hanashimasu. I'm just fascinated with the culture.'

'The girls?' she said, regretted it, blushed.

'No, no, no,' Harold chuckled. 'Goodness gracious me. Why do you say that? The girls? Gracious me.'

'Sorry. I shouldn't have. It's just that I, er, I'm sorry.'

'No, no, don't be.' He chuckled again. 'I'm just fascinated by the arts of calligraphy, tea making, meditation. You know, all the wee things that make one slow down in the world. Appreciate the moment.'

'Yes, I know.'

There was a pause, and they both sipped their tea. It was strong, given a perfect degree of substance by the milk, and very clean. Simultaneously they sighed, and then they laughed.

'So what was it that resonated with you?' said Harold.

'It was what you said about curating the world for the next generation. Curating the world. That's a beautiful way of putting it.'

'You think a lot about that?'

'I'm very aware – more than most, it seems – of the dire trajectory that the world is following.'

'Ah, climate change.'

'Yes, but that's only part of it. Climate change, population growth, water scarcity, food scarcity. The world is coming under the most extraordinary pressure, and over the next forty years we'll have to do something to face those challenges. Otherwise there'll be all-out war. The apocalypse.'

'I agree entirely. I've thought long and hard about this. It haunts me, as it should haunt any thinking human being. But I am always led to the same conclusion; what could I, an academic past his sell-by date, do about it? It is the responsibility of the political class, the business elite, to hammer out a solution for all this. Sure, I can vote, I can write to my MP, but is that really going to make any difference?'

'That seems rather defeatist.'

'No, no, not defeatist. These thoughts feed my interest in making the world a more beautiful, softer, more humane place on the microcosmic level. Making a cup of tea properly is a step towards saving the world. Bumbling around in my camper van. Inviting people in for cups of tea, discussions like this one. It may not make a great deal of difference to the whole, but it's the most I can do.'

'Be the change you want in the world.'

'Aha! A quotation! There's always a quotation, isn't there. I know this one. I know this one. Now let me see . . .'

'Gandhi.'

'Oh yes, of course. Gandhi. Of course. How could I forget? I should really write these things down.'

They sipped, again, simultaneously.

'Well,' said Harold, 'what about you?'

Hsiao May took a deep breath. 'As you know,' she said, 'I'm all about insects.'

'I know.'

'Insects are my academic interest, my research interest. But they're also the basis of my personal philosophy. No, not philosophy. Theory.'

'Theory?'

'Guiding principles.'

'How so?'

She was nervous now, for a reason she did not understand. 'Let me open my cool bag. There. You see?'

Within the white interior, in addition to the cans of Diet Coke, there were various brown paper bags, various Tupperware tubs.

'What are these?' said Harold carefully.

'These are . . . I believe these to be an important component of humanity's survival.'

Harold raised his eyebrows then knitted them, thoughtfully.

'Imagine,' said Hsiao May, 'if there was a way to feed people on livestock that could happily thrive in their millions in very confined spaces. That were higher in protein, pound-for-pound, than any conventional animals. That were rich in micro-nutrients, iron and zinc. That were distant enough from us in the food chain not to pass on any diseases. That were cold-blooded, making them energy-efficient, as they didn't have to expend energy warming themselves. That were cheap to produce, cheap to breed, cheap to feed. That were natural recyclers, thriving on food by-products, cardboard, even manure. What would you say?'

'I'd say how does it taste?' said Harold.

'Delicious. Delicious. With the right recipes, delicious.'

'I'd say is it safe?'

'Absolutely.' She pulled out the smallest paper bag, lighter than it appeared, and laid it on the yellow sofa. 'Here,' she said, prising it open. 'Tenebrio molitor. A beetle larvae. Commonly known as mealworm. Pan-fried with sea salt and cracked black pepper. A great snacking food.' She took out a pinch and popped it in her mouth. 'Would you like to try?'

Harold hesitated, then reached over and placed a small

amount in the palm of his hand. Then he raised it carefully to the light.

'Not as I expected,' he said thoughtfully. 'If you sold me a packet of these in the pub, I'd be none the wiser.'

'Exactly. No yuck factor.'

'But it is actual mealworm?'

'It is actual mealworm.'

'How does it taste?'

'Try it. Look. It's perfectly fine.' She ate a handful now, by way of demonstration.

'You're sure it's safe?'

'Of course. I eat it all the time. It's an ideal snack. Healthy too.'

Harold hesitated again. Then he took a sip of tea. The little cluster of mealworm, yellowish and crusty, sparkling with crystals of salt, lay waiting in his palm. He replaced the teacup and raised the mealworm to his face. Then he cupped his hand, brought it to his mouth; the mealworm pattered on to his tongue, tumbled into the corners of his cheeks. He chewed. Hsiao May watched in anticipation.

'Well?' she said.

'Hmmm,' said Harold. 'Tastes a bit like sunflower seeds. And a whiff of wild mushrooms.'

'Exactly,' said Hsiao May. 'You see? Eco-friendly and delicious. Now have a look at this.' A second bag joined the first; she dug her hand into it. 'Roasted crickets,' she said. 'You roast them as you would a potato. Then when they're nice and crispy, you pull off the ovipositors and legs.'

'Now this,' said Harold, taking one in finger and thumb, 'looks more like an insect.'

'Do you think so?'

'Yes, I do. Goodness, I barely want to touch it.' He dropped it into the bag.

'Now isn't that interesting,' said Hsiao May, rolling a cricket in her fingers. 'Why do you think you had that reaction?'

'I don't know. It's evolutionary, perhaps. Insects tend to be rather dirty.'

'Most of the world eats them. Always has. In India, in South America, in Africa. Children roast tarantula in Venezuela. Tenebrio molitor is factory farmed in China.'

'Tenebrio molitor?'

'The stuff you've just eaten.'

'Oh.'

'The Oaxacans are quite happy to eat grasshoppers, but believe that prawns are foul.'

'Is that so?'

'Yes. It makes sense if you think about it. Lobsters, prawns, shellfish; they are scavengers. They are also arthropods, but they feed on the garbage of the ocean. Insects, which usually consume fresh vegetation, are actually far cleaner.'

'I see.'

'Do you know how you bait a lobster?'

'Meat?'

'Putrid flesh.'

'No.'

'Yes. Insects are more hygienic by far. Crickets, actually, are even mentioned in the Bible as a foodstuff. So are locusts and grasshoppers.'

'Really? Where?'

'Deuteronomy.'

'Now isn't that interesting.' He reached into the cabinet, past the bottle of Balvenie, and took out a battered, leather-bound bible. 'Could you give me the chapter and verse?'

'Of course,' said Hsiao May, without so much as a pause. 'Leviticus 11:22-3.'

Harold lurched awkwardly to his feet and hunched around the dim light bulb, holding the ancient pages of the bible – his father's bible – to the glow. There was a silence.

'I see,' he said suddenly. 'Now isn't that fascinating? "Even these of them ye may eat: the locust after his kind, and the bald locust after his kind, and the beetle after his kind, and the grass-hopper after his kind." All these years and I'd never noticed those little verses before. Fascinating.'

He closed the bible, put it back beside the whisky, sat down.

'So,' said Hsiao May, 'your reaction derived from ingrained ethnocentrism.'

'Did it?'

'Absolutely. I see it all the time.'

'Ingrained ethnocentrism.'

'I'm not being critical. I don't mean to belittle culturally assumed attitudes. They have a visceral hold over all of us.'

'I suppose they do.'

'This touches on what I'm going to be talking about at the conference. The need to bypass cultural ethnocentrism by transforming bugs into a foodstuff. Psychologically. In the popular imagination.'

'How?'

'Lots of ways. By changing the language surrounding it.'

'The language?'

'Yes. Off-putting terms such as bugs, insects, termites, worms and so on can be substituted for other more friendly ones: micro-livestock, chapulines, tenebrio.'

'I see.'

'Also by making it look less buggy. Insect flour, for instance. Or insect hot dogs. Or insect steak.'

'Insect steak?'

'It could work, so long as you get enough of them. So long as you choose the right species. A lot of them are too viscous with-out the exoskeleton.'

Hsiao May paused, marshalling her thoughts. It was going well, she could sense it. Harold had already eaten some meal-worm. And he was reacting to her arguments objectively. Perhaps it wasn't so difficult to change people's perceptions after all. If they had enough intelligence.

'Honey,' she said. 'That's bee vomit.'

'I suppose it is.'

'In the nineteenth century, the Society for the Propagation of Horse Flesh as an Article of Food had French chefs prepare a banquet of what they called *chevaline*. It was a resounding success.'

Harold's brow was furrowed now. 'Was it?'

'Four-fifths of all animals are insects.'

Harold got to his feet and rummaged carefully in a cupboard. Instinctively, Hsiao May stopped speaking. Then Harold closed the cupboard and sat down.

'Sorry,' said Hsiao May, 'I've been going on a bit.'

'No, no,' said Harold. 'It's lovely to get somebody on to their passion.'

'It certainly is a passion. With good reason.'

'Indeed.'

'Sorry, anyway.'

'Don't mention it. Please.'

'So . . . would you like to try a cricket?'

'That's very kind of you, but I'm . . . I'd . . . I think I'd rather have a Rich Tea. Can I tempt you?'

Hsiao May smiled and felt herself blush. 'A Rich Tea would be lovely,' she said.

Natalie

In the dream, there had been nothing but darkness. It had been moving, shifting, changing, writhing, and although she could make out nothing with her eyes, she could feel it. At times the darkness became heavy, and she felt as if she was going to be crushed. At times it became thin and air-like, and she felt sure she would lose track of everything. At times it seemed comprised of snakes of all different sizes, all seeking to insinuate their way into her being. At times it smelled of the medicine of her childhood; rotten apples; burnt onions. It stank, and offended her, and tasted of everything that was foul; there were horrible noises of grinding and scraping, and these times were perhaps the worst of all.

When she woke up, it was to the most blinding of headaches. It was pitch-black. She did not know where she was. The smell of skunk was in her nose, in her throat, in her lungs, in her skull. Her mouth was so dry that she couldn't even swallow. After lying there, compressed and uncomfortable for a couple of minutes, she hauled herself up and sat, rocking slightly. Her hand found her face. Wet with drool, water in her hair. God, she was so stupid.

Where the hell were Stevie and Dave? She had to get out of this suffocating car. She opened the door and emerged into the cold. There was a clattering sound by her feet and she saw that her new phone had fallen out of her pocket. She picked it up. The top right-hand corner was scuffed a little now, but it seemed to be working OK. It was then that she became aware of a patina of whitish crust on her hands. She spent some time spitting, wiping, scraping with her sleeve.

When the sobs had subsided, she felt no better. She looked round; nobody in any of the nearby cars had noticed. She dried her eyes, sniffed, then stood with feet braced against a wave of giddiness. It passed. And when it passed, in that new clarity, she became aware of a noise that had been skirting the edges of her consciousness. She turned and squinted through the fog, catching sight of the footballing figures ghosting in and out of view. And there were Dave and Stevie.

A chill passed through her body and lodged in her abdomen. She squeezed her nails into her palms. She walked around the car and started towards them; she was going to say hi, whatcha doing, where'd'ya go, how long have I been out? She was going to ask if they had any water. But then she stopped, and felt that she didn't want to be seen at all. She slipped back behind the vehicle and watched them for a few minutes. Then she turned away.

Something was not right, that much she knew. In the centre of her chest the darkness of her dream remained, weighing her down. She didn't know what was wrong. Dave was all right, Stevie was all right. Shouldn't she be flattered that she turned him – them – on so much? This was uni, after all. She had to live a little, otherwise what was the point? It would have been unfair of her to have turned round and rejected him all of a sudden. She didn't want to get a reputation as a player right at the beginning. Those things stick, don't they? It had been bad of her to pretend to be asleep those last few times. But she just couldn't face it. She didn't want to carry on with him, and that was the honest truth, but she didn't know how to deny him.

This was all her own silly fault. Why was she being so uptight? Here were two guys who were really into her, especially Stevie, and what was she doing? Being stupid and pathetic. Why did she feel so shy? Why so unsure of herself? Where had her self-confidence gone? And why had she started to feel so revolted? There were guys uglier than Stevie.

Now no tears came. She was desperate for a drink of water;

she dared not approach Davie and Stevie or the other footballers, nor the men in the white van over there. She saw a
woman sitting in a camper van with an older man. They looked
approachable, but just as she was making up her mind to knock
on the window, she saw the way they were speaking, and didn't
dare to invade their privacy. It was as if the universe was turning its back on her.

Beyond the barrier, at the side of the motorway, there was a
stretch of wasteland that shouldered up into a hill, dotted with
clumps of trees. In front of it, Natalie noticed a figure sitting on
some sort of metal box. A vaguely familiar man, wearing a
uniform of some sort; on the ground in front of him was a
bottle of water and a Waitrose carrier bag. In Natalie's mind's
eye, a shaft of sunlight cut through the night and illuminated
the bottle, causing the pure refreshment inside it to glint, the
condensation on the outside to sparkle. By chance, or perhaps
by way of that strange phenomenon that causes people to sense
when others are looking at them, the man glanced up and
smiled. And she recognised him as the driver of the Waitrose
van that she had visited with Stevie and Dave earlier that night,
so long ago.

'All right?' he said.

She came to a stop in front of him. There was a moment's
silence.

'Sorry,' she said. 'I just, like, wondered if I could have a little
bit of your water please?'

'Help yourself,' said Jim, shuffling along the top of the box.
'Have a seat.'

Natalie did so, reached for the bottle.

'Phew,' said Jim, 'that's some aroma.'

'Aroma?'

'You smell like Bob Marley. No offence.'

'None taken.'

How could she take offence? There was something easy about
Jim's manner, something accepting; as soon as Natalie sat down

next to him she felt a sense of camaraderie, the two of them looking out at the world together. She twisted off the lid and drank, and the water was life-affirming and sweet. Then she regarded him as closely as she dared. He was old, in his forties perhaps, lean, and with eyes that seemed to be watching intently everything and nothing at once.

'Have you come far?' said Jim.

'I've been at a festival.'

'Going anywhere urgently?'

'No, not urgently.'

'Still cold?'

'I'm OK now.'

'Good.'

'What's in the bag?' said Natalie, noticing with some embarrassment that she had drunk almost half the bottle of water.

'Oh, bits and bobs,' said Jim. 'Help yourself. There are M&Ms, some chocolate digestives, a couple of bags of Haribo. Doritos. Stuff like that.'

'What can I take?'

'Whatever you want, love. There's always more where that came from.'

She took a packet of Oreos and helped herself to a couple.

'How come you're sitting out here?' she said.

'Got bored of sitting in the van. Realised it wasn't any safer in there anyway. So thought I might as well get some fresh air, like.'

Natalie offered the open end of the Oreos packet to Jim; he took a biscuit.

'What about those boys you were with?' said Jim. 'Assuming you were all together. You didn't go to the festival on your own, did you?'

'No, no. They're my friends.'

'Where are they? Passed out, stoned?'

'No,' said Natalie, 'they're playing football. See, over there?'

'Oh, those guys. That's some sight, like,' he said. 'Football on the M25.'

'My friends are those ones on the left. See? Dave and Stevie.'

'Dave and Stevie,' repeated Jim. 'Either of them your boyfriend?'

'It's complicated.'

'Always is, like.'

'Stevie, you know, he's sort of up for it. But I'm not.'

'That don't sound too complicated to me,' said Jim. 'It sounds pretty straightforward.'

'But I just think, well, I don't know. I think it's my fault. Whatever.'

'What's your fault?

'This whole thing.'

'You're not in love with him, like?' said Jim.

'No! I mean, he's all right. But the thing is, I sort of maybe led him on?'

Jim frowned.

'That don't sound right,' he said.

'I'm not, like, a slapper,' said Natalie quickly. 'But when he came on to me at first, like, I didn't say no. So how can I say no now?'

'Sorry,' said Jim. 'Sorry, I don't mean to embarrass you.'

'Whatever.'

Natalie brought the water bottle to her lips and found it to be empty. Her head was fuzzy. The world looked creepy in the darkness, in the street lamplight, in the mist. She looked towards Dave and Stevie. They were running around like banshees, Stevie especially, flailing, competing. She looked away.

'We went to the festival and it ended up, like, me and them in a tent,' she said. 'Everyone else dropped out. And on the first night, you know, we got pissed and it, well, you know. I thought, like, fuck it. You only live once. Whatever.' She felt herself blushing uncontrollably. What was she doing, telling all this to a complete stranger? 'I'm sorry,' she said, 'I sound like I'm a dirty sket.'

There was a pause. 'I can't pretend to know what that means, but it don't sound right to me.'

Natalie's blushes increased, but she went on. 'It was my fault, anyway,' she said. 'I let it carry on.'

'What?'

'I, like, didn't have a choice. I just . . . I mean you can't just turn round and sort of say, sorry, guys, like, I didn't know what I was doing, I was drunk, now go fuck yourselves.'

'Why not?'

'We were staying in the same tent.'

'So what?'

'So I couldn't just . . . it would have been . . . rude.'

'Rude?'

'Just . . . oh God, this is making me sound like such a twat.'

'Not you,' said Jim. 'Them.'

'I know it sounds bad and everything,' said Natalie. 'I thought so too, especially when they started giving me nicknames and stuff.'

'What nicknames?'

'It's nothing. It was only one nickname, actually. OK, all right. It was Piece of Meat. It's sort of like their sense of humour, you know.'

'Piece of Meat?'

'Yeah, but it sounds much worse saying it like that . . . it was like a joke to them. Whatever.'

Jim shook his head. 'I'm sure it's none of my business,' he said, 'and God knows I'm in no position to give advice, with my own life the way it is. But if you ask me, you've got to stand up for yourself, like.'

'Do you think so?'

He looked around for inspiration. 'I may have only known you five minutes, but I can see you're a decent girl. You're young. You just don't know yourself, that's all. And that's not a crime.'

'But it wasn't Stevie's fault,' said Natalie, 'it was mine. That's exactly what I'm saying.'

'Look,' said Jim, 'if you want to tell them where to get off, like, I'll give you a lift home. When this traffic moves.'

'Where to get off?'

'You know what I mean. If you want to . . . if you want to, just tell them to fuck off.'

'I couldn't do that,' said Natalie.

'Why not?'

'It would be . . . I'd have to . . . all my stuff's in their car.'

'That's what I said. I'll give you a lift. Be a chance to . . . you know, good deed for the day.'

'Thanks,' she said. 'I mean, that's great and everything, but, it's just that I don't really know you.'

'You're right,' said Jim. 'Anyway, the offer's there.'

Natalie buried her face in her hands for a moment, then shook her head and got to her feet.

'You've been very kind and everything,' she said, 'and I'm not saying I don't trust you or anything. You're right about everything. But Stevie and Dave are my friends. My uni friends. They're part of my world, you know? And I don't even know you or anything. I can't explain. But thanks for the advice and everything, you know . . . but, like I say, this was all my fault to begin with. I've probably not sort of explained it properly. I've probably made them out to be bastards when actually they're OK. Whatever. What I'm saying is . . . it's not that I don't sort of believe you or anything. But I just can't do what you're saying. That's it. I just can't.'

Penalty

Then the ball caught a deflection off Dave's shin and looped, spinning, into the air. It was now 5 a.m., and a grey light was spreading softly across the sky. The boys were back on the tarmac again, in the theatre of play, and once again were playing two-on-two with a single goal; Kabir had been nominated as goalkeeper, and he had accepted the position grudgingly.

Neither Stevie nor Dave had played football for a long time. Although Dave had played for his school First XI, his adolescence had been given over to the pleasure of the spliff, and this does not an athlete make. Stevie, of course, had never been much good. His left foot stuck out sideways when he ran, and his elbows flailed; in the playground he had always been stuck in some obscure position in midfield; and when he exerted himself he made a strange hissing sound, as if he were powered by steam. They were both, of course, easily outclassed by Shahid and Mo, as they had been all night.

The ball took flight. Shahid found himself at the right place at the right time for the volley, but it wasn't going to be easy with that spin. Nevertheless, such opportunities come only rarely, and his football brain had taken over, meaning that time had slowed down and the angles were appearing with great clarity to his mind's eye. He was faintly aware of the whoops coming from the white van on the other side of the motorway; the two men had been cheering and heckling, drinking from a bottle, and although it was bizarre to be responded to in this way on a night-time motorway – and although he had been wrong-footed by it at first – as the game had gone on, his brain had processed the cheers and boos and begun to relate to them in the same way he related to the noise of the fans each Saturday at London APSA. The ball came down before him as if on angelic wings. He took a right-footed crescent swing and caught the sweet spot. It shot like a dart from his laces, cut a clean curve through the dawn sky and disappeared past Kabir before he could even move. It continued without bouncing, glanced off the uppermost edge of the motorway barrier beyond and burrowed deep into the shrubbery.

'Ten-two,' shouted Shahid jubilantly, exchanging hand slaps with Mo, 'ten-fucking-two!'

'No,' said Stevie shrilly, 'ten-three. Ten-three.'

'You haven't got three goals, brah.'

'We have. We have. The first two Dave scored off solo runs, remember? The third was mine. The one that caught a deflection and shit.'

'Oh yeah, right you are,' said Shahid. 'The own goal.'

'Not own goal. Deflection.'

'Right. Deflection. A memorable goal, that one.'

'Yeah, it was a memorable goal,' said Stevie, his voice rising. 'It was a memorable goal.'

Shahid grinned. With every goal that he scored, he was feeling better. This reaction proved he was getting under their skin. He wanted more. He wanted to beat these fuckers until they bled: no revenge, but revenge enough.

'Yeah,' said Kabir, 'but how do we get the ball back?'

'Just go and get it, brah,' said Shahid. 'I'll get the next one. Promise.'

Kabir hesitated, then disappeared into the shrubbery.

'Look,' said Mo, 'why don't we change the teams around? One of us and one of you. Otherwise it's not fair.'

'Might be a good idea,' said Dave.

'I'm not agreeing to that,' said Stevie quickly. 'We're not going to give up like that.'

'You're not giving up?' said Mo. 'We've been beating the shit out of you all night. It's ten fucking two.'

'Three.'

'Sorry, yeah, three. Whatever, we're spanking you.'

'So?'

'So, whatever. We can carry on playing if you want. It's just getting a bit boring, that's all.'

'Look, brah,' said Shahid, 'if a pasting's what they want, a pasting's what they'll fucking get. Right, mate?' He fixed Stevie with a long, mocking look.

'Look, Stevie, it's only a kick-around,' said Dave. 'There's no point playing if we're just going to be slaughtered.'

'Don't be so fucking pathetic,' said Stevie. 'We'll change our tactics. We just need a few more goals and before you know it we'll be snapping at their heels.'

Shahid heard him and laughed. 'Snapping at our heels,' he repeated to Mo, 'they reckon.'

'Butt out of this, all right?' said Stevie. 'We're having a team talk.'

Shahid and Mo faded into the mist.

'Let's just leave it, OK?' said Dave, his voice lowered. 'I'm getting tired, anyway. Look, dude, the sun's rising. Can't you hear the birds? And I'm fucking sweating.'

'Seven goals?' said Stevie, 'you want to give up for the sake of a seven-goal lead? You girl.'

'Something's not right here,' Dave replied. 'I don't like it.'

'Don't like what, dude?'

'I don't know. It feels funny. They're hard bastards, they are. And the guys by the van? They're making me antsy.'

'You're just being paranoid,' said Stevie. 'It's the skunk.'

'Thanks for reminding me. I've got the munchies.'

'Forget the fucking munchies.'

'We were lucky to get three goals, anyway,' said Dave. 'We didn't deserve any of them. Especially that last one. We only scored because of the fog.'

'Don't be such a fucking girl.' Stevie turned, walked a few paces, walked back. 'Here's what we'll do. Whoever gets the ball, the other one draws the defenders away and the first one has a shot. We need to get some shots in.'

'That won't work.'

'Then when we get the chance, we need to go down. Call for a penalty, or at least a free kick.'

'You're saying we should play dirty?'

'It's not dirty. All the footballers do it. It's gamesmanship.'

'Fuck.'

'And then back to shots.'

'Stevie, it's just a kick-around.'

'You got any better ideas?'

'Yeah, let's just call it off.'

'I said better ideas. That's not a better idea. That's a gay idea.'

'Fuck sake,' said Dave, under his breath. Then there was the sound of the ball bouncing on the tarmac again and Shahid and Mo stepped into view.

'Game on!' said Stevie, clapping his hands. 'Let's go.'

The goalie kicked the ball high in the air, and it fell kindly to Stevie. He made an effort to trap it but it squeezed under his foot and was nicked by Mo, who backheeled it to Shahid. He accepted it smoothly, held it up, stroking it from side to side, waiting. Dave went in for a tackle but Shahid easily sidestepped him, ran a few paces towards goal, stopped, flicking the ball back and forth; then Stevie went in hard and barged him out of possession. Shahid swore in bewilderment. Now Stevie had a clear attempt at goal, but was unable to capitalise on the advantage; he lost control of the ball and it bobbled off down the motorway. Nevertheless, a cheer went up from the two men by the van.

'Oi-oi! Get stuck in, my son,' yelled Rhys. 'Get fucking stuck in. Ha ha.'

'En-ger-land,' sang Chris, 'Engerland, Engerland, Engerland.'

'That was a foul,' said Shahid. 'Free kick.'

'Bollocks,' said Stevie. 'Come on.' He ran down the middle lane, retrieved the ball, dribbled it back. 'Come on.'

Blinded by anger, Shahid went in hard. But he lost his composure and missed; Stevie managed to both release the ball to Dave and avoid getting chopped down. Mo was out of position. Dave lined it up and let fly; the ball whizzed across the tarmac and skidded inside the far post. The goalie made a half-hearted effort, too late.

'Goal!' shouted Stevie. 'Ten-four!'

'Get in!' shouted Rhys and Chris. 'Engerland, Engerland, Engerland.' Stevie turned towards them and punched the air. Their laughs and cheers increased. 'You're shit and you know you are . . .'

'Look,' said Shahid, taking a few steps towards the van, 'come on, why don't you two come and play? Show us how it's done? Have a fucking game.'

'Shahid,' said Mo nervously.

'Nah, mate,' called Rhys, 'you're all right.' Then, in an aside to Chris, he said something else.

Shahid turned back and saw that the goalie had returned with the ball. He raised an arm. 'Come on, mate,' he said, 'give it a boot.'

'Let's play first to fifteen,' suggested Stevie, panting hard.

'You're on,' said Shahid. 'First to fifteen.' He felt hollowed out, as if something had been knocked out of him.

'Engerland, Engerland, Engerland. Ha ha.'

Kabir booted the ball into the air; they jostled for position beneath it, and when it came down they scrambled to trap it and it bobbled away to the left. Shahid gave chase, controlled it neatly. Mo went out wide, waving his arms and shouting, 'Square ball! Square ball!' Shahid went to pass it but dummied, drawing the ball back between his legs. But he had overestimated Dave, who had not read the dummy in the first place; when he saw the ball being dragged back, he stuck a clumsy toe in and it skittered free.

Stevie, approaching at a brisk trot, couldn't believe his luck and rushed in the direction of the goal. Shahid went in for the challenge; the ball ricocheted between their shins and squirted out to Dave. Mo put in a half-hearted tackle from behind, but it was too late. Dave had fed the ball back into the path of Stevie, who was continuing his advance like a juggernaut, hissing like a steam train, and he struck it first time. Kabir rose to meet it, but his bare hands were unable to grip the shining leather, and it spun from between his palms and dropped behind.

'Goal! Goal! Ha ha ha!'

'En-ger-land, En-ger-land, En-ger-land!'

'Fucking hell, Kabir,' said Shahid. 'What sort of fucking goal-keeping was that?'

'He was offside!'

'We're not playing offside, you nonce! This is two-on-two!'

'Yeah but that was just fucking goal-hanging!'

'Ten-five! Ten-five! Fucking yes!'

'Yeah, nice one mate, nice one.'

'Ruuule Britannia! Britannia rules the waves. Britain never, ever, ever, shall be slaves. Ruuule Britannia . . .'

'They reckon they're at a fucking England match,' said Shahid, to nobody in particular. 'Oi! You ain't at a fucking England match, you know!'

'Fuck off. You're not English any more! You're not English any more. You're not English, you're not English, you're not English any more . . .'

'Take it easy, man,' said Mo. 'Calm down, OK?'

'I am fucking calm,' said Shahid. 'But those cunts should shut the fuck up.'

'Just ignore it, OK? They're just pissed up. Ignore it.'

'This doesn't feel right, dude,' said Dave, drawing a jubilant Stevie aside. 'I'm telling you.'

'What you on about? It's ten-five! We've got them on the run. Now whoever gets it next, try and get a foul. Try and get a penalty. OK?'

'But . . .'

'Game on, game on!' Stevie clapped his hands again.

'Stevie, you don't say "game on" in football.'

'Game on! Let's play ball!'

'Stevie! Fuck sake.'

Kabir elected to throw the ball out this time, and Stevie and Mo both went up for the challenge. Mo won easily, and nodded it down to Shahid, who trapped it with velvety precision. Dave crabstepped up to him, legs apart, trying to corral him away from goal. In a heartbeat Shahid had skipped past him; Stevie cut across, threw himself at the ball; then he went down, rolled over twice, shrieking.

'What?' Shahid was saying, his arms raised as if in fright. 'I didn't even touch him. I didn't touch him.'

Dave stooped. 'You all right, mate?' he said, for all the world unsure whether Stevie was faking or not.

Stevie sat up gingerly. 'That's a fucking penalty, that is,' he said.

'What?' said Shahid uncertainly. 'I didn't even touch you.'

'Like fuck,' said Stevie. 'That's a penalty. That's a penalty.'

'Free kick, free kick,' said Mo, pointing to a spot in the tarmac a couple of feet from the dashed line that separated the slow lane from the middle. 'Free kick.'

Stevie got painfully to his feet.

'It's so a penalty,' said Dave, warming to his friend's theme. 'Look, it's only a few yards from goal.'

'That's outside the area,' said Mo.

'Bollocks it is,' said Dave. 'It's not like there's any markings or anything.'

'I didn't even do nothing to begin with,' moaned Shahid childishly. 'Fucking hell.'

'Penalty,' Stevie announced. He took the ball and placed it perpendicular to the goal; when nobody protested he was surprised.

'Kabir, man,' said Shahid, 'let Mo go in goal. He's better at penalties than you.'

'But I've been playing in goal all night,' said Kabir, his arms going limp. 'At least let me stay in for the pen.'

'Don't be a twat,' said Shahid. 'You'll only let it in.'

Kabir rolled his eyes and exchanged places with Mo, who took up a position in the centre of the goal, crouched a couple of times, and clapped his hands together.

Stevie stepped back from the ball and looked Mo straight in the face. He knew in his gut he could do this. The fog was dispersing now, chasing its feathery tail across the surface of the land and down to the various rivers and streams that nestled silently in the shadows. Adrenaline was warping his thoughts. He was going to conquer this game in this weird no-man's-land. He took another step back for good measure.

'Go on, my son!' came a shout from behind him. 'Queen and fucking country! Ha ha.' He turned, glanced across at the two men by the white van, and acknowledged them awkwardly with a flutter of the hand. The thinner one pumped his fist, jutted his chin; the fatter one swigged from the bottle. He turned back. The ball. The massiveness of the tarmac. The goal.

'You'd better fucking save this, Mo,' said Shahid.

Dave stepped closer. 'Hit it low,' he said into Stevie's ear. 'He won't be able to dive on this surface. Plus there's no crossbar.'

Stevie filled his lungs and began his run-up, letting out his hissing noise. With a grunt, he struck the ball. Not a great shot; not low, not high, but chest height, which was the easiest to save. And at the very moment the ball left the canvas of his trainer, Rhys split the air with a bellow: 'Goooon!'

Mo had already started moving to save the shot, but his concentration was pricked by Rhys's shout; for an instant he took his eye off the ball, and fumbled the catch. It slipped out of his grasp back into the path of Stevie, who booted it, with unnecessary force, past the goalkeeper and into the greying light.

In jubilation, Stevie ran in a curve away from the goal, arms in a V, pursued by a grinning Dave. The cheers from Rhys and

Chris were loud and barking; they began chanting for England again. Shahid clutched his head. At the top of his voice, which was hoarse and strained, in a tone of pure frustration, he yelled the goalkeeper's full name: 'Mo-*hammed!*'

There was the briefest of pauses. Then, mindlessly, as if meeting one war cry with another, with a single synchronised voice Rhys and Chris both gave vent to their demo chant: 'Whose streets? Our streets! Whose streets? Our streets!'

'Right,' said Shahid, 'that's it. That's fucking it.'

'Leave it,' said Mo, trying to restrain him, 'just leave it.'

'Fuck off. There's more of us than them. Oi! Come and have a game, you fucking Nazi cunts! Show us what you're fucking made of! Be fucking men!'

'Whose streets? Our streets! Whose streets? Our streets!'

Then Chris turned his back, loosened his belt, and mooned the Asian boys, slapping his butt-cheeks with his hands. The line had been crossed. Led by Shahid, the three of them strode across the slow lane, across the middle lane, across the fast lane, closing in on the two men in the shadow of the white van. The fog had all but disappeared now, and they could see each other with renewed clarity.

Rhys and Chris readied themselves.

'Let 'em fucking come,' said Rhys softly. 'Let 'em get within range, innit. When I chuck this bottle at 'em, we leg it round the back of the van and get out the toys. Then we'll let 'em fucking have it.'

As if in a dream Dave watched Shahid and his friends go; suddenly it dawned on him what was about to occur. 'Fuck!' he said, grabbing Stevie's arm. 'Come on, back to the car.'

'What? What?' Stevie replied, still intoxicated by his penalty.

'It's about to kick off, dude,' said Dave urgently. 'I mean it. Come on, I'm not getting caught up in this shit. Come on!'

Pulling Stevie after him, Dave hurried to the barrier, climbed awkwardly over it, and made his way back to the car. He shoved Stevie into the passenger seat, slid behind the wheel, and locked all the doors. There they sat in the gloom, craning their necks, watching the spectacle unfold.

'Hey,' said Stevie. 'Where's Piece of Meat?'

'Fuck knows,' said Dave. 'Oh shit! Fucking hell! Check that out!'

M25

Hsiao May and Harold were sitting now within that state of natural comfort engendered by a good cup of tea. Harold got up to clear the cups into the sink, and in so doing managed to take another little sip of whisky, just to keep the wolf from the door. Hsiao May didn't seem to have noticed. He sat down heavily on the sofa, letting out a sigh of satisfaction.

'It's so lovely to finally make your acquaintance,' he said, 'it really is.'

'Likewise,' said Hsiao May. 'So do you spend much time in here? I mean, do you go on long holidays or anything?'

'From time to time,' Harold replied. 'It's a lovely feeling to be able to carry your house with you, like a wee snail.'

'Yes,' said Hsiao May, 'I can see that.'

'I have been known on occasion to do a full circuit of the M25,' said Harold. 'Sometimes more than once.'

'Really?'

'It's a topic of especial interest to me. The M25. It is one of my passions.'

'Of course, sorry, you did mention.'

'Not at all.'

'How many circuits have you completed in one go?'

'Oh, I don't know.'

'You must know.'

'Without counting stops for petrol? Toilet breaks?'

'Without counting them.'

'I don't know. Four? Five?'

'That's a lot, Harold.'

'I know.'

'It must have taken a long time.'

'Sometimes I can spend a whole afternoon just driving round and round. Other times, if the weather's good, I find somewhere to park the old van, have a little nap perhaps, then get out and explore the environs at a leisurely pace. I find it . . . very therapeutic. Goodness, that must seem terribly odd.'

Hsiao May thought for a moment. 'You know,' she said, 'I think I understand.'

'Really?'

'Yes. It must be . . . well, therapeutic. As you say.'

'Yes.'

'A living history.'

'Exactly.'

'A microcosm. A cross-section of millennia of life.'

'Precisely. That's very perceptive of you.'

'Do you have a favourite section?'

'Of the Orbital?'

'Yes, of the M25.'

'Oh, I don't know. I'm a bit embarrassed about it.'

'Why?'

'I don't know. Um, I suppose it's just a bit nerdy.'

'Of course it's nerdy. You're an academic.'

'I suppose so.'

'I'm just as nerdy as you. More so.'

'Well, I don't know what to say to that.'

They laughed, filling the camper van with the sound for which it seemed to have been designed.

'There are just so many fascinating bits,' said Harold after a time. 'Take Junctions 7 to 9. There you have the top of Reigate Hill, the highest point on the Orbital, at 700-odd feet. And to the west you have the village of Merstham. Limestone from there was taken to build London Bridge, Windsor Castle, and Henry VII's chapel in Westminster Abbey.'

'What else?'

'Well, Junctions 1 and 2 are good. Dartford Tunnel crossing, you know. Cyclists used to be taken across in a specially adapted London bus, but these days they're ferried over in a police Land-Rover, free of charge.'

'Seriously?'

'Aye, it's one of those last vestiges of good old British eccentricity. Then there's the QEII Bridge. It's absolutely wonderful. In each of the concrete pylons is a two-man lift used for the sole purpose of replacing the light bulbs. And from the centre, you have a marvellous view. There's a redbrick packaging factory, piles of containers owned by Eldapoint and Maintainer, which are supposed to be for sale or rent. On a clear day you can see the roofs of the Lakeside Shopping Centre, and the huge pink Proctor & Gamble detergent factory, fully automated. And in the shadow of that vast thing is the ancient church of St Clements.'

Hsiao May reached into her cool bag and brought out a can of Diet Coke, but she did not open it.

'And then, further round, from Junction 3 onwards, you have Lullingstone, with its late second-century Roman villa, complete with bathhouse, central heating and mosaics. And then you have the deer parks, and the Henry VIII tiltyard, you know, which was used for jousting . . . And it was the site of a fake airfield during the Second World War, with aircraft made of wood and canvas, intended to take the heat away from Biggin Hill. Rumour has it that at one point, a solitary German bomber flew overhead and dropped a wee cardboard bomb on it. And they say the Germans don't have a sense of humour.'

'A cardboard bomb?'

'Exactly! Exactly! You know, the heir to Lullingstone Castle is the most wonderful chap by the name of Tom Hart Dyke. He's a plant hunter, and has created an extraordinary garden of rare plants in the grounds. Once he was captured by guerrillas on the Panama–Colombia border. You may have seen it on the news?'

'It rings a bell . . .'

'He's recently made a wee volcano too. In the grounds.'

'A volcano?'

'Aye, a wee one. With a smoke machine that blows scented fog.'

'Scented?'

'I know! You see, it's all so fascinating. He is the most charming man. And it's all so beautiful too, with the constant drone of the Orbital in the background. Like a continual stream of transience, permanent and primordial, like a river. Only made by man, that's the thing.'

'It sounds magical.'

'Aye, it is. And there's the site of the old Saxon burial ground at Junction 7. Two hundred graves had to be moved when the Orbital was built. The ground in that area is Gault clay, which, when it dries, cracks to reveal rainbow-coloured fossils. Their colour fades when they're exposed to air, you know.'

Hsiao May was starting to feel a little dizzy.

'Further round you have the Clackett Services. Those monstrous lorry parks? Modernity itself, so ugly. But they're crossed by a Roman slave road, which used to run from London to the great ironworks in the Sussex forest. Just north of the Services they found a Roman temple. You see, the whole gamut of human history's brought together in the Orbital.'

'I do see.'

'And junction six – goodness, junction six is special. Most people miss it, but if you keep your eyes open you'll see a wee cutting across the road, which indicates the very point where it is intersected by the Greenwich Meridian. A brass rod in the grounds of Waltham Abbey nearby places it exactly. It is almost spiritual.'

Hsiao May nodded, opened her Diet Coke and took a sip. The bubbles, the flavour, in this unfamiliar context, were a sweet, old-fashioned infidelity.

'But I suppose my very favourite spot is just north of Junction

6. The Godstone Vineyard. It lies at the mouth of an enormous disused quarry, hidden by trees. In summer one can sit with a drink on the veranda and watch the traffic stream past a Bronze Age tumulus.'

'I'd . . . I'd love to join you,' said Hsiao May. 'One day. Not necessarily soon or anything, but . . . one day. If that's all right. It really does sound fascinating.'

'Would you? Would you really? Goodness, that would be special. To have a companion would be lovely.'

Hsiao May noticed that her hands and feet were trembling.

Harold stopped now, a strange expression on his face, as if he had just caught a glimpse of himself in the mirror. 'Goodness gracious,' he said, 'I should apologise. I've been rambling.'

'You haven't at all. It's your passion.'

'I'm embarrassed now. Christ, I've lifted the lid.'

'On what?'

'On my nerdy, lonely life.'

Hsiao May leaned forward. 'It's not nerdy and lonely,' she said. 'It's magnificent.'

Suddenly, over Harold's shoulder, framed in the rectangle of the window, Hsiao May saw something. She put down her can of Diet Coke. 'What's that?' she said. 'I think something's going on.'

Harold followed her gaze. Shouts could be heard now. Then figures came into view, and something struck the side of the camper van.

'Christ almighty,' said Harold.

'Are the doors locked? Are the doors locked?'

With some effort, Harold squeezed through to the front again and made sure that they were.

'What on earth are they doing?' said Hsiao May. 'Do you think they'll come here?'

'Get down low,' said Harold, drawing her back onto the sofa. 'Let's try not to draw attention to ourselves.'

'Shall we call the police? Shit, I left my mobile in the car. We're so exposed.'

'Mine is somewhere in the glove compartment,' said Harold. 'But I have no idea if it works.'

'Shall we try?'

'Someone else surely will have alerted the police. Let's leave it. I think we should lie low. And what I need to do is protect you.'

Squatting awkwardly on the floor, he put his arm around her. And she did feel protected. As if nothing could possibly defile the charm of this camper van. And even if it did, as if nothing could possibly get past Harold.

Over the hill

Monty and Shauna sat on the bench, legs stretched out insouciantly, gazing up at the night sky in easy companionship.

'So you like your wine,' said Monty.

'You noticed?' Shauna replied ironically. 'I keep meaning to cut down. Not supposed to be healthy.'

'I never know what to think about all that. Seems like there's always a new health warning coming out. And they usually contradict each other. Red wine, for one.'

'I know! You're so right. I think it also depends on your lifestyle too. My colleagues booze all the time. And my friends. It makes it completely impossible to give up. The peer pressure. Don't you find?'

'Yeah, I know what you mean,' said Monty, with feeling.

'I still don't completely understand what you do actually,' said Shauna. 'What was it again?'

Monty glanced at her sidelong, saw her lit dully by the early dawn, grey upon grey upon grey. What to say? If he told her he was a manual worker and left it at that, he would be selling himself short. Couldn't he just tell the truth for once? What harm could it possibly do? Nobody could hear them. It wasn't like they were under surveillance or anything. So far as he knew.

'I'm a labourer,' he said.

'OK . . .'

'But I'm also, um, I'm in a sort of organisation.'

'Sort of organisation?'

'Yeah. But at the same time, I'm not really part of it at all.'

'What's that supposed to mean? Are you in the Territorial Army? A few of my school friends ended up doing that.'

'No. Not the army.'

'So what is it then? You have to tell me, Monty, otherwise it's not fair. I've been telling you about myself all bloody night.'

'Well, OK. Where shall I start? I'm involved in a kind of . . . in an international organisation. Um, that sounds like I'm an arms dealer or something. God.'

'It does sound pretty dodgy,' said Shauna gaily, and Monty thought he saw a flicker of excitement in her eyes. 'It's delicious. Tell me more.'

'Do I have to?'

'Yes, Monty, you do jolly well have to.'

'Well, if you put it like that. Right. So, basically what I do is travel to foreign countries and meet other members of the organisation, and we organise things. Meetings and suchlike.'

'Oh my God, you're a terrorist.'

'Don't be stupid.'

'But not an Islamist terrorist. You're something horrible and left-wing. You're a Marxist terrorist.'

'Nothing as exciting as that.'

'You're a radical animal rights campaigner.'

'Nope. I'm allergic to horses for a start. And cats. And badgers, probably.'

'You're a militant gay-rights activist.'

'Do I look gay?'

'What's wrong with looking gay?'

'Nothing, but are you saying I look gay?'

'I'm not saying that. Don't be so paranoid. But you've got a dodgy job. I can tell.'

'God, can we change the subject?'

'You see? You have got a dodgy job.'

'All right, all right. Let's talk about something else. Let's talk about this traffic jam.'

'Yes, now that would be an exciting thing to talk about. That would be riveting.'

'When do you think it's going to move?'

'Fucked if I know. I can't imagine it moving an inch. Ever.'

'It'll move sooner or later, don't worry. They're probably clearing the road as we speak.'

'It feels to me like we're going to be here for ever. For ever and ever. In which case, I'm glad we bumped into each other. You're a good person to chat to, Monty. Even if you won't tell me what you do.'

'Thanks. So are you. But you know, speaking of the jam, maybe we'd better walk up to the top of the hill. So we can see the traffic when it moves.'

So they got up to go, Shauna with her big bottle of water and paracetamol. The fog had cleared completely now, and had left a patina of dew clinging to the grass, which darkened their shoes, their ankles, as they climbed. Before long, they were out of breath and speaking in short bursts.

'Fucking hell, this is knackering,' said Shauna. 'Can we take a break?'

'Come on, we're almost there. We'll take a break at the top. Maybe we'll be able to see what's up now the fog's cleared.'

'Taskmaster.'

'Come on. You can do it.'

'Bloody hell. I'll have to spend a week in a spa after this. And I don't mean the grocery shop. Anyway, I know what job you do.'

'What's that?'

'You're in the police. You're one of those undercover cops. Aren't you?'

There was a silence.

'If I give you an answer to that,' said Monty, 'will you promise not to ask me any more details? At least, not until I've quit?'

'OK.'

'Then the answer is yes.'

*

They neared the brow of the hill. This evening had taken a turn that Monty never would have expected; he had never seen himself as someone who would stumble into a friendship with a stranger. It was actually comical, in a way. No doubt about it, tonight the rudder had fallen off his life. But how beautiful this girl was! How funny. How characterful her smile, how bright and perceptive her eyes. Fuck me, he thought. I'm behaving like a teenager. Here he was, almost at the top of the hill, and he didn't know what his next step would be.

For her part, Shauna was feeling better. Throwing up earlier had cleared out her system. The painkillers had dealt with her headache and her thirst had been assuaged by the water. To cap it all, here was a man beside her. He was rather strange, rather cagey, she had to admit, and she knew that she should be wary of strangers. But this felt different – more substantial. Like muesli is to Cheerios, she thought. Though that was about the least romantic metaphor ever. Like gold is to fool's gold. How cheesy could you get? Like a good English Stilton to a Dairylea. Cheese? Her mind was spinning. The idea of Hubster seemed laughably inadequate now; inadequate, superficial and rather pathetic. She smiled at herself and shook her head. Here was some totally random labourer-cum-undercover-cop, a James Bond fantasist probably. Not her type at all. What would her friends say? Her parents? Yet her every instinct was telling her to grab him with both hands and never him let go.

He was probably sticking around out of pity. He was probably married or something. He was probably a nutter. An escaped convict. A highwayman. A frisson of excitement. She looked at Monty sidelong. Oh God, she thought. Oh God.

Then they arrived at the brow of the hill, with the nightish dawn above them and the undulating land spreading out all around. Monty commented that the traffic hadn't moved, and Shauna shrugged ironically. She sat on a low-hanging branch on the edge of the copse, her chin cupped in her hands, and Monty leaned against a tree. Then something caught their eye:

further down the hill a figure could be seen emerging from the woods and walking down the slope.

'Wow, he's been in there all along,' said Monty.

'Who?'

'That guy down there. See him? I saw him coming up earlier.'

'The black guy?'

'Yeah.'

'Weird. Wonder what he's been doing?'

'Your guess is as good as mine.'

It was then that they heard the shouts.

'Fuck,' said Monty. 'Look down there.'

'What? Where?'

'Look. Look. Looks like it's getting hairy.'

'Down there? Oh yeah, I see. Shit. They won't, will they?'

'I should have known it. Rhys could never sit still for that long without getting into a fight. Jesus.'

'How do you know those people?'

'They're my friends. Well, not my friends. Not my friends at all, actually. I was giving them a lift in my van. Part of my work, you know. I hate the cunts really.'

'And it's your van?'

'Yes. Oh fuck, look. Shit.'

'Oh God. Shouldn't you go and help?'

'What can I do from here?' he said. 'But I'd better make a phone call. A really quick one. OK?'

'Don't leave me here. It's creepy as fuck.'

'I'll just be over here. OK?'

'Oh my God. What are they doing, what are they doing? Shit, I can't watch. Monty, call the police! Call the police!'

'That's what I'm doing.'

'I can't watch. God, Monty, I can't watch any more. I can't watch.'

Battle

Rhys, his blood quickening, with a hoarse cry of 'cunts', drew back his arm and hurled the half-full bottle of brandy in the direction of the oncoming footballers. It rotated on its axis in the air then smashed on the tarmac. Shahid and his friends, disoriented, let out a volley of shouts.

'Now,' said Rhys. 'Fucking now!'

In their haste to get to the back of the van, Chris, who was still fastening his belt, stumbled. Rhys hauled him to his feet and dragged him round the side. They had lost precious seconds, but now the back door of the van was before them. Chris could almost see the weapons: the bats, the chains, the mace. He could almost feel the grain of the wooden handle in his palm; the cool, shifting links of the chain; the hiss of the mace gas as it spurted under his finger from the canister. He gripped the handle of the back door, pressed the button, pulled. In his mind's eye it opened. But the handle did not give. The back of the van regarded him blankly. In desperation, he gave it two hard yanks; a rattle; a kick. Then he butted it with his head.

'Fuck!' he yelled. 'What the fuck?'

'Monty must've locked it,' said Chris.

'That fucking cunt,' said Rhys. 'Where are the keys?'

'He's got 'em. Monty's got 'em.'

'Cunt, I'll fucking kill him. Quick, round the front.'

Stones were falling from the sky around them now like over-sized hailstones. The bastards were picking them up from the central reservation. Rhys cursed himself for not predicting that hurling the bottle would evoke this sort of response. One glanced off the van roof and ricocheted onto the side of a camper van, making a clunk, leaving a scar. Another hit Rhys on the shoulder. Pushing Chris in front of him, he tried to make it back to the front door, hoping to get in and reach the weapons cache somehow from there, or at least grab the wheel-lock which lay in the passenger footwell. But immediately he saw it was too late.

Shahid stood fixed in time, his lips pulled back from his teeth and his fist at head height, watched by a hundred pairs of eyes on the motorway. Then the spell was broken. He let out the bellow of a maddened bull, and punched with all his strength. When his knuckles hit Chris's temple he was surprised; surprised when the head bobbed in a way that spoke of sleep. The fat face looked delicate to him then, that formation of nose, those eye sockets. It had taken on an expression of disappointment, as if realising how easily it could be crushed.

Rhys pushed in front of his brother, shoved Shahid back. There was blood on Chris's face, Rhys could see it out of the corner of his eye, and he was whining like a pig. Rhys reached into his pocket and brought out the object that he always carried with him.

When he thrusted, Shahid twisted instinctively. The blade passed through his T-shirt, sliced an L-shape in his chest, but the twisting motion entangled it in the fabric and the weapon sprang from Rhys's grasp. It fell, spinning, and bounced once, twice, on to the tarmac of the M25. Mo and Kabir, sensing a fleeting advantage, flew at Rhys. Disorientated, he defended himself from the blows however he could, throwing his arms out wildly. He stumbled backwards and slammed into the side of the Chrysler; there was a loud bang, followed by a pattering sound, as his elbow shattered the side window of Ursula and Max's car.

Suddenly there was a high-pitched scream: 'My baby, my baby, my baby!'

Ursula burst from Popper's passenger seat and hurled herself at the fighting men. As the bodies heaved and tussled she caught a glimpse of her daughter, crying as she had never cried before, eyes wide, hands agitating the air, covered in a constellation of glass.

Shahid found himself on the tarmac on his hands and knees. Dazed, his T-shirt sodden with blood, he blinked. There, between his hands, in parallel with the white dashes on the surface of the motorway, was Rhys's knife, its handle pointing towards him.

Hero

In the front seat of his silver Golf, Popper sat hunched over the steering wheel, every muscle in his body tensed, sweat glistening in the crevices of his face. His eyes were fixed on the spectacle that was unfolding before him. He watched the woman grappling with the men. He watched her receive a blow to the face, watched her stagger backwards, then push forward again. His breathing was shallow, he was trembling uncontrollably, and his legs felt hollow, as if they could never support his weight. What was happening to him? Where was his courage? His signet ring was making a ferocious tapping sound as his hands on the steering wheel shook. He groped around inside of himself for the old battle instinct, the fighting instinct, the bravery that was as much part of him as his ability to breathe. But he was clutching at water; it ran through his fingers, was sucked away in great lugs.

He saw the woman fall to the ground. Again she got to her feet, plunged back into the fray. Unable to bear it he averted his eyes, pressed his forehead into the top of the steering wheel, bile rising in his mouth.

Ursula tried again to pull the nearest man away from the Chrysler. Suddenly a hand gripped her shoulder and threw her aside. A youth, his T-shirt thick with blood, snaked his way between the bodies and she saw the flash of a blade as he struck. There was a godawful howl, seeming to come from everywhere and nowhere, from the motorway itself, from the landscape. Several more movements. Still she could not see Carly. Worse, she could no longer hear her cries.

She dashed back towards the seething knot of men, tried to break her way through to her baby. Then, by some unseen force, the group changed shape. Now between herself and Carly was a lean, short-haired man with wild eyes. Blood was streaked across his face, and blossoming on his shirt, and his lips were curled back from his teeth. With one hand he was brandishing the knife, creating a circle of space around himself with wicked little jabs; somehow he must have wrestled it back from his attacker. Without thinking, she stepped into the cavity, begging him to move aside; he thrust out his hand and gripped her by the throat.

And then a new figure approached from behind, pushing people aside, throwing blows wildly. Within seconds he had beaten his way through to her. Faced with the knife, he hesitated not for a moment. In another instant she was free and unharmed, leaning in through the window to Carly and the newcomer was wrestling ferociously with the knifeman. They swung round once, twice, in the constricted space between the cars; then there was a single, anguished bark. Ursula turned to protect the children. The knifeman lay on the ground, writhing slightly, losing blood. Several feet away from his hand lay the knife. In the background, the three footballers were running off into the night, one of them stumbling. And there in the centre was the man who had saved her life, clutching the side of his neck.

'Max!' cried Ursula. 'Max!'

Carpe diem

'We should have done something,' said Shauna.

'I did. I called the police,' said Monty. 'Look, here they are now. You can't just step into these situations. Rule one. It's not safe.'

'But they're your friends.'

'I keep telling you, they're not my friends. They're, well, they're my enemies. I . . . I'll tell you about it. I promise I'll tell you about it. But now's not the time.'

'That man. I can't believe how he stepped in.'

'He was much further down the hill than us. By the time we arrived, it would have been all over. Anyway, he must be the woman's husband or something. Look, they're in a huddle. Those must be their daughters.'

'What's he doing? He's kicking something away.'

'The knife, I think. Yes, the knife.'

'He's hurt. Look, he's holding his neck. We should get down there.'

'Look, here comes the cavalry. Thank God nobody's blocking the hard shoulder.'

A little further along the motorway, a sudden movement caught their eye. A beaten-up, ancient Peugeot estate was trying to manoeuvre out of the queue. Forward and backward it went, jolting and jerking crazily; then at last, with a squeal of tyres, it broke free, sped down the hard shoulder and into the distance. Within seconds, a police car was giving chase, siren blaring. The motorway tapered round a bolt of land, and both vehicles disappeared from view.

'Well, that was a bit stupid,' said Monty. 'They're fucked now. Must've been in a right panic.'

'Wouldn't you have been?' said Shauna.

'Me?' said Monty, 'I suppose I would.'

As a slit of sun appeared on the horizon, Shauna took another dose of paracetamol. A floodlight had been set up on the motorway below them, bathing the scene like a stage; after some discussion, the medics carried the injured men off the carriageway where they had more room to administer help.

'The cops seem very interested in your van,' said Shauna. 'They're all over it.'

'I'm not surprised.'

'Aren't you going to go down there and talk to them?'

Monty thought for a moment. 'Do you know,' he said, 'I don't think I am. To tell you the truth, I'm sick of it. I don't want to go down there and get myself involved with that shit. Do you know what I mean? Is that terrible?'

'I don't know about that, but I don't want you to go either.'

They sat in silence on the edge of the copse, drinking water. Below them, Ursula could be seen frantically going from Max to Carly and back again, with the occasional gesture of concern for Bonnie; she seemed to not want the children to see Max in his current state, prostrate and cared for by medics, and yet she did not want to leave his side. A policewoman was trying to calm her. A few metres away, Rhys and Chris were receiving treatment under the gaze of two police officers. Statements were being solicited from the drivers of nearby vehicles. After a time a tow truck threaded its way along the hard shoulder. It came to a stop beside the white van, and the driver had a conversation with the policemen. Then, after some complicated manoeuvres involving five or six cars, the white van was hooked up to the tow truck and removed from the scene.

'Isn't that your van they're taking?' said Shauna.

'They're welcome to it,' Monty replied. 'That's my old life they're towing away.'

'So what will your new life consist of?'

'I have no idea. But it will have nothing to do with Rhys and Chris Baker, or anybody associated with them. I've had it.'

Time passed. Another tow truck was on the scene now, and efforts were being made to hook it up to the Chrysler. Ursula was going through the boot, frantically packing a bag of essentials. A policewoman was looking after Carly and Bonnie, who were sitting by the side of the road and eating. They were both wrapped in silver hypothermia sheets. Max was being bundled up in a red blanket, in the glare of the open ambulance door. Rhys and Chris had already been loaded into another ambulance, and, in the company of two policemen, had been driven away. The scene looked strangely sad and desolate, like a disused children's playground.

'How are you going to get home now?' said Shauna, after a time.

'I honestly don't know.' Monty looked down at his calloused hands.

'Well,' she said. 'Carpe diem and all that. If the traffic does move, I'll give you a lift. If it'll help at all.'

Monty looked at her. 'I wouldn't want to take you out of your way,' he said.

'Don't worry,' she replied. 'You won't.'

'But I feel I should tell you something first.'

'Oh?'

'My real name's not Monty. It's Mark.'

'Mark. I have to say, that's actually a big improvement.'

Ambulance

The scene was like a renaissance painting, everybody posed in symbolic positions; but such paintings were never painted in these colours, Max thought. Here he was, prostrate on a plastic bed, surrounded by medical equipment, strapped down because of the jolting vehicle. Here was Ursula, half-crouching, half-kneeling, holding his hand, her face turned upwards as if in supplication. Her other hand was cradling Carly, whose face was buried in her coat, although her two little eyes were open and staring at him, two little bright spots of innocence. There was Bonnie, withdrawn into her shell, clutching tightly a biscuit, not eating; there was a policewoman next to her, holding her hand. And there was the ambulance man, dressed in Lincoln green, purple plastic gloves on his hands, keeping a watchful eye on the affair.

There was no pain now. They had given him something for it. But so bright! He had never known such illumination as this. Without warning, though in such a way that he should have expected it, the locus of his consciousness seemed to divide. For a few minutes he was not only Max, he was also Ursula and Carly; he could feel their individualities as vividly as his own, and this made his heart open with such blissful suddenness that it made him want to cry.

'Max,' Ursula was whispering, 'are you feeling . . . OK?'

'I'm fine,' he said, hearing his voice deep in his ears. 'I feel fine.'

'I'm so sorry,' she said.

'You don't have anything to be sorry about.'

'I do. About . . . this. About . . . everything.'

Her hand was inside his, a little white slip of a thing within the thick wrap of his fingers. With his thumb he stroked her palm, and this made tears spring to her eyes.

'No,' he said. 'It's me that's sorry. I'm sorry. I'm so sorry . . .'

'You'll be fine,' she said, 'they said you're going to be fine. It's just blood loss, that's all.'

'Carly, don't worry,' said Max. 'Daddy is going to be fine. Do you want to hold my hand?'

Carly nodded timidly.

'Dad,' she said, 'are you feeling poorly?'

'Yes, a little poorly, darling,' he said, 'but I'll be fine tomorrow.'

'Why are we in an ambulance?'

'Because Daddy needs to go to hospital for a little while. So the doctors and nurses can make him better.'

A dull pain passed from his neck down his spine, a little toy train. Then it was subsumed in the folds of whatever drugs he had been given before. The ambulance rocked slightly as it went around a curve, and Max felt as if his eyes were rolling around in his head. But they were not; they never left Carly and Ursula.

'Why are you not well, Daddy?'

'Because I had a cut. It's not a bad cut. It's under this big plaster.'

'Can I see it?'

'Not now, darling.'

'Why?'

'Because it has to be under the plaster. That will help it get better. I'll show it to you tomorrow.'

'Carly, darling,' said Ursula, 'let Daddy relax now. He needs to relax, OK darling?'

Carly nodded.

'Carly, sweetheart,' said Max, 'I love you, sweetie. I love my Carly so much.'

'I love my daddy so much,' Carly replied, as she always did.

'You holding my hand is making me feel better,' said Max. 'It's making me feel happy.'

'Don't talk now, Max,' said Ursula. 'You should conserve your energy.'

'I'm fine,' said Max. 'I feel fine . . . I love you, Carly. I love my little girl.'

Carly said nothing this time, but he could see, amid all the confusion and fear, a new reassurance appear in her eyes.

'It's been tough recently,' he said to Ursula, 'but I'm sorry. And I love you too.'

'I know,' said Ursula. 'I love you. Underneath it all, it's the deepest thing.'

'We are soulmates,' said Max. 'I haven't said that for years. Do you remember?'

'Yes, I remember,' said Ursula. 'And it's still true.'

'Remember that shitty hotel in Thailand? With the cockroaches?'

'Yes, I remember. And that dodgy instant coffee.'

'I would die for you.'

'Please don't say that, Max. Don't say that.'

'You make me happy. Even when we're fighting. You're always there. You're part of my soul. You're what keeps the world together. You're my . . . you're . . . you're . . . I'm sorry.'

Ursula took her hand from his, wiped her eyes, her face, with a tissue. Then she blew her nose, and this made them all smile through their tears. Now her hand was back in his, beside Carly's, and he was stroking it with his thumb again.

'I have so many regrets,' he said, and the words were loaded with a different pain, one that came from a deeper source. 'It's unbearable.'

'We both do,' said Ursula. 'But we have a future. That's where we're going to live.'

'The future,' said Max. 'Our future . . . do you think we can manage it?'

'We can try,' said Ursula.

'We need to find a new way of . . . of . . . of being.'

'We can do it. We can change whatever needs to be changed.'

'There's so much I need to tell you. We need to talk for ever.'

'There will be time. But you should relax now. Gather your strength.'

'I'm tired.'

'Just relax. Is it painful?'

'I'm so tired.'

Ursula turned to the ambulance man. 'Is it OK for him to sleep?'

The man nodded. 'Let him get some rest,' he said. 'It's the medication making him drowsy. It'll be all right.'

'You should rest,' said Ursula, softly. But Max was already asleep, still holding her hand.

Friends

'I think it's over,' said Harold. 'I think we're safe.'

He knelt on the sofa and parted the curtains a fraction. Then he opened them wide, exposing the cars, the motorway, the dawn.

'You can see the aftermath,' he said. 'Look.'

Hsiao May joined him on her knees on the sofa.

'God,' she said, 'those poor men.'

'It's very magnanimous of you to feel compassion for them,' said Harold.

'Do you not feel compassionate?'

'Of course. That of God in every man and all that.'

'Exactly.'

'Nevertheless, it speaks very well of you. Cup of tea?' said Harold, getting to his feet again.

'I couldn't, honestly. We've only just had one.'

'I could drink tea until the cows come home.' He paused, his weight on the balls of his feet, indecisively. 'I hope the van isn't dented,' he said at last. 'That stone, or whatever it was, seemed to hit it rather hard.'

'We'll have to get out and have a look,' said Hsiao May. 'Do you think it's safe to go out?'

'Let's not bother,' said Harold. 'Either it's dented or it isn't. Getting out won't make a difference. Are you sure you won't have a cup of tea?'

'Absolutely sure, thank you.'

'Fine.'

He busied himself with the tea making, and they knew it was

for the last time. Then, as the kettle boiled, he turned, abruptly, to face her. 'Look,' he said, 'I'd like to ask you something. Do feel absolutely free to say no if that's how you feel. No pressure in the slightest.'

'OK,' said Hsiao May softly, her heart skipping in her chest.

'It's just that, after the extremely stressful experience we've both had, I feel rather wound up. In the cupboard is a small bottle of whisky. Would you mind terribly if I had a swig?'

'Aren't you supposed to be driving?'

'Yes, yes. I'm only talking about one wee dram. Not nearly enough to put me over the limit. I mean, if it makes you feel uncomfortable . . .'

'It's OK with me,' said Hsiao May. 'So long as you keep it modest.'

Harold smiled sheepishly, and in a matter of seconds had taken his Balvenie from the cupboard and administered himself a dose. 'Ah,' he said, wincing with pleasure. 'That's hit the spot.'

Then he continued with his tea making.

Hsiao May knew that the end of the jam was near. Something had changed in the air; the atmosphere had become restive and charged. She gathered up her cool bag, noticing with some shame the four empty cans of Diet Coke that stood side by side on the narrow worktop. It was now or never; she could feel it. *Why you always so shy?* said her mother's voice. *You need grab life like you mean it. Or, mark my word, you will be old and lonely with nobody to care for you. You want be old and lonely with nobody to care for you? No. Nobody want be old and lonely with nobody to care for them. So you must go for it. Take the opportunity when it comes up. Nobody will take it for you.*

She cleared her throat. Harold, who was adding the finishing touches to his tea, looked up expectantly.

'Harold . . .' she said.

'Aye?'

'I – I was wondering . . .'

She was interrupted by a commotion outside, the sound of somebody shouting. No, not shouting, just speaking loudly; and, on reflection, not with aggression but excitement. They both looked out the window. A figure was approaching along the line of cars: a man in a faded T-shirt, with – they saw as he came under the glow of the nearest light – a soft-looking, nondescript face.

'Oh,' said Hsiao May. 'It's him.'

'Him?' said Harold. 'Who? Him? Do you know that man?'

'Yes. I mean, no, not really. He knocked on my car window earlier. Creeped me out a bit, to be honest.'

Tomasz came closer and closer, and now they could hear his words more clearly now. 'We're going to move!' he was calling. 'Five minutes, everybody! Five minutes!'

Following him, several metres behind, was an incoming tide of noise, as engines everywhere were turned on. Exhaust began to plume into the air once more like the breath of warhorses. The people who were in the open ducked quickly back into their vehicles. Lights flicked on in reds and whites; people stretched and fastened their seatbelts.

As Tomasz passed the camper van, he caught Hsiao May's eye and held his hands out to her momentarily like a gondolier. 'Won't be long now!' he called. 'Won't be long at all!' This last word he turned into a sort of yodel. Then he had passed the van. He diminished, and diminished, and was gone, leaving behind him the growling engines, the people getting ready, the atmosphere that precedes a race. But still nothing had moved.

'You'd better be getting back,' said Harold. 'Wouldn't want to have your car stranded once this lot starts to move.'

'Yes,' said Hsiao May, wishing for just a little more time. 'You're right. But don't you think it might be a false alarm? After all, nothing's moved yet. And how would that man know anything?'

'Might be,' mused Harold. 'But I wonder if it would be better not to take the chance? If it proves a false alarm, you'd be more than welcome to come back.'

Hsiao May got to her feet, picked up her cool bag. 'It's been lovely,' she said haltingly.

'An absolute pleasure,' said Harold. 'This has been the most charming traffic jam I have ever experienced. And I've experienced quite a few.'

They laughed. She took a few paces to the door, and rested her hand on the handle. Then, finally, she turned. 'We should, we should see each other again. I don't know. What about . . . I know, I could cook you dinner one evening this week. Are you free?'

The words hung in the air. Harold seemed to be studying her closely.

'It wouldn't need to be bugs,' she added hastily. 'I can cook other things too. Steak? Do you like steak? Pasta? I could do Chinese. Or Japanese, if you like that. Yes, I can do Japanese. Japanese?'

Harold winced slightly, in the same way he had after taking a slug of whisky. 'This might be a wee bit awkward,' he said. 'I mean, I don't want to assume anything . . . I have thoroughly enjoyed meeting you, Hsiao May, and I would love to come to dinner with you. I am extremely flattered to have been asked.'

'But?'

'But my dear, you do know I'm a homosexual?'

'A homosexual?'

'Yes.'

'I – I didn't, actually.'

'I'm sorry. I'm not suggesting for a minute that your invitation was a romantic one. But I just thought it best to be clear.'

'Of course. Thank you.'

'Well, then,' said Harold.

'I would still love you to come for dinner,' said Hsiao May. 'As a friend.'

'I'm sorry, now I feel a bit silly. But I just thought it best to be straight with you. So to speak.'

'Friends would be fine.'

'Great.'

She turned, pressed down on the handle. The door swung open, a portal into a harder world. She stepped into it and closed the door behind her.

No

There was a succession of sharp knocks on the car window. Dave and Stevie, who were already on edge, jumped in their seats. There, in the dawn light, was Natalie, gesturing for them to open the door. Stevie let out a high-pitched whoop of relief.

'Jesus,' he said, 'almost shat myself. Open the door. Stupid fucking cow.'

Dave opened the door and Natalie regarded them coolly.

'Where have you been?' said Dave. 'It's all been properly kicking off here. Properly kicking off.'

'We've been in the thick of it,' said Stevie.

Natalie did not speak.

'I'm telling you,' said Stevie. 'There was a proper fight. A stabbing, it looked like. Look, the police are still there. And the ambulances. People were going down all over the place and shit. It was mental. Where were you?'

Still Natalie did not respond.

'What's wrong with you?' said Stevie. 'Get in the car.'

'No,' she said quietly.

'What?'

'I said no. I'm not getting in that car. Open the boot.'

'What?'

'Open the boot.'

'What for?'

'Just open the boot.'

Dave shrugged, reached down and heaved up the lever that released the boot. Natalie walked around the car and they could hear her scrabbling at the back. Then the boot slammed and she reappeared, her rucksack on her back.

'What are you doing?' said Stevie.

'Going home,' said Natalie.

'Home? What? Who with?'

'Never you mind.'

'What about the traffic?'

'When it moves. Whatever.'

'She's crazy,' Stevie said. 'She's finally fucking gone crazy.'

'No, I haven't,' said Natalie. Something in her voice made Dave and Stevie look up. 'And I'm not . . . I'm not, like, a piece of meat.'

Stevie laughed nervously. Then he fell silent. Then he laughed again.

'I'm not a piece of meat, and I'm not stupid,' said Natalie.

'I never said you were.'

'You treat me like I am.'

'Look, Natalie, take it easy.'

'I'm not a piece of meat.'

'We were only joking, OK? It was a joke.'

'It wasn't funny.'

'I can't help it if you've got a sense of humour failure.'

'I'm not a piece of meat.'

'OK, OK. I get it.'

'It's you. You're, like, like, really mean.'

'Mean?' said Stevie, laughing again. 'Who the hell says "mean"?'

'You've been really mean to me all weekend. You know what I'm talking about.'

'I haven't got to listen to this,' said Stevie. 'If you want to fuck off with some freak you've met by the side of the road, be my fucking guest. In fact, you know what? I don't want you back in this car. You can just fuck right off.'

'It's not your car,' said Natalie. 'It's Dave's.'

'OK, whatever.'

'No,' said Natalie, looking surprised at her own words. 'You can fuck right off.'

'What did you just say?' said Stevie.

'I said you can fuck right off, Stevie. You told me to fuck right off. I'm saying no, it's you that should fuck right off.'

'What are you on about?'

'You know what your problem is? You've never, like, had a girlfriend because you're a scrawny fucking runt. I should've seen it coming. But that's all over now. I can totally, like, see you for the mean little fucking creep you are.'

'Someone's put you up to say this. You couldn't've thought of this yourself.'

'I'm not stupid. I'm not a piece of meat.'

'You're a broken fucking record, that's what you are.'

'I'm not. And you, Dave, you're ... I don't know, you're weak. You're both, like, weak, actually. Cowards.'

Dave tried to respond but found he had nothing to say.

'Well, then,' said Natalie. 'See you around.'

She began to walk away. She could see Jim sitting at the wheel of his van, watching her. In a burst of courage, she turned back. 'One more thing,' she said. 'You both have really small cocks. And I'm not, like, even joking now. Proper tiny!'

Dave swung the door closed and sat in silence. Finally he stole a glance at Stevie who was sitting hunched in his seat, his fingers pressed over his eyes. 'Fuck her,' said Stevie. 'Fuck her.'

The move

The traffic began to move. Popper turned the key in the ignition, and the Golf sprung immediately to life. With a vast growl
and turning-on of lights, the motorway awakened. Popper's
Golf moved, and the camper van moved, and the Smart car
moved, and the Prius, and the Ford estate, and all the other
cars. Around him surged a wave of emotion of which he was
oblivious, and in the distance a flurry of exultant honking
caught on, then died away.

The line of traffic moved for a few seconds in formation, a
human settlement migrating, and then, as if newly awakened to
their autonomy, the cars began to go at their different speeds,
and weave into different lanes.

People's minds turned once again to the future, near,
middling, and far. Shauna was driving slowly now, slower than
she could ever remember, talking to Monty as if they were old
friends. Hsiao May, alone in her Prius, overtook her easily and
gradually faded from sight. Harold, for a while, chuntering
along in his camper, sat behind Shauna and Monty; but within
a few minutes he had fallen way behind. The footballers, now,
were in custody, being taken to the nearest police station; Rhys
and Chris were arriving at hospital, accompanied by the police.
Natalie, in the front of Jim's van, was cruising at a high yet
constant speed in the fast lane, rushing smoothly into the future
as she opened another packet of Oreos. Stevie and Dave, still
cursing under their breath, worried that their car was about to
break down. Max, in the ambulance with his family, slipped in
and out of consciousness. And Popper made headway in the

middle lane, driving his car consistently, moving neither to the left nor the right.

Once again anonymity reigned. Once again cars, and the people in them, moved too quickly for colours and patterns; once again this was a world of glimpses, grime, and the relentless roar of machines, capped by a sky that was moving from pink to grey to yellow to blue. Another day.

Acknowledgements

Thanks as ever to my agent, Andrew Gordon, David del Monté and my friend Danny Angel, who read the book more than once and gave me invaluable feedback. Thanks to James Jeffrey and Musa Okwonga, both of whom offered some very helpful thoughts on the character of Popper. Thanks to all at Polygon. And with much love to Isobel, Libi, Isaac, Imogen and the rest of my family.

Two sources were fascinating and helpful in equal measure when writing this novel. The first was a small but excellent book called *M25: Travelling Clockwise* by the late Roy Phippen, a cabbie with a passion for the London Orbital. The second was an article written by the brilliant Dana Goodyear for the *New Yorker* magazine in August 2011 entitled 'Grub: Eating bugs to save the planet'.